THE
WALK
ON

THE WALK ON

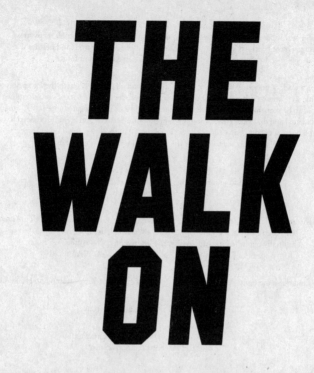

THE TRIPLE THREAT · BOOK I

JOHN FEINSTEIN

A YEARLING BOOK

This is a work of fiction. All incidents and dialogue, and all characters with the exception of some well-known historical and public figures, are products of the author's imagination and are not to be construed as real. Where real-life historical or public figures appear, the situations, incidents, and dialogues concerning those persons are fictional and are not intended to depict actual events or to change the fictional nature of the work. In all other respects, any resemblance to persons living or dead is entirely coincidental.

Text copyright © 2014 by John Feinstein
Cover photograph copyright © 2014 by Grady Reese/Corbis
Photograph of football copyright © 2014 by Shutterstock

All rights reserved. Published in the United States by Yearling, an imprint of Random House Children's Books, a division of Penguin Random House LLC, New York. Originally published in hardcover in the United States by Alfred A. Knopf, an imprint of Random House Children's Books, New York, in 2014.

Yearling and the jumping horse design are registered trademarks of Penguin Random House LLC.

Visit us on the Web! randomhousekids.com

Educators and librarians, for a variety of teaching tools, visit us at RHTeachersLibrarians.com

The Library of Congress has cataloged the hardcover edition of this work as follows:
Feinstein, John.
The walk on / John Feinstein. — First edition.
p. cm. — (The triple threat ; book 1)
Summary: After moving to a new town his freshman year in high school, Alex Myers is happy to win a spot on the varsity team as a quarterback but must deal with the idea of not playing for two years since the first-string quarterback is not only a local hero, he is also the son of the corrupt head coach.
ISBN 978-0-385-75346-3 (trade) — ISBN 978-0-385-75347-0 (lib. bdg.) —
ISBN 978-0-385-75348-7 (ebook)
[1. Football—Fiction. 2. Coaches—Fiction. 3. High schools—Fiction. 4. Schools—Fiction. 5. Moving, Household—Fiction. 6. Divorce—Fiction.] I. Title.
PZ7.F3343Wal 2014
[Fic]—dc23
2013044495
ISBN 978-0-385-75349-4 (pbk.)

Printed in the United States of America
10 9 8 7 6 5
First Yearling Edition 2015

THIS IS FOR MY CHILDREN:
DANNY, BRIGID, AND JANE,
WHO INSPIRE ME EVERY DAY.

1

"Twelve is taken. Make the team and then you can worry about a number. But you aren't going to get twelve."

Alex Myers was standing in front of the equipment cage in the locker room at Chester Heights High School. School didn't open for another week, but football season began on the last Friday in August, so tryouts and practice started early. Alex had two days to show the coaches that a freshman should be practicing with the varsity.

The school had more than two thousand students, so it also had a junior varsity team. But the JV team only played four games and didn't start practice until mid-September. Alex wanted no part of that. Plus, he knew he was good enough to play for the varsity. In fact, his plan was to *start* for the varsity.

His plan, however, was not going well.

As instructed, he had reported to the equipment cage at nine o'clock to be issued a jersey, uniform pants, pads, and a helmet. All of these were on loan for the two days of tryouts. Players were told to bring their own cleats. There were about a dozen kids in line in front of the cage when Alex arrived. Most of the other kids knew one another, so they were talking while they waited. No one seemed to even notice he was there, except for the tall, gangly African American kid standing right behind him.

"You look like you're new too," he said, putting his hand out. "I'm Jonas Ellington."

"Alex Myers," Alex said, grateful that he wasn't actually invisible. "Yeah, I am new. Where are you from?"

"New York. My dad got a job down here in January. My mom, sisters, and I moved at the start of the summer. What about you?"

"Boston. I just got here last week with my mom and sister. . . . My parents are getting a divorce. My mom has family in Philly, so she decided she wanted to be close to them. *I'd* rather be back in Boston, close to my friends. But I didn't get a vote."

Jonas shook his head. "Dude, I'm sorry about that. I have friends whose parents have split and I know it's rough. Do you know anybody down here?"

"You," Alex said, and they both laughed. "And my cousins, but they're six and four."

"Well, you got me," Jonas said. "What position you play?"

"Quarterback," Alex said. "I can play DB too, but at a school this big I doubt too many guys play both ways."

Jonas made a face. "You might want to think about hon-ing those DB skills. The starting quarterback is the coach's son. Unless he gets hurt, *no one* is taking a snap but him."

Hearing this bit of news, Alex felt something turn in his stomach. He decided to change the subject—at least for the moment.

"Let me guess," he said. "You're a wideout." Jonas was about six two and probably didn't weigh much more than 150 or 160. If he played anyplace else, he was likely to get broken in half.

"You got it," Jonas said. "I can play corner too if they want because I'm fast. But I'm thinking you'll be throwing to me a lot the next couple days."

"Works for me," Alex said as they reached the front of the line. That was when he made the mistake of asking for number 12. He was handed a jersey with 23 on it and started to turn back to point out that wasn't a quarterback's number. But when he saw the glare on the old equipment man's face, he thought better of it.

"In case you're wondering," Jonas said as he accepted his gear from the man in the cage, "the guy who wears twelve is—"

Alex put his hand up. "You don't even have to tell me," he said. "The starting quarterback."

■ ■ ■

A few minutes later, Alex found out the quarterback's name—or at least his last name: Gordon. When the fifty or so kids who had shown up for the tryouts jogged from the locker room to the practice field, they were greeted by a half dozen coaches, one of whom was clearly in charge.

"Everyone take a knee," the coach-in-charge said.

Alex put his helmet on the ground in front of him and leaned one hand on it, noticing that everyone else did the same. Jonas was right next to him.

"I'm Coach Gordon," the coach-in-charge said. "I've been the varsity coach here at Chester Heights for fourteen years. And this is Coach Merton." He turned to an older, shorter man whose face seemed stuck in a permanent scowl. "Coach Merton is our junior varsity coach. A few of you will make the varsity, but most of you will end up playing for Coach Merton.

"We have forty-one varsity players returning from last season. They will all be here starting Thursday. This is your chance to show us that you deserve to play with the big boys this season.

"After we watch you play and drill the next two days, we'll post two lists in the locker room on Wednesday. The first list will be those who make varsity. My guess is we're talking no more than five of you. We played in the state semifinals last season and we have fourteen starters back from that team—so we already have a rock-solid group.

"The second list will be players guaranteed a spot on the JV. If you are on that list, you'll report for the first JV practice on September. . . ." He paused and turned to the scowling coach. "Remind me what day it is, Coach Merton?"

"September fourteenth. The first JV game is September twenty-fourth."

"Right," Coach Gordon said. "If you are *not* on the second list and you want to take another crack at making the JV, Coach Merton will have another tryout once school starts.

"Everyone with me?"

They all sort of nodded, which apparently wasn't good enough.

"First lesson of Chester Heights football, boys," the coach said. "When I ask a question, there are two answers: Yes sir or No sir. If the answer is No sir, you stand up and tell me why the answer is no—or if you don't understand something, ask me to explain it. That goes for every coach on this field too. Everyone understand?"

This time they all shouted back. "Yes sir!"

Alex glanced at Jonas, who shook his head just a tiny bit and was clearly thinking the same thing: were these tryouts for the football team or the Marines?

■ ■ ■

A few minutes later, after they had been led through a series of stretching exercises by a strength coach whose name Alex didn't hear, they were told to report to their position coaches.

"You may think you're a two-way player, but chances are you won't be—and definitely not for the next two days," Coach Gordon said. "Decide what you think your *best* position is and report to that coach as I introduce him."

When he introduced Coach Hillier, he said that quarterbacks and wide receivers should report to him under the south goalpost. Alex was relieved when Coach Hillier started walking.

"Did you have any clue which way was south?" Jonas said softly as they and about a dozen others followed Hillier.

Alex grinned. It was good to not be the only new kid. "I

figured it was the way the coach was walking," he answered, and they both laughed quietly.

Once they were all assembled, Coach Hillier, who looked to be the youngest coach on the field, surprised Alex by not telling them all to take a knee. When he spoke, his voice was much less of a bark than that of either Coach Gordon or the strength coach.

"Okay, fellas, let's start by getting to know each other a little bit. I'm Tom Hillier, and in real life I teach English literature and I also help out with the weekly student newspaper. I probably won't be able to memorize all your names in the next couple days, but I'll give it a shot. So let's go around the circle here and each of you can tell us your name and what position you intend to play."

There were fifteen of them in all: ten who said they were receivers, four who said they were quarterbacks, and one who introduced himself by saying, "I'm Tellus Jefferson and I'm a pretty good quarterback. But I know I'm not taking playing time from Matthew Gordon Junior, so I'll catch passes from him if that will get me on the field."

It was the first time Alex heard the star quarterback's name. Matthew Gordon. Senior was the coach. Junior was the quarterback. And Alex was the new kid in town, with exactly one friend.

■ ■ ■

The good news was that his one friend could clearly play.

Coach Hillier had each quarterback throw eleven passes apiece—one to each receiver, since Tellus Jefferson opted to catch rather than throw. First he had the receivers run simple down-and-in routes of no more than ten yards. Then there were out patterns to the sidelines—comeback routes where they ran straight downfield for about fifteen yards, stopped, and then came back toward the quarterback.

These throws were easy for Alex. Coach Hillier had told the four QBs to not put everything they had on their passes—he wanted them to get their arms loose before they threw anything with real zip. For a few minutes, Alex forgot about the snarling equipment man and the drill-sergeant coach and lost himself in the pleasure of throwing the football.

He could still remember the first time he'd talked his father into playing catch with him with a baseball. He was six. His dad had stood a few yards away and said, "Okay, son, show me what you've got."

Alex had unleashed a hard peg that his dad caught, but he staggered backward a little as it hit his glove. Alex could still see the surprised look on his face. His dad moved back and Alex whipped the ball to him again. By the time they found a comfortable spot, Alex's dad was at least twice as far away as he had been starting out. He could still hear his father telling his mom, "Linda, I think we may have an athlete on our hands. Your son's got a gun on him."

He could also still see his mother putting her hands on her hips and saying, "A gun? I thought you were playing catch."

"An arm, Linda, an arm. Alex has an amazing arm."

Those were happier days, before his dad stopped coming home for dinner every night because he didn't want to fight traffic from downtown Boston to Billerica during rush hour. It was also before his parents started arguing about how much his dad was working and how little time he seemed to have for his family.

Not focusing on what he was doing, Alex put a little more on his next throw than he needed to and he could see the receiver shaking his hands in pain after he had dropped the ball.

"Easy, Alex," Coach Hillier said softly. "No need to show off just yet."

Throwing had always been easy for Alex, whether it was a baseball, a football, or even a basketball. Now, with Coach Hillier feeding him one ball after another, he felt completely comfortable and he knew, even not putting that much into it, that he was throwing the ball harder and more accurately than the other three quarterback hopefuls.

He could also tell that Jonas was the best of the receivers. His cuts were sharper, his long legs covered the ground easily, and the ball seemed to disappear into his hands when he caught it. When one of the other quarterbacks threw a ball high and wide on a stop-and-go pattern, Jonas simply reached above his head with his left hand, gathered the ball into his body, and made a virtually impossible catch look easy.

"Nice catch, Jonas!" Coach Hillier shouted.

The coach was catching on to the names quickly. At least, Alex hoped, the ones that mattered.

After they had gone through several rounds, Coach Hillier said, "Okay, QBs, I only want you to make three throws the next round—except for you, Winston." He turned to the smallest of the four quarterbacks, who'd struggled to make the simplest throws. "You just take the last two, okay? Since we've only got eleven receivers." Winston nodded. No doubt he knew already that he would be lucky to make the JV list.

Coach Hillier told the receivers he wanted them to run straight fly patterns—running straight down the field as fast as they could. "When you get to the 35, check to see if the ball is in the air," he said. "QBs, your target is between the 40 and the 45."

Each receiver lined up on the goal line. Luke Mattson made the first three throws. All three of his passes wobbled in the air, and the receivers had to slow up to wait for them to come down at about the 38. Jake Bilney was next. He did better. His throws were accurate, but he had to kind of hoist them in the air to get them near the 45.

Alex stepped up. He noticed that Coach Hillier had Jonas ninth in line, meaning he would be Alex's third and last receiver. Alex took the toss that Coach Hillier was making to start each play—sort of a standing snap—then dropped back a couple steps and easily targeted the 45-yard line, the ball dropping gently into the receiver's hands. Coach Hillier looked at him and just said, "Nice," in a voice so soft Alex was pretty sure he was the only one who could hear it.

It was the second compliment he'd given—the first being to Jonas for the one-handed catch.

Alex's second throw was a copy of the first, except that the receiver dropped the ball.

"Good throw," Coach Hillier said, as if to let him know that he had known the ball was where it was supposed to be.

Alex smiled as Jonas lined up to go out for his third throw.

"Okay if we send him a little deeper?" Alex said.

Coach Hillier smiled. "Sure." He turned to Jonas. "Don't look back until you get to the 45." Turning back to Alex, he said, "That far enough for you, ace?"

Alex didn't know if the ace reference was sarcastic or not, so he just nodded.

Jonas sprinted downfield as Alex took his three-step drop. When Jonas crossed the 40, Alex stepped up and released the ball. It left his hand in a tight spiral just as Jonas began to look over his shoulder for it. He ran under it and gathered it in as if the ball had been dangling at midfield, waiting for him.

Alex turned toward Coach Hillier, who had his arms crossed and was clearly trying to suppress a smile.

"How far you think you can throw it?" he asked.

"About sixty," Alex said. "Maybe sixty-five if I had to."

Coach Hillier raised an eyebrow just as a sharp whistle blew from midfield. The position drills were over.

"After the lists are posted on Wednesday," he said, "come see me. We need to talk."

The rest of the morning was pretty routine. Everyone ran the forty-yard dash twice. Alex was easily the fastest quarterback and the fourth fastest overall, behind one of the running backs, one of the defensive backs, and Jonas—who blew everyone away by running 4.53 twice. That time was fast for a *college* wide receiver, much less a high school freshman. Alex could tell by the way the coaches looked at their watches that they were impressed.

He was too. He had run 4.79, which he knew was a good time for a quarterback, but it didn't seem to draw much attention. Which was fine—his legs weren't his strength, his arm was.

After about ninety minutes, Coach Gordon called them all together again. "We'll do a little hitting tomorrow," he said. "And we'll scrimmage some, now that we have an idea of what you guys can do. See you same time tomorrow." He paused. "Don't be late—that's one way to guarantee you don't make either list."

Clearly, the Marines frowned on tardiness.

In the locker room, Jake Bilney, whom Alex had judged to be the second best of the quarterbacks, introduced himself.

"You're obviously new here," Jake said after offering a handshake. "Where'd you come from?"

"Boston," Alex said. "Just got to town a couple days ago."

Jake smiled and looked around the room. "Well, let me be the first to welcome you," he said. "But I gotta warn you, I might be the last."

"What do you mean?" Alex said, a little bit puzzled.

Jake looked around the room again, then lowered his voice. He was leaning against a locker in a casual pose, but when he spoke his tone was anything but casual.

"Has anyone told you about Matt Gordon?"

"You mean Matthew Gordon Junior?"

Jake smiled. "Yeah, he goes by Matt because he *hates* being called Junior and everyone calls his dad Matthew."

Jonas, who had just come out of the shower with a towel wrapped around his waist, couldn't resist jumping in. "I thought his first name was Coach."

Jake turned at the sound of his voice. "You're the fast guy. What was your forty time, like four flat or something?"

"Four-five-three," Jonas said. "I'm Jonas Ellington."

"You're new too, right?"

"Uh-huh. From New York," Jonas answered.

Jake nodded. Other kids were buzzing past them, but no one seemed to be paying any attention.

"Around here, his first name *is* Coach. But in the news-papers and on the Internet his full name is 'Coach Matthew Gordon.' Or, more often, 'Renowned Coach Matthew Gordon.'"

"Not a fan?" Alex said.

"Actually, I am," Jake said. "He's a very good coach. Check his record. Two state titles; the semis last year with a very young team. A lot of people think he'll coach a col-lege team sometime soon. He just turned forty last season—I remember because there was a big party for him. Matt and I are friends, so I got to go. I haven't ever really played for him because I was on JV last season, but I've spent a lot of time at his house. He's tough, but he knows football."

"So you played JV last year?" Alex said.

"Last *two* years," Jake said. "And I figured I'd be Matt Gor-don's backup this year because the two guys behind him both graduated. Then you showed up."

Alex tried to hide his smile. Just as he had sized up the other quarterbacks, clearly Jake Bilney had sized him up.

"Well, I don't know about that—" he started to say before Jake cut him off.

"Come on, Myers, I could see it on your first throw. What was that baseball movie? *The Natural?* That's you. Coach Hillier saw it too. But there's no way Matt Gordon's not play-ing. The offense is set up for him and he's very good."

"Better than Alex?" Jonas asked.

Jake shook his head. "Can't throw like him," he said. "I'm not sure I've seen anyone in this *league* who throws like that. But Coach runs that 'read-option' offense that Robert

Griffin the Third made famous. Matt's not as fast as RGIII, but he's fast enough and he's very strong. Plus, he throws it okay when he has to."

He paused. "Although he did throw two interceptions in the state semis when we got behind." He smiled. "Of course, Coach blamed the receivers—said they didn't run their routes right. The fact that they were seniors and he never had to see them again may have had something to do with that."

"So you're saying I won't get a fair chance to start, no matter what I do?" Alex said, abandoning any pretense of modesty.

"No, I'm not saying that," Jake answered. "I'm saying that in this offense, Matt's a better quarterback than you are. He's also the leader of this team. You'll find that out."

He paused. "So I'm saying that you can start—at another position. But not at quarterback."

■ ■ ■

Alex was tempted to call his dad for advice because he'd always been the one to understand any sports-related problem. His mom had no interest in sports, even though both her children were athletes and loved going to games. She occasionally went with the rest of the family on excursions to Fenway Park and the TD Garden and to Boston College for both football and basketball games, but she rarely paid much attention.

Alex's sister, Molly, who was two years younger, was actually more passionate about the local teams than Alex—if that was possible—and she was the one who kept bugging their dad to take them to a Patriots game. His answer was always the same: "Life's too short. It's not worth the effort getting in there or getting out. We've got a great view on TV."

Dave Myers didn't seem to mind paying twenty-five dollars to park his car at Fenway—but then the Red Sox were his first love. Alex was a Celtics-first guy: he loved watching Rajon Rondo when he wasn't hurt. Then came the Patriots: he aspired to be Tom Brady in every possible way.

Both Alex and Molly had bonded with their dad through sports. He had never been a pushy jock dad, even though both kids had shown potential at a young age. Molly was fast and tall—already nearly five seven at age twelve. She was a star soccer player and a good tennis player but perhaps had the most potential in track. Alex, who had shot up to six one at the end of eighth grade, was more into the team sports: football, basketball, and baseball. When he was younger, he and his dad had played golf together, and walking the course had always been a good time to talk. But that had happened less and less as their dad grew more absent from home.

Now Alex wondered if he should call his dad and fill him in on what was going on at his new school. He finally decided against it because he really didn't *know* what was going on. There was no sense making a big deal out of something that might not be a big deal.

■ ■ ■

The second day of tryouts was very different from the first. There were no speeches and no introductions and it was apparent that the coaches had established a pecking order among the players based on what they had seen the first day.

When the coaches had the players spend the last forty-five minutes of the morning scrimmaging, Alex and Jake Bilney took most of the snaps at quarterback. Every once in a while the other QBs got in for a play or two, but it was almost always to call a running play. Alex thought that Jake was a better runner than he was a passer. He seemed to make solid decisions about when to keep the ball or pitch, a sign of both smarts and the experience he had gotten from running the JV offense. But his throwing wasn't nearly as good.

Needless to say, the offensive sets were very basic, but Coach Hillier spent a few minutes with Jake and Alex, giving them a couple of read-option calls. That meant it was their decision after taking the snap to run, pitch to a back, or drop back to throw. On one play, Alex saw some daylight to the right as he took the snap. He thought he might run through the hole, but when he noticed that one of his linemen had whiffed on his block, he quickly changed direction, dropped back, and found Jonas wide open behind the entire defense. Alex was standing there admiring his work when he heard a whistle blow.

"Coach Hillier, what's this young man's name again?" Coach Gordon said, walking toward Alex.

"Alex Myers," Coach Hillier said.

"Myers, once you commit to a play, you follow through on it, do you understand?" Coach Gordon said. "If your blockers don't know what you're doing, they can get caught downfield and we end up getting penalized!"

"But, Coach, none of them were across the line when I dropped back—"

Coach Gordon held up a hand and looked not at him but at Coach Hillier.

"Coach, I expect you to make it clear to this young man that at Chester Heights *no one* argues with the coaches."

"Yes sir," Hillier said quietly, making it clear that even the coaches at Chester Heights didn't argue with *the* coach.

Alex was baffled. He had made a perfect play and been yelled at for it. And then, his position coach had been yelled at for something *he*—not the coach—had said.

Alex managed to get through the rest of the scrimmage without making any more good plays that got him in trouble. Everyone was exhausted by the time Coach Gordon and his omnipresent whistle brought them back to midfield.

"I want to thank all of you for putting in the work you did the last two days," he said. "Most of you"—he paused, and Alex could feel his eyes searching him out—"came in here with a great attitude. Cut lists will be posted at 10 a.m. tomorrow."

He turned and started walking in the direction of the locker room. Alex looked for Coach Hillier, but he was following Coach Gordon. Alex stayed where he was, on one knee, staring after them while everyone else got to their feet, eager to get out of the August heat and into a shower.

He felt a hand on his shoulder and looked up to see Jonas.

"Don't sweat it, man. He's just one of those coaches who wants everyone to know how tough he is," Jonas said.

"Yeah, but what if he cuts me to show how tough he is?"

Jonas laughed. "Are you kidding? You are far and away the best player out here—it wasn't even close."

"You're just as good—if not better."

Jonas shook his head. "I'm good, I know I'm good, but you, my man, are a star."

"Can't be a star if you aren't on the team," Alex said. "And you certainly can't be a star if you're the last guy the coach wants to see starting."

"You mean because his son is the starting quarterback?"

Alex stood up. "What do you think?"

"I think you're a little bit paranoid," he said. "But only a little bit."

Alex didn't want to look uncool by showing up before ten o'clock the next morning to check the cut lists. He also didn't want his mom around in case the news was bad, so he told her he would ride his bike to school. It wasn't that far, but he wasn't a hundred percent sure he knew the way.

That was his mother's concern.

"You might get lost," she said. "Then what?"

"If I get totally lost, I can call you on my cell," he said. "Or I can ask for directions. Somebody will know where the high school is."

She suggested printing out Google Maps directions, but he waved her off. "You want me looking down at the directions while I'm riding?" he said.

"No," she said.

"I have to learn how to get there. Might as well do it today, when getting lost won't mean being late for anything."

She finally gave in.

"Okay," she said. "As long as you promise to call and let me know when you get there."

He sighed. "How about a text?"

"Deal," she said.

■ ■ ■

It was ten o'clock by the time he left. He figured that should give the other players time to have been there and gone so he could look at the list in relative privacy.

The last twenty-four hours had been tough. One minute he knew that Jonas was right: no way could Coach Gordon cut him. He didn't think of himself as cocky, but he did think he'd been the best player at tryouts. Then the next minute he'd swing back the other way. Of course Gordon would cut him. He had his son to play quarterback, Jake Bilney would make a reasonable backup, and he wouldn't have to worry about Alex outshining both of them. Alex had no idea if he was better than Matt Gordon, but he was very curious to find out.

Finding the school turned out to be easy. It was ten-twenty when he pulled into the back lot of the school and parked outside the locker room door. He put the lock on his bike, dutifully texted his mom that he wasn't dead, and was heading for the door when several kids he recognized from tryouts came out.

Judging by the looks on their faces, they hadn't made varsity—or maybe even JV. No one said hello. They all looked away from him and kept walking—which he was beginning to think was the traditional Chester Heights greeting.

He pulled the door open and walked up the stairs, trying not to go too fast, then turned left to where the football coaches' offices were. He suddenly remembered that Coach Hillier had told him to come talk to him after the cut lists went up. He wondered if that offer still stood and if he'd meant *today*.

Just outside the doors that said CHESTER HEIGHTS LIONS FOOTBALL — LEAGUE CHAMPIONS 2012 — HEAD COACH: MATTHEW GORDON, he saw a bulletin board. He was delighted and relieved that no one else was around. There were two white sheets of paper tacked to the board underneath a sign that said FIRST VARSITY PRACTICE: THURSDAY, AUGUST 21. FIRST JV PRACTICE: TBA.

The sheet on the left said VARSITY. The sheet on the right said JV.

The list on the left was much shorter than the one on the right. Heart in his throat, Alex scanned it quickly. There were four names:

BILNEY, JAKE
ELLINGTON, JONAS
HARVEY, STEPHEN
MYERS, ALEX

Alex was almost hyperventilating by the time he got to his name—which had probably taken about five seconds. There it was, though—last, but that didn't matter. He wasn't at all surprised to see Jake Bilney on the list because Jake said last year's backup quarterbacks had graduated. Jonas was a lock—at least in Alex's mind—just as Alex had probably been a lock in Jonas's mind. Stephen Harvey was a linebacker—Alex wasn't even sure if he was a sophomore or a freshman—who had run a faster forty than any of the defensive backs, even though he was bigger than all of them. He made sense too.

There were twenty-seven names on the JV list—Alex counted—which meant that twenty of the fifty-one players who had tried out had been told not to even bother to come back when JV practice started.

Alex reached for his phone. He figured Jonas had already been there, but he wanted to be sure he knew. But before he could get the phone out, he felt a hand on his shoulder. He looked up and saw Coach Hillier standing there with a smile on his face.

"Congratulations," he said. "You're a Lion."

"Coach, thanks," Alex said, letting the phone slip back into his pocket. "I was about to come in and see you. . . ."

"Right. I told you to come in after the lists went up, didn't I?"

He looked around the hallway for a second and then waved a hand. "I'm the only one that's in today," he said and started walking. "Come on, let's go back to my office."

Coach Hillier pointed to a chair opposite his desk and said, "Have a seat. You want something to drink? Water? Coke? Gatorade?"

"Um, a Gatorade would be great."

"Care about flavor?"

"No. Anything's fine."

Coach Hillier disappeared for a moment, then came back carrying two Gatorades. He flipped one to Alex as he walked around the desk to sit down. He had been wearing a cap and sunglasses throughout the tryouts so this was the first time Alex was really seeing his face. He had what Alex's mom called "the look"—dirty blond hair that was just a little bit on the long side, blue eyes, and an easy smile.

"You did well the last two days," Coach Hillier said. Then he smiled. "That's kind of obvious, though, isn't it? Fifty-one kids try out and you're one of four who make varsity."

"I'm just glad I made the cut," Alex said. He liked Coach Hillier and didn't want to come off as cocky.

"There was no way to *not* put you on varsity," Coach Hillier said. "Not with the way you throw." He leaned forward in his chair. "Is your throwing motion natural? I mean, have you always thrown that way or have you gone to camps?"

"That's the way I've always thrown," Alex said.

"Good. If anyone ever says they want to change it, tell them no—this is the way you do it."

He paused. Alex was nodding, not sure if he was supposed to say anything.

Coach Hillier leaned back again.

When he spoke, he dropped his voice a little and the friendly smile was gone.

"Alex, you've got the best arm I've seen here in ten years," he said. "We've had three QBs who got D1 scholarships—one who may start at Pittsburgh this season. Matt Gordon is almost sure to make four. None of them has an arm like yours. Your throws look effortless; you move well. For a freshman, your footwork is terrific—though it'll get better. You can be a star."

"Thanks, Coach—"

Coach Hillier held up a hand. He wasn't finished.

"But not here. Not the next two years. Unless Matt Gordon gets hurt, you'll never see the field as a quarterback." He stopped, clearly considering his next words. "You ever repeat that to anyone, I'll deny saying it. I just think you deserve to know what's going on. I read the questionnaire you guys all filled out with your permission forms. I know you just moved here, so moving is probably out of the question right now. But you might be able to get a waiver to play at Woodlynn or Brookhaven or another Philly suburb. I know the coaches there and I'm almost certain you'd start right away for any one of them."

Alex was stunned, not sure what to say in response. The quarterbacks' coach at Chester Heights was telling him he could be the best QB the coach had ever seen at the school—but he shouldn't stay.

"What does that mean—a waiver?" he said.

"You could switch to another school nearby if you say you want to take a course that we don't offer here," Coach Hillier said. "Woodlynn has Latin—we don't. Brookhaven has AP History and AP English—we don't. Your grades are good. Latin would be an easier sell because you'd be taking it right away, but the other ones could work too."

Clearly, he'd been thinking about this. Alex had a dark thought, and before he knew it, he was voicing it.

"Coach, did Coach Gordon put you up to this?"

Coach Hillier almost came out of his chair. He shook his head and laughed.

"Are you kidding?" he asked. "First, he's not worried about you and whether you or Matt should be playing. Matt's *very* good—especially in this offense. And, for the record, he's a good kid too. He's worked really hard. He's probably put on twenty pounds of muscle in the weight room in the last year and he's going to be very tough to tackle.

"Second, when he looks at you, he sees plenty of talent. He also sees someone who can be good two years from now, when Matt's in college. And if, God forbid, Matt got hurt, you'd be a very good stand-in for him.

"Although, when practice starts, you're going to be third on the depth chart."

"Third?"

Coach Hillier nodded. "Jake Bilney's more experienced than you. He's a junior."

"I know, but . . ."

"But you're better than he is? Of course you are. Doesn't matter. Coach Gordon believes in seniority and, being honest, he probably doesn't want you getting too many reps in practice. As it is, people are going to notice the first time you throw the ball."

"But that isn't fair."

Alex was starting to get angry. Coach Hillier was very calm about all this. He didn't feel the least bit calm.

"You're right, it's not. That's why I called you in here. I think you deserve to know the situation. If you stay here, it's not going to be a fair fight. Your time will certainly come, though I suspect you don't want to wait two years.

"But you're up against a quarterback who may be all-state this season."

"And he's the coach's son."

"His pride and joy," Coach Hillier said.

There wasn't a hint of a smile when he said it.

After his talk with Coach Hillier, Alex decided it was time to call his dad. His mom wouldn't understand about depth charts, and not getting a chance to play, and the possibility of transferring in order to play more. In fact, she would be very much against that idea: change schools for football? No way.

He stopped at a McDonald's on the way home and ordered a hamburger and French fries. After finishing them, he punched in his father's direct dial number at work. He was actually a little surprised when his dad picked up right away.

"Did you make it?" his dad said.

"Who told you?" Alex asked.

"Your mom sent me a text this morning."

"I made it."

"I told her you would. No way would any coach cut you, Alex. You've got a great arm—always have. It's a good start for you down there. I know it hasn't been easy making the move."

It was the first time his father had acknowledged how tough it had been for Alex to leave his friends and his old school . . . and his father. Rather than go there, he dove into the story of the two Matthew Gordons, ending with Coach Hillier's suggestion he might want to transfer.

"How good is the Gordon kid?" his dad asked.

"I haven't seen him yet, Dad," Alex said, slightly exasperated because he thought he'd made that clear. "And anyway, it doesn't matter. He's starting, no matter what."

There was a pause. Alex thought his father was thinking. Then he heard another voice in the background.

"Dad, you still there?" Alex asked.

"Yes . . . sorry . . . Alex, I think this is a wait-and-watch thing right now. See how it goes when practice starts. Then let's talk again."

"You need to go, don't you?"

"I do. I'll . . . call you later."

Alex hung up the phone feeling no better—maybe slightly worse—about the situation.

■ ■ ■

The guy in the equipment cage wasn't a lot friendlier the next morning when Alex reported for the first varsity practice than he had been on the first day of tryouts.

The new kids had all been told to be there by nine o'clock so they could be properly fitted for pads, a helmet, a jersey, pants, and shoes. Everyone else had apparently already been through that drill, so they didn't have to arrive until nine-thirty. The entire team was due on the field at ten.

"Name," the equipment guy said, looking down at a list and not at Alex.

"Myers."

The guy didn't looked up, but Alex saw him put a check next to his name.

"What's your height and weight? Don't need it exact; they'll get that later. In the ballpark."

"I'm six one, 170," Alex said.

The guy finally looked up and Alex decided to seize the moment.

"It's Alex, by the way," he said, putting out his hand. He was, after all, a member of the varsity team now.

The guy shook his hand—reluctantly. "Quarterback, right?" he said.

Alex could see on the list that next to each name was a position.

"Right," he said. "What's your name?"

"Bill O'Connor," he said. "You can call me Mr. O. That's what all the kids call me."

"Nice to meet you, Mr. O."

If Mr. O thought it was nice to meet Alex, he didn't show it.

"What's your shoe size?" he asked.

"Ten," Alex said. "Ten wide."

Mr. O disappeared for a couple of minutes, then returned with all sorts of equipment. "If the shoes don't fit, bring 'em back and we'll try another pair," he said. The uniform was number 16. It wasn't 12—which Alex knew was taken—but it was an improvement from 23.

"Lockers are alphabetical by class," Mr. O said as he handed over the gear. "Freshmen are in the last row."

Alex thanked him and walked to the back of the locker room. Jonas was already there. The last "row" consisted of six lockers stuck behind the rest of the lockers. There were two other kids changing when Alex walked up carrying all his new clothing.

"Hey, QB," Jonas said, clearly glad to see him. "I think you met Steve Harvey at the tryouts."

Harvey looked up and nodded at Alex. "It's Stephen," he said, glancing coldly at Jonas. "No one calls me Steve."

"Sorry," Jonas said.

"No big," Stephen said.

"And this is Marty Lunt," Jonas said.

"Marty's fine," Lunt said, grinning in Harvey's direction as he and Alex shook hands. "So's Lunt or Hey you, for that matter."

Marty Lunt was a stocky kid, no more than five nine but probably close to two hundred pounds. Alex guessed he had to be a fullback or a center.

"I don't remember seeing you at tryouts," he said.

"I wasn't there," Marty said. "I'm a repeat ninth grader. I actually practiced with the varsity but didn't play last year. Coach and my dad decided I needed another year to put on some more weight so I could play center. I wanted to be a fullback, but my hands are brutal. I can snap a ball, but I can't hold on to one. Right, Stephen?"

The two apparently knew one another.

"You never held it when I hit you, that's for sure," Stephen said.

"When did you guys play against one another?" Alex asked.

"Stephen's a repeater too," Marty said. "We played against each other in practice last year. He had to go to tryouts because we have a lot of linebackers. We only have two centers right now, so I was all set."

Alex found the idea of repeating a year of high school for football interesting . . . in a bad way. He knew that "redshirting" was a common practice at the college level: players often sat out their freshman year to get bigger or to learn about the college game or to mature. If they didn't play at all, they still had four years of eligibility remaining. He hadn't realized anyone did the same thing—albeit under a different name—in high school.

"Are there a lot of repeaters on the team?" he asked.

"Maybe twenty to twenty-five guys across the four classes," Marty said. "From what I hear about you, Coach might want you to be a repeater. That way you'd have three years to play after Gordon graduates."

That thought set off alarm bells in Alex's head.

"What did you hear about me?"

"That you're really good," Marty replied. He nodded at Jonas. "Your boy here's been talking you up."

"He *is* good," Stephen Harvey said, surprising Alex. "I bet they do try to get him to repeat. It's not like he's going to play this year."

Alex started to say something but thought better of it. He needed to get dressed.

■ ■ ■

Mr. O had told Alex that he should try his pads on to make sure they fit but that the team wouldn't be practicing in pads until Monday. Alex was the last one among the freshmen dressed, but Jonas lingered after Marty and Stephen had headed out.

"You think any more about what Coach Hillier said?" he asked quietly as Alex was pulling off his pads after determining that they fit. Alex had called Jonas after talking to his dad and told him everything.

"Yeah," Alex said. "But I'm staying for now. I want to at least see how good Gordon is before I run away from competing with him. Plus, I went online and the changing to another school thing isn't all that easy."

Jonas nodded. "Yeah, I can see that. But will they *let* you compete? That's the question. I haven't seen Gordon yet, but he can't be better than you."

"Different than me," Alex said. "He's a runner, a bull. They were eleven and two last season. He must be pretty good."

They heard a voice from the front of what was now a crowded locker room. "Everyone on the field in five minutes."

Alex couldn't see which coach the voice was attached to, but everyone began surging in the direction of the door.

"Ready?" Alex asked.

"Born ready," Jonas said.

Alex laughed, picked up his helmet, and followed Jonas, ready—he hoped—for his first varsity practice.

■ ■ ■

He and Jonas had just made it outside into what was already a hot, sunny morning when Alex saw someone slowing in front of them. He was wearing, Alex noticed, number 12.

"Myers?" he said, turning to put out a hand as Alex and Jonas approached.

"Yeah," Alex said, trying to sound casual as he returned the handshake. "Alex."

"Matt Gordon," the other kid said. "I heard you just transferred in. Where'd you come from?"

They were still walking in the direction of the field as they talked.

"Boston," Alex said. "My parents split and my mom wanted to be closer to her family."

"Sorry," Gordon said.

He was bigger than Alex—a couple of inches taller and, as Coach Hillier had said, a good deal heavier. Even without pads on, he had broad shoulders and, in the short-sleeved jerseys they were all wearing, Alex could see his arms were cut.

"Stuff happens," Alex said. "At least we didn't move to Wyoming or something."

Gordon looked at him and smiled. He was about to say something else when a whistle blew.

"Better hustle," Matt said, breaking into a trot. "My dad takes no prisoners."

At the sound of the whistle everyone who had been walking started to trot, run, or in some cases, sprint. It took Alex and Matt Gordon about seven or eight seconds to get from the goal line—where they'd been when the whistle blew—to midfield. They dropped to one knee along with everyone else.

Coach Gordon stood with his hands on his hips, waiting until everyone was in position and quiet.

"There are eight of you who are new to varsity this year," Coach Gordon said.

For a moment, Alex thought he was going to ask each of them to stand and introduce himself to his new teammates. He was wrong.

"So all of you get one warning: when I say practice begins at ten o'clock, that means you are here, waiting for me and for your coaches, at ten o'clock. Not the other way around.

"The rest of you know that rule. I'm guessing about twenty of you were not here on a knee when I blew the whistle."

He looked directly at his son. "Gordon, you're the offensive captain of this team and you weren't here. Would you please tell the newcomers what happens to players who aren't on time for practice?"

Alex could see Matt Gordon visibly sag a little bit. "Steps, sir."

"How many reps?"

"Up and down five times. That's first offense. Second offense, we do it ten times and we do it at six o'clock the next morning. If it happens a third time—well then, we need to have a talk."

"Okay, all of you returning players who weren't here on a knee when the whistle blew, head for the steps. Gordon, Detwiler, you lead the way."

A tall, husky African American kid stood up and said, "Um, Coach, I was here."

"Are you the captain of the defense, Detwiler?"

"Yes sir."

"Were all the players you are supposed to lead here?"

"No sir."

"Then you can lead them to the steps."

"Yes sir."

"Let's go," Coach Gordon said. "We're wasting time."

Matt Gordon stood and, along with Detwiler, led about half the team in the direction of the stands on the far side of the field. Alex had read online that Lions Field seated about eight thousand fans. He estimated there were about thirty-five rows of seats leading to the top of the stadium. In this heat, up and down once would be no fun. Five times would be exhausting.

As Alex and the lucky group that didn't have to run watched, Alex heard Jonas, who had been just behind him in the circle around Coach Gordon, hissing in his ear.

"Your new best friend wasn't joking," he said.

"What?"

"Gordon said his dad didn't take any prisoners."

"You've got that right," Alex said, just as the whistle blew again.

■ ■ ■

The non-runners began to stretch under the supervision of the strength coach—who introduced himself as Coach Gentile—while the runners headed up and down the steps. Everyone stole looks as they stretched, and Alex could see the group slowing noticeably with each new trip back up.

He laughed as a thought crossed his mind: I could be the starter and transferring might *still* be a good idea.

Once the runners rejoined the group, they were given a little extra time to stretch and then everyone got a brief water break. It was very hot, but not as humid as it had been, and that provided a bit of relief.

Then they were all sent to work with their position coaches, going through drills like those from the first day of tryouts. Each drill lasted five minutes. The coaches called them periods. At the end of each period, a horn blew and everyone turned to their coach to find out what was next. Conditioning drills came first and were the same for everyone. Then each coach had position-specific drills for his group of players.

Alex watched Gordon closely. For all the talk about his ability as a runner, Gordon actually had a strong arm. But as the drills continued, Alex noticed it wasn't that *accurate* an arm. His shorter throws had plenty of zip but were occasionally a little high or a little wide. His longer throws also had plenty on them, and he had no trouble throwing the ball past midfield, but they rarely found their target. Each quarterback made ten long throws during the drills: Alex completed nine of his, Bilney four, Gordon one.

If Coach Hillier took note of this, he certainly didn't say anything. He was back in a cap and sunglasses, so it was impossible to detect any reaction to what they were doing. He kept up a steady stream of encouragement for everybody—as did the other coaches working around the field. Their chatter, along with players shouting the usual encouraging clichés, made for a steady stream of noise throughout the drills.

One thing that was apparent to Alex—and everyone else—was that Jonas was the best receiver in the group, even with all the upperclassmen there. It wasn't just his speed; it was his hands. On a couple of Gordon's off-target short throws, Jonas simply reached out with one hand and gathered the ball in. He almost never made it look hard. Gordon's only long-distance completion was to Jonas. It looked like Gordon had overthrown it, but Jonas found an extra gear and raced to the far side of the 50 and pulled the ball in.

Gordon turned to Bilney at that point and asked, "Where'd *that* kid come from?"

"Freshman," Bilney said. "Just moved from New York."

Gordon said nothing in return as Coach Hillier flipped the ball to Alex for his next throw. But as Jonas returned to the goal line, Alex heard Matt say, "Nice catch, dude. You made me look good."

One hour into his first practice Alex had one thing figured out: the younger Gordon was a much nicer person than the older one. He almost wished it was the other way around.

Friday, the second day of practice, ended with the entire team lined up across the goal line to run a hundred-yard dash. Alex couldn't see the point of the exercise—except maybe for those who would be returning kickoffs. For everyone else it was just an excuse to make them go all out in the torturous heat one more time.

"Anyone slows up or gives up will run some steps," Coach Gordon said. "You've all got the weekend off, so I expect you to give me everything you've got left." He almost seemed to smile. "First guy across the line is excused from next week's run."

Apparently, this was some kind of weekly ritual.

Alex found himself—coincidence?—between Matt Gordon and Jake Bilney. Glancing down the line, he could see that most guys had lined up by position. That was part of the ritual too, he guessed.

"Don't beat us too bad," Gordon said softly as they started to lean into a starting position.

"What makes you think I'm going to beat you?" Alex asked, although he expected to dust both of them.

"Gut feeling," Gordon said just as his father said, "Take your mark."

The whistle blew and they were off. Alex wasn't going to let up no matter how nice a guy Gordon seemed to be. As he reached midfield, he could feel himself tiring. He could also see out of the corner of his eye that he was near the lead, although someone—he was guessing it was Jonas—was several yards in front of everyone else.

By the time he reached the 10-yard line he was gasping and he could almost feel the pack closing in on him from behind. He put everything he had left into the last ten yards and crossed the goal line somewhere near the front. He was a little surprised when both Gordon and Bilney crossed not so very far behind him.

No one spoke for a few seconds because everyone was leaning over, trying to get their breath back. Alex noticed that one of the linemen was on the ground, holding his leg. One of the trainers was jogging over to him.

"Cramp, Lucas?" Coach Gordon said.

"Think so, Coach," Lucas answered in a pained voice as the trainer reached him and started to work on his right leg.

Alex noticed Jonas, a few yards away from him, standing up straight, looking like he could run another hundred without breathing hard.

"Ellington, you're excused from the hundred next week," Coach Gordon said.

He turned to Coach Raye, who coached the linebackers. "Jeb, who'd you have in the top five?"

Coach Raye had a clipboard in his hands and he glanced down at it. "Ellington, Washburn, Josephs, Myers, and Eisenberg."

Alex had finished fourth. Washburn was, like Jonas, a wide receiver, and Josephs was the starting tailback. He didn't know Eisenberg, which made him think he probably played defense—a cornerback, he guessed.

"Okay," Coach Gordon said. "Everyone take a knee right here.

"School starts Monday. As you older guys know, we want you taped and on the practice field by three-thirty. That gives you forty-five minutes from your last class, since you are all excused from last-period study hall or club meetings—*as long as you keep your grades up*—to get over here and get ready. If the trainers get behind taping and someone is late as a result, they'll let us know, but it usually isn't a problem. Seniors get taped first, then juniors, and so on.

"Monday and Tuesday you'll meet with your position coaches before we practice so we can give you playbooks and teach you the basic offense and defense. Older guys, there's a few wrinkles the staff worked on over the summer, so don't think you know it all.

"On Wednesday and Thursday we'll be in pads. We need to get the feel of being hit again, so be ready. On Friday we'll have a scrimmage under game conditions. The following week we get into our regular game-week routines, and two weeks from today we play our first game.

"Everyone got it?"

They all answered, "Yes sir."

"You gonna be ready?"

"Yes sir!"

"Any questions?"

None.

"Okay, then, let's get in. Captains . . ."

Matt Gordon and Detwiler—whose first name was Gerry, Alex had learned by looking at the depth chart on the locker room bulletin board—stood and walked to the front of the group. They put their arms up together and the rest of the team stood and formed a circle around them, everyone putting an arm in the air and leaning into the circle.

"State champs—on three," Gordon said.

He counted three and they all yelled, "State champs!"

With that, they all headed for the locker room. Next time he made this walk, Alex thought, the first day of school would be over. He wondered if the non-football-players would be any friendlier than the football players had been.

■ ■ ■

The answer, it turned out, was not so much.

Alex's mom insisted on driving him to school, even though he would have preferred to ride his bike.

"First day, you let me drop you off," she said. "After that, we'll see."

There was a first-day assembly scheduled for seven-thirty. Alex was out of the car and walking in the front door of the school—which he hadn't even seen yet since all the athletic facilities were located behind the main school building—by seven-fifteen. He wanted time to find his locker and to find Jonas, who was also planning to arrive a little early.

As he walked into the building, the first thing he saw was a giant banner that said WELCOME TO THE LIONS' DEN!

Not the most encouraging welcome, really, but he was now, he guessed, a Lion. He started down a hallway, glancing at the locker number and combination that had been sent to his house with all the other registration stuff. But the locker numbers here were nowhere near what he needed. He saw a tall, dark-haired girl walking in his direction. She was wearing a bright white button on her shirt that said ALLY BELYARD—SENIOR CLASS COUNCIL.

Okay, Alex thought, she should know her way around.

"Excuse me," he said. "Can you tell me where the freshman lockers are?"

Ally Belyard, senior class council, barely slowed. "Third floor—at the end. Take the steps and turn right."

Then she was gone before Alex could ask where the steps were. But he kept walking and, sure enough, there were steps about halfway down the hallway. He went up two flights, turned right, and saw a gaggle of kids standing in front of lockers— many of them trying out their locks to be sure they worked.

One of those working a combination was Jonas.

"How long have you been here?" Alex asked as he walked up.

"About a minute," Jonas said. "Took me three tries to get someone to tell me how to find this place."

Alex laughed. Turns out Ally Belyard actually *was* helpful.

"Where do you think 194 is?" he asked, looking again at the paper in his hand.

"Can't be far, I'm 182. . . ." Jonas twisted the lock one more time and pulled on the handle. The locker swung open and he smiled in triumph.

He took a couple of notebooks from his backpack and put them in the locker. "Come on, I'll help you find yours and then we can go figure out where the auditorium is."

"I'm sure," Alex said, "there will be dozens of people willing to help."

■ ■ ■

It turned out they didn't need any help. They just followed the crowds back down the steps to the first floor. Most of the classrooms were on the second, third, and fourth floors. There were labs in the basement. The auditorium took up a large chunk of the first floor—not surprising since, at least on this morning, it had to accommodate almost two thousand kids, plus faculty and staff.

Alex and Jonas found places near the back, at the end of a row, which made Alex happy because he had Jonas on his right and an aisle on his left.

At exactly seven-thirty, a bell rang and a balding, middle-aged man walked onstage to a small podium with a microphone.

"Returning students of Chester Heights—welcome back!" he said, drawing a response of cheers, hoots, and a few scattered boos that sounded fairly good-natured to Alex.

The man smiled and put his hands out for quiet as if the applause had been too loud to be believed. "New students of Chester Heights—welcome!"

More of the same—probably, Alex guessed, from the same kids.

"For those of you who are new, I'm Joseph A. White, your principal. This is my twelfth year at Chester Heights and I can honestly say I believe it will be our best year *ever!*"

"Why would he think that?" Jonas whispered. "Because we're here?"

"That's gotta be it," Alex said.

Mr. White droned on for a while about how wonderful the teachers were, how proud he was of the seniors who had graduated the previous spring, and how everyone should make sure their parents made it to Back to School Night. Alex felt a twinge at the mention of parents, plural, but then remembered that his father had been working on Back to School Night the last two years anyway. . . .

"Those of you who are old, help those of you who are new," Mr. White said as clearly bored students began to whisper to one another. "All of you new kids, freshmen or otherwise, don't hesitate to ask questions. Everyone is here to help."

About four people among two thousand clapped.

"And *now*," Mr. White said, apparently coming to the best part of his speech, "I want to introduce to you the man all of us here at Chester Heights High look to for leadership, the man who is going to lead us to another league championship *and* to the state championship this year, our very own, COACH GORDON!"

Alex suspected that Gordon was one of those coaches who actually believed his first name was Coach. Now, as he watched *Coach* Gordon make his way to the podium, smiling and waving like a politician, he was convinced of it. The room was filled with cheers, and the coach put his palms down for quiet.

"Welcome back, Lions!" he said, causing some of the students to growl like lions.

Again he held up his hands for quiet.

"Last year, as you all know, we *did* win our fourth league title in six years!"

More growling and a lot of cheering.

"This year, that will *not* be enough. This year we *will* get that state championship! I've only seen the team practice for two days, but I can tell you we have the makings of greatness! This is going to be a team you can all be proud of!"

"He's not nearly this enthusiastic when he talks to his players, is he?" Jonas said as more cheers washed over the coach.

"Now, as most of you already know, we open our season a week from Friday, right here at home at seven o'clock against Mercer Academy. This will be a major challenge for the Lions! Which is why we need all of you at the pep rally and at the game!"

This time it was Alex's turn to whisper to Jonas. "This *isn't a* pep rally?" he said, causing Jonas to laugh.

"Does everyone hear me?" Coach Gordon asked.

"YES!" came the answer.

"Can I get a roar?"

"ROAAAAAR!"

He put a fist into the air and walked off the podium to a standing ovation from many of the students.

"Get to your classes as quickly as you can," Mr. White said, coming back to the microphone. "No one gets marked late today. Let's have a great year!"

Roar, thought Alex.

6

Alex managed to get through the first day of classes pretty much unscathed. The halls were crowded, but the rooms were marked clearly, and when he did make a wrong turn, someone eventually pointed him in the right direction.

The only thing that made it difficult was the sheer size of the place. His middle school in Billerica had had three grades and about a thousand students. Chester Heights had twice as many students, was at least twice as big, and had kids in all different shapes and sizes. He had been one of the big kids at Billerica Middle School. Now he was a lowly freshman, and despite his height, he felt like an ant dotting the massive hallways as he moved from class to class.

He had what he figured were the standard freshman classes: Algebra, Geology—better known as Earth Science— American History, English 1, and French, which he had opted for over Spanish back in middle school. His mom spoke good

French and wanted her children to do the same, even though his father pointed out that both Spanish and Chinese would probably be more valuable to them long-term.

"It can't possibly be a bad thing to know how to speak French," his mom had said.

That was the end of the argument. Most arguments between his parents ended that way—at least in Alex's memory: Mom won and Dad threw up his hands and said, "Yes, dear."

And so Alex trudged into his last class of the day in room 407, wondering just how much French the other kids in the class spoke. The teacher was—according to the PowerPoint presentation she began the class with—Mademoiselle Schiff. The PowerPoint was fairly typical: there would be a vocabulary quiz every Friday, written assignments most nights, and a book to be read—in French—by the end of the year. It was the final line on the screen that terrified Alex the most: "These are the last words you will read in English in this class."

"*D'accord?*" Mademoiselle Schiff said when the lights came back on.

That much, Alex understood. Mademoiselle Schiff was easily the youngest teacher he had encountered all day— Alex guessed she was no more than twenty-five. She was petite and blond and, Alex saw pretty quickly, no-nonsense.

In French, she asked each student to introduce themselves to their classmates. Alex managed to get through "*Je m'appelle Alex Meyers*" without incident. In fact, Mademoiselle Schiff said, as he sat down, "*Monsieur Myers, votre accent est très bien.*"

Alex had been told he had a good accent before. It was his vocabulary that he was worried about.

He was glancing at the clock, wondering why it was moving so slowly, when the final student stood up to introduce herself. As soon as she did, Alex forgot about the clock.

"*Je m'appelle Christine Whitford*," she said in an accent that, even in a few words, Alex could tell was better than his. But it was not her accent that got his attention.

She was about five six, he guessed, and she had long jet-black hair. He could see her eyes sparkling from across the room, and when she smiled in response to being complimented on her accent, Alex was convinced that the entire room got brighter. He had to meet Christine Whitford—if only to see if she was half as pretty up close.

When the bell sounded, Alex was out of his seat quickly. He gathered his books, stuck them in his backpack, and then timed his exit so that he would be a half step behind Christine Whitford.

"*Votre accent est superbe!*" he said, pulling up alongside her in the hallway.

She gave him a sideways glance and the hint of a smile.

"Do you try to talk to all the girls in French?" she asked.

"Only the ones that speak French," he said.

"You heard me speak three words," she said.

"But you spoke them *so* well," he said. "The teacher even said so."

She shook her head and laughed.

"Let me guess," she said. "You play football."

That brought him up short. "Why do you say that?" he said.

"Only a football player would just walk up to a girl and be so obvious," she said.

"Obvious?" Alex said. He thought he'd been doing pretty well. . . .

They were walking through the crowded hallway, slowing for people in front of them. Walking next to her, Alex realized that Christine wasn't as tall as he had thought. She was probably closer to five four than five six, but man was she cute. Now she pushed her hair back from her shoulders and smiled her mesmerizing smile.

"I'm right, aren't I?" she said. "At the very least you're some kind of a jock. I'm guessing football."

"Well," he said, trying to sound modest as he bragged, "I'm on my way to practice right now, if you want to know the truth."

If she was impressed, she didn't show it. "Well, that explains it, then."

"Explains what?"

"You're a freshman, you made the varsity football team, you think you're God's gift."

Wow, she was tough.

"How do you know I'm a freshman?"

"*Everyone* in that French class is a freshman," she said. "Unless you flunked French One last year and you're a sophomore."

"I didn't flunk anything," he said defensively as she grinned.

They had reached the end of the hallway and someone was calling her name. Alex was relieved to see it was another girl.

"You better go," she said. "You don't want to be late for practice."

Alex didn't have a comeback for that. Christine's friend walked up, didn't so much as glance at Alex, and said, "Come on. Meeting starts in five minutes. Let's go."

"Meeting?" Alex said, not wanting her practice crack to be the end of the conversation.

"School newspaper," Christine said. "If you aren't a varsity athlete, last period is for study hall or student clubs and activities."

She smiled and her eyes sparkled again. "Maybe if you ever get to play, I'll write something about you."

Okay, he figured, *now* who was flirting? He decided not to repeat that thought—he didn't want to come across as a cocky football player—but still he couldn't resist a comeback.

"Maybe you will," he said. "*If* I decide to let you interview me."

Her friend was tugging on her arm, but she clearly didn't want to let him have the last word either.

"What position do you play?" she asked.

"Quarterback," he said.

She laughed. "Quarterback? In that case, I guess I won't be talking to you at *all*. Unless I do a story on what it's like to sit on the bench all season."

The look on Alex's face must have given him away completely, because her gotcha grin faded. "Don't feel bad," she said. "You're a freshman. Matt Gordon won't be here forever."

She and her friend turned and walked down the hall.

For a split second, Alex felt lost. Apparently, everyone in this school knew who Matt Gordon was and that he was *the* quarterback on the football team.

He watched Christine Whitford disappear into the crowds and the hallway got noticeably darker. . . .

■ ■ ■

When Alex walked into the locker room a few minutes later, it was already packed. The soccer team also used the locker room and this was the first day of soccer tryouts. Alex considered himself lucky to have an assigned locker, even if it was buried in the back of the room.

Jonas was already in his practice gear—everything but shoes and socks, since he still had to have his ankles taped—when Alex came around the corner.

"I was getting worried about you," he said, looking up. "You get lost or something?"

Alex shook his head. "No," he said. "I was trying to talk to a girl."

That got Jonas's attention. "Really?" he said. "How'd that go?"

Alex put his hands together as if he were gripping a baseball bat and made a swinging motion. "I whiffed," he said, even though he wasn't completely sure that was true.

"Really?" Jonas said again. "First day of school and you asked a girl on a date? You're a lot braver than me."

"Nah, I'm not *that* brave. I was just trying to talk to her."

"So how do you know you struck out?"

Alex shrugged. "I could just tell."

Jonas gave him a look. "Did she just walk away from you or did she talk to you?"

"She talked to me. She said she could tell by the way I came up to her that I was a football player."

Jonas laughed. "Dude, you didn't strike out. You just didn't get up to bat yet."

Someone was bellowing at the front of the room. "All football players, check the depth chart on the wall by the door on your way out. Know which group you are with— ones, twos, or threes—before you hit the field."

Alex knew that ones were first-stringers, twos were second-stringers, and threes were third-stringers. Coach Hillier had said he'd be a three—behind Gordon and Bilney— but he harbored a small hope that he had shown enough the first couple days of practice to find himself second when he looked at the chart.

"I already looked," Jonas said, apparently reading his mind. "You're third."

Alex opened his locker, hoping to make it harder for Jonas to read his disappointment.

"What about you?" he asked.

"Second at both wide receiver spots," he said. "The starters are both seniors. I get it. I'm not worried."

Alex knew he didn't need to worry. He'd thrown to all the receivers the previous week, and while the two seniors in question were both good, they couldn't come close to matching Jonas's speed or his hands. His hands were what set Jonas apart.

Jonas would play from the first game and he would play a lot because the coaches would understand he gave them a better chance to win. The same wouldn't be true, he knew, at the quarterback position.

"You better hustle and get dressed," Jonas said. "They're taping the sophomores now."

Dress now, sulk later, Alex told himself.

■ ■ ■

Being the third-string quarterback wasn't too bad for Alex. During drills, he got as many reps as Gordon and Bilney. Practice was more intense than what he was used to from middle school. There were more coaches and everything was scripted: there was no fooling around going from one drill to the next. Even water breaks were managed closely: two minutes and they were done. No lingering.

Even so, it was football practice and Alex felt at home. It was a good way to end an awkward first day at a new school.

Day two was easier—or at least practice seemed to come sooner. Matt Gordon continued to be both friendly and encouraging. At one point, when Alex hit Jonas perfectly in stride on a deep fly pattern, he patted Alex on the shoulder and said, "Great throw, Goldie."

Alex looked at him and said, "Goldie?"

Gordon grinned. "Yeah," he said. "Goldie with the golden arm."

It was tough not to like Gordon. He was clearly the team's leader, and there was no doubt that the respect the other players had for him came from his ability and his personality and had nothing to do with the fact that he was the coach's son. If anything, everyone liked him despite the fact that he was the coach's son.

Alex's comfort level took a nosedive when the team began scrimmaging. By his count, the team ran fifty plays during the last hour of Tuesday's practice. The ones got about thirty plays, the twos around fifteen. Alex didn't know the exact number. He did know the exact number of snaps he took: five. On three of them he was told to hand the ball off.

On one, Alex took the snap and started to run right. The slotback came from the right side of the formation, and Alex faked a handoff to him as he ran by. Keeping the ball on his hip, Alex got around the corner and ran about ten yards before pulling up.

Quarterbacks weren't tackled during scrimmages so no one really bothered to chase him down.

"Good job," Coach Hillier, who was calling the plays, said as Alex jogged back to the huddle. "Okay, let's end on a high note: X left, Z right, and go."

He looked at Alex. "You got that?" he asked.

Alex nodded. He'd taken his playbook home to study and they had spent time before practice going over the basic plays. The two wide receivers were designated as X and Z. In this case, they were Tim Cummings and Freddy Watts, the third-stringers at those positions. "Go" simply meant that both would run deep and Alex would try to hit one of them. In a game, the slotback would be the "check-down" receiver, meaning if no one could get open deep, the quarterback would look for him over the middle on a short route. In a scrimmage, Alex would throw the ball deep, no matter what—especially since this was his one chance to show the whole team what he could do.

What was apparent, as Alex dropped back, was that the

defensive coaches hadn't expected Coach Hillier to call a go route for the third-team quarterback. The defensive backs were pinched in, clearly expecting another running play or perhaps a short pass. Both Cummings and Watts blew past the defenders and all Alex had to do was decide which one of them to throw to.

He finally decided on Watts—who was on the left— because throwing to the left, as a right-handed quarterback, was a little bit easier for him. The ball was in the air for more than fifty yards before it floated down into Watts's waiting arms. The throw felt perfect coming out of Alex's hand and he could almost hear a collective "Ooh" come from the ones and twos, who were assembled on the sidelines watching the last play of the afternoon.

Watts gathered the ball in and ran into the end zone, holding it in the air as if he had just scored a key touchdown.

"Nice throw," Alex heard Coach Hillier say behind him.

Jonas jogged from the sideline to give him a high five. So did Matt Gordon.

"Good job, Goldie," he said, just as a sharp whistle cut through the air.

It was Coach Gordon, standing at midfield. They circled him and took a knee. Coach Gordon looked at Watts, who had been accepting high fives of his own as he came back up the field.

"Eighty-four," he said, calling Watts by his number. "You ever hear of Bear Bryant?"

It took Watts a second to realize the coach was talking to him. Someone nudged him, but it was too late.

"Eighty-four, are you listening?" Coach Gordon said. "I asked you if you knew who Bear Bryant was."

Watts shook his head. "No sir."

"Well, you better Google him tonight and be able to answer the question tomorrow. Bear Bryant once said, 'When you get into the end zone, act like you've been there before.'

"We don't celebrate touchdowns here, eighty-four. We *expect* them. So, since all of you offensive players think a completed pass by the *third* string *against* the *third* string is such a big deal, you can all run those steps a couple of times. Just in case you forget the next time."

He turned to his son. "Gordon, get 'em going."

Matt Gordon was on his feet. "Let's go, offense," he said, sounding just a little weary. They'd been on the practice field for just under two hours. Everyone was craving a shower. But that would have to wait. As they jogged to the steps, Bilney fell in next to Alex.

"Damn you, Goldie," he said, sounding serious. "If you weren't so good, we'd be in the locker room by now."

Alex didn't really hear him because Coach Gordon was still talking behind them.

"Good job today, defense—except for you threes. See you tomorrow."

And then he added one more thing. "Coach Hillier, a word."

As they started up the steps, Alex couldn't resist a glance over his shoulder. Coach Gordon was talking to Coach Hillier. He did not appear to be congratulating him on calling a good play.

Alex figured Coach Gordon had called Coach Hillier over as the offense went to run the steps because he hadn't liked the last play call of the day. Jonas thought he was being paranoid.

"Nah, that wasn't it," he said as they walked out of the locker room. "It was about something else. He was mad at Watts for showboating."

"That's why we ran," Alex said. "It's not why he was getting on Coach Hillier."

"You need to chill," Jonas said. "It was one play. Good throw, but just one play."

"You know what they say about being paranoid?" Alex said.

"What's that?"

"You aren't paranoid if someone's out to get you."

Jonas laughed. "Alex, no one *needs* to get you. Fair or not, you're the third-string quarterback."

He was right. And that was considerably more upsetting than whether or not he was paranoid.

■ ■ ■

School began to get old for Alex pretty quickly. Homework started after the second day of classes, which meant his mom started her usual role as enforcer. He had to get it done before he could do anything else.

His dad called on Tuesday night just as Alex was finishing his reading for history.

"You're two days in. What do you think?" his dad said as a conversation starter.

"Dad, football started last week," Alex said.

"I know, Alex," his dad said. "I was talking about school."

Alex felt a slight wave of resentment. For years, his dad had driven him to practice whenever possible. He rarely missed one of his games and, much to Alex's relief, had never been one of those parents who yelled at him or at his coach or at referees or umpires. After games, they would talk through what he had done well and what he had to work on, and he knew how proud his father was of his successes.

Now he felt like he had slipped out of sight, out of mind. Alex had called his father almost a week earlier to tell him about his frustrations. This was the first time he'd called back.

"Well, Coach Hillier was telling the truth," Alex said. "I'm third-string, so I'm not getting too many reps when we scrimmage."

"And the starter is the coach's son, I know," his dad said. "That's going to be a tough one. For now, though, you've just got to stick with it. I've talked to your mom and we agree that transferring isn't the answer. Your time will come."

Alex knew his parents talked about how he and Molly were doing on a regular basis, so he wasn't surprised the transfer issue had come up. Still, maybe it was the phone or maybe he was being paranoid—again—but his father sounded almost disconnected. Alex changed the subject.

"When are you coming to see us?" he said.

"I'm hoping to make it down for your first game next week."

"Well, that would be great. But be prepared to watch me watch the game."

"Doesn't matter. I'm coming to see you and Molly, not a football game."

That made Alex feel a little better.

"We miss you, Dad," he said softly.

"I miss you guys too," his dad said.

■ ■ ■

Although Coach Hillier didn't say anything to him, Alex's suspicions about the last play call on Tuesday were pretty much confirmed over the next few days. The scrimmages were all the same. The ones got about sixty percent of the snaps, the twos about thirty percent, and the last few plays were for the threes.

The play calls for the third offense were about as conservative as possible: a couple of straight handoffs, a counter to the left slot, a counter to the right slot, and then—maybe—a quick pass over the middle, or some version of a screen. Alex could have been half-asleep and done what was needed on those plays.

On Wednesday, when Coach Hillier had called "X slant right"—a quick toss over the middle to Freddy Watts—Alex had said, "Coach, how about if we try loop 99," a very deep curl pattern that he knew he could convert a lot more easily than either Gordon or Bilney.

Coach Hillier didn't even look at him. He just said, "On two," indicating the snap count for the play he had already called.

So on Thursday, when Coach Hillier lined them up for the last play of the day and called "Z slant left"—basically the same play they had run the day before, only with the other receiver coming from the left side instead of the right—Alex decided he'd had enough.

As they broke the huddle, he walked a couple steps out of his way so he could get into Jonas's ear. Jonas was in with the threes because Watts had rolled an ankle during drills and the threes were a man short.

"Run loop 99," he whispered.

Jonas glanced back at him as if he were crazy. "What?" he said.

"Just do it!" Alex hissed.

Coach Gutekunst, the defensive coordinator, was shouting at them. "Hey, fellas, how 'bout it? We'd like to get done here before dark."

Alex jogged to the line, then stepped back into the shotgun formation that the Lions used about half the time. He called three numbers. They were meaningless—all that mattered was that on the third number the ball was snapped to him.

He dropped back and saw Tim Cummings—the Z receiver—make a sharp cut about eight yards behind the line of scrimmage and then come open. He ignored him. Because his blockers had been expecting a short, quick pass, they had let up on their blocks early and Alex had to roll to his right to avoid a couple of rushers—who appeared to be surprised that he still had the ball.

Jonas was a true friend. He had to know that running loop 99 was going to get them both in trouble, but he was doing it anyway. He sprinted about thirty-five yards down the field, then looped back to the middle, coming back a couple of yards to meet the pass. Alex had pulled up and fired a bullet that stayed straight as a string until Jonas gathered it in. Jonas took a couple more steps and then rolled on the ground before popping up as whistles sounded all over the field.

Alex was still admiring his work when he heard Coach Hillier's voice in his ear.

"What the hell was that, Myers?" he demanded angrily. "What do you think you're trying to prove? You run what I call—do you understand?"

He was right in Alex's face, his nose almost brushing against Alex's face mask.

"Do you hear me?" he repeated.

"Yes sir," Alex said, deciding this wasn't the time or place to argue. As he finished his two-word answer, he heard Coach Gordon's voice cutting through the late-afternoon humidity.

"Coach Hillier, did you call loop 99 on that play?" Coach Gordon was standing twenty yards away, hands on hips.

Coach Hillier looked at Alex for a moment, then back at his boss.

"Yes sir, I did," he said. "I wanted to see Ellington run the route."

Coach Gordon's hands were still on his hips, as if he were deciding whether to question Coach Hillier's honesty. He turned away, blew his whistle again, and said, "Everybody take a knee."

Alex was about to thank Coach Hillier for covering for him, when Coach Hillier put his arm around him.

"You *ever* do that again, you won't see a practice field for a week—if ever," he said into his ear so it looked to everyone else as if he were giving him a coaching tip. "I didn't do that for you; I did that so the entire offense wouldn't have to run. They don't deserve to be punished because you and your buddy are trying to show off."

"It wasn't Jonas's fault."

"He went along with it. He runs the play I called and there's no problem. I want the two of you in my office at six tomorrow morning."

"Six? But, Coach—"

"One more word and it's five-thirty," Coach Hillier said. "My daughter's a swimmer. I'm up at four-thirty every day, so just try me if you think I'm kidding."

"It's not fair to Jonas," Alex said, not ready to give up, even though Coach Gordon had started to talk.

"You're right," Coach Hillier said. "He can come at six. You be there at five-forty-five."

With that, he turned and walked away.

■ ■ ■

Linda Myers wasn't the least bit pleased when her son informed her he had to be at school at five-forty-five the next morning. She was even less happy when he told her why.

"Look, Alex, I know you're frustrated with this Coach . . ."

"Gordon," Alex said.

"Right, Gordon. I know he's been difficult and I know this thing with his son is a problem."

"His son's not the problem. He's a nice guy."

"Alex! Let me make my point. You said you *like* Coach Hillier. So why would you ignore his instructions? He's absolutely right. You can ride your bike to school in the morning. I shouldn't have to get up at five because you let your ego get in the way of common sense."

She turned and walked out of the room. Alex sighed. That was his mom: all common sense, with zero knowledge or understanding of any sport. He thought for a moment about what his dad might say—not that it mattered, since he wasn't here. He figured his dad would understand why Alex had done it, but he'd tell him it wasn't a very good idea and he shouldn't do it again.

Thinking about that, he laughed. "What are they going to do?" he said aloud. "Make me third-string?"

■ ■ ■

He was out the door and on his bike by five-twenty-five and pulled into the virtually empty back lot of the school by five-forty. As he locked his bike, he saw Coach Hillier come out the back door with a cup of coffee in his hand. Apparently, they'd be heading for the steps before Jonas arrived.

"Come on inside, Myers," Coach Hillier said, waving at him with his free hand.

Or not.

Alex followed the coach through the locker room door and then up the steps and down the hallway to where the football offices were. No one else was around this early. Coach Hillier walked into his office and waved Alex to a seat.

"You drink coffee yet?" he asked.

Alex shook his head. "No."

"Good."

He had a file open in front of him on his desk.

"I guess you've had a tough few months," he said, tapping the file. "Parents split, you move away from all your friends, start in a new school, and the one thing you're really good at, you're stymied because the coach's son happens to start at your position."

Alex knew that his reason for moving to Philadelphia couldn't be in his file. Then again, he hadn't hidden it from anyone, so it wouldn't be hard for Coach Hillier to find out about it. He smiled, glad to have a sympathetic ear.

"It's been kind of rough," he said. "I'm sorry about yesterday. I just wanted to show people what I could do."

"I know," Coach Hillier said. "Trust me, people around here know you're talented. But you can't pull stuff like that. I can't even make a case for you moving up to second team if the other coaches think you're some kind of troublemaker."

"I understand, Coach. You're right. I just feel bad I got Jonas in trouble. He shouldn't have to be here so early to run."

Coach Hillier nodded. "Yeah. He made a mistake, but it

says a lot about him that he stuck with you even though he knew it almost certainly meant trouble for him." He sat back in his chair and sipped his coffee. "So I told him to stay home and sleep."

He looked at the coffee cup. "This is cold," he said. "Let me get a hot cup and then we'll go outside and run."

For a moment Alex had thought he might get a reprieve. Coach Hillier seemed to read his mind. "I'm glad you know you made a mistake," he said. "But I can't let you off the hook. Put on some shorts and a T-shirt. I'll meet you outside in five minutes."

Alex understood. "Yes sir," he said.

He got changed and headed out. The sun was up, but it would still be cool outside—that was about the only good thing about running at six a.m.

As he pushed open the door, he almost hit someone who was apparently about to pull it open.

"Sorry," he said, stepping back.

"You better be sorry." The door swung open and there, with a Starbucks cup in his hand, stood Coach Gordon.

8

"Well, well, if it isn't Chester Heights' number-one show-off," Coach Gordon said when he saw Alex. "Off to run, I hope? Where's Coach Hillier?"

"He went to get more coffee," Alex said.

"You owe him an apology," Coach Gordon said. "Don't think for a second I don't know you did that on your own."

It occurred to Alex that apologizing to Coach Gordon might be a good idea—if only to make life a little easier for Coach Hillier. But he couldn't bring himself to do it. What's more, he decided, it almost certainly wouldn't make any difference.

"Well, enjoy your run. Knowing Coach Hillier, he'll let you off easy—three or four circuits. If it were me, it would be more like ten."

Alex had a number of responses for that, but he held his tongue.

"Yes sir," he said.

Coach Gordon looked him up and down for a moment. "Myers, how tall are you?" he asked.

"About six one."

"Are you fourteen or fifteen? Did you hold back a year?"

"No sir. I'm fourteen."

Coach Gordon considered that for a moment.

"Well, you might want to give some thought to doing that. Lot of kids do it now, you know. Gives them another year to grow. And, in your case, you'd have three years to play once Matt graduates, instead of two."

"I don't think my parents would like that idea," Alex said. "Being honest, neither do I."

Coach Gordon shrugged. "Your mistake to make," he said.

He pushed past Alex and headed for his office. Alex wondered if all successful football coaches were complete jerks. Then he turned and walked toward the field as the sun continued to climb into the eastern sky.

■ ■ ■

Alex didn't really mind the running. The hard part of the punishment had been getting out of bed before sunup. Once he was finished, he felt good. His father had told him once that athletes—regardless of their ability—always felt better after a workout because of something called endorphins, which were some kind of enzyme released in your body that energized you.

He felt energized after his fifth lap up and down the steps.

"Problem with you, Myers, is you're too young and too strong to know this should hurt," Coach Hillier said. "Next time I'll put you on the clock and demand a certain time from you each trip up and down."

"Won't . . . be . . . a . . . next . . . time," Alex said between breaths.

"Good."

Coach Hillier put a hand on his shoulder. "Look, Alex, I know you've got plenty of talent and loads of potential. Believe it or not, Coach Gordon knows it too. He's just not going to tell you that anytime soon."

"Why not?"

"It's not his way."

Alex took a long gulp of air.

"He just asked me coming out of the locker room if I'd consider staying back a year so I can have three years of eligibility after Matt graduates."

"What'd you tell him?"

Alex gulped air one more time. The sun was up by now, and even though it wasn't hot yet, it felt warm after his stair climbing.

"I told him I didn't like the idea and I didn't think my parents would like it either. I'm a good student. Why would I want to go to high school for an extra year?"

"It might increase your chances to get a college scholarship."

"Do you think I'll need an extra year to have a chance to get a scholarship?"

"It's hard to tell. You're just a freshman."

Alex's breathing was back to normal now.

He smiled at Coach Hillier.

"Well," he said. "I think I'll be okay."

This time, it was Coach Hillier's turn to smile.

"Christine was right about you."

That got Alex's attention. "Christine?" he said. "As in Christine Whitford?"

"Mm-hmm."

"What did she say? When did you talk to her?"

"At our first meeting for the school paper. She introduced herself after the meeting and asked if I would read some of the stories she'd written while she was at Whitman."

"Whitman?"

"That's the middle school a lot of the kids here went to last year. I had mentioned when I introduced myself to the new kids that I was one of the football team coaches. She said, 'I met one of your new players today.'"

"She did? Did she say anything about me?"

Alex wondered if the burning in his cheeks as he waited for the answer had anything to do with his workout. He suspected not.

"She said you were extremely confident."

"Did she say it like that was a good thing?" Alex said, knowing he was being reeled in but unable to resist.

"Not really . . ." Coach Hillier turned to walk away. "See you at practice. Run the plays I call."

He left Alex standing there knowing that the burning in his cheeks had *nothing* to do with the workout.

■ ■ ■

Alex ran all the plays as they were called for the next several days in practice. There weren't many and none of them called for him to throw deep. Every once in a while as he stepped into the huddle and called another short pass, Coach Hillier would give him a look as if to say, *Stay cool and do what you're told.*

He did as he was told. The more he watched both Gordon and Bilney, the more upset he became that he wasn't getting the chance to show what he could do. The funny thing was he liked both Gordon and Bilney—especially Gordon. It would have been easier if they acted like jerks, because then he could *really* get mad. But neither one was like that. In fact, one afternoon after Gordon had taken about half his reps, he turned to Coach Hillier and said, "Coach, why don't you give Alex a few of my reps? I'm a little bit sore."

"Sore from what?" Coach Hillier said quietly. "Are you hurt, Matt? Do you need to see the trainers?"

"No, but I just thought . . ."

"Let your coaches think, Matt. You just play."

Alex wasn't exactly sure what to think about Coach Hillier. At times he would stand behind him after a play and offer words of encouragement or suggestions. On occasion he would step in to show him how he could run a play better. He quietly suggested that he slide his thumb slightly upward so he would have more control of the ball, and Alex was amazed at the difference such a subtle change could make. His throws instantly had a tighter spiral and seemed to get where they needed to get with just a tad more zip on them.

Then there were moments when Alex knew he'd made a good play, made an adjustment during the play that the other quarterbacks couldn't make, and he would be greeted with silence. It was almost as if it were okay for Coach Hillier to encourage him—but only up to a point.

As they walked off the practice field, Alex thanked Gordon but it was Bilney who responded.

"He did it because you need extra reps, Goldie," he said. "If we struggle on offense and I come in, I'm Matt lite—same type of player, just not as talented. You come in, our offense is entirely different."

Alex looked at Matt. "That true?" he asked.

Matt, who hadn't broken stride, shrugged. "Jake knows his football," he said. He put a hand on Alex's shoulder. "I also like you."

"Can we break up the lovefest?" Jake said. "Go in there and be a star one night, Goldie, and *then* see how much Matt likes you."

"I'd still like him—in fact, if he wins a game for us, I'll flat-out *love* him," Matt said. "But he's not taking my job. Not yet anyway."

They were coming up on the locker room door. Jake smiled.

"If my last name was Gordon, I could say that too," he said.

"If you were any good, you could say that," Matt said. He was smiling, but for the first time since he had met him Alex heard a little bit of an edge in Matt Gordon's tone.

"Yeah, that too," Jake said, and the tension broke. They all laughed and Alex pulled the door open.

■ ■ ■

The only thing more frustrating than football practice was French class. Alex had no chance to even try to sit close to Christine Whitford because she seemed to arrive every day with an entourage of four or five girls who would all sit together. One day he beat her to the door and pretended to be reaching into his backpack for something in the hallway. When she walked out the door, he looked up as if surprised to see her.

"Hey, I hear my coach is your editor," he said, reaching for an opening.

"*Your* coach?" she said with a smile, not slowing her walk down the crowded hallway. "Doesn't he coach everyone on the offense? Or is he personally assigned to you?"

Alex had managed to fall into step with her.

"He coaches all the quarterbacks," he said, trying to sound as casual as possible.

"So he coaches Matt Gordon, Jake Bilney, and you."

She clearly knew something about football.

"You follow the team closely?" he asked.

"I'm going to be one of the people covering the team, so I've been studying the depth chart." She glanced at him. "I'd come and watch practice, but Coach Gordon won't let anyone watch. He seems to think closing practice makes him more important."

"Yeah, well, that's the way he is," Alex said.

"You don't like him?" she said.

Uh-oh. If she was asking him on behalf of the *Weekly Roar*, he had better be careful.

"I didn't say that," he said.

She gave him an actual smile—which made him a little bit dizzy. "I'm not quoting you for the paper. I'm just curious."

They had walked down one flight of steps to where the freshman lockers were. But she was continuing down while

Alex was heading to his locker. She stopped one step below him, which meant Alex was looking almost straight down at her.

He dropped his voice as he answered. "He seems to think Lombardi could have learned from him."

She smiled. "As in Vince Lombardi?"

"Yeah, him."

"You're funny," she said.

She turned and headed down the stairs.

The good news about Chester Heights High as far as Alex was concerned was that the academics weren't all that challenging. He liked his teachers and he also liked the fact that they didn't seem to believe in burying their students in homework.

The exception to this—naturally—was Mademoiselle Schiff. She hadn't been kidding that first day about not speaking any English in class. She walked in every day and began speaking French so fast that Alex was often lost after *"Bonjour, mesdemoiselles et messieurs."*

Alex needed no more than an hour most nights to deal with his other subjects—unless he had reading in history and English, which he often enjoyed—but he usually needed another hour just for French. He lived in fear of getting behind, especially in vocabulary, because he didn't want to look foolish in class—or, more specifically, in front of Christine Whitford.

The only good news was that he was no worse than just about everyone else in the class when Mademoiselle Schiff called on him. He almost always had *some* understanding of what she was asking, and fortunately, whenever a student began to stumble, she would move on to someone else before it became embarrassing.

The one person who never seemed to get flustered was—naturally—Christine. She was Hermione Granger, except her expertise was in French, not magic. Her hand was always up, she was clearly a step ahead of everyone else, and of course, her accent was flawless—at least to Alex's ear.

On the day before the opening football game, Christine shocked Alex by calling to him as he was walking out of class.

"Alex," she said, surprising him for several reasons: One, that she was apparently speaking to him. Two, that anyone was speaking to him because, other than Jonas and a couple of the other football players, almost no one had spoken to him since his arrival. And three, that she called him by his first name. On the rare occasions when anyone other than Jonas spoke to him, he was Myers or, from Matt Gordon and Jake Bilney, Goldie.

Hearing her voice, Alex knew it was Christine instantly. He paused, then looked back and saw her approaching. The weather was still quite hot, so she was wearing a T-shirt, shorts, and flip-flops, pretty much like every other girl. Unlike a lot of the other girls, she wore no makeup. She didn't need it.

"What's up?" he asked, hoping he sounded calm—even though he wasn't.

"So I'm one of the people covering the football game tomorrow night," she said. "Mr. Hillier told me yesterday."

She had fallen into step with him.

"How many people cover the game?" he asked.

"Four," she said. "Plus two photographers. I'm the only freshman."

"Congratulations," he said, wondering if her starting a conversation with him meant he kind of had the upper hand. Should he go for funny or sincere?

"Thanks," she said. Then she lowered her voice. "Is it true that Coach Hillier thinks you're better than Matt Gordon?"

He stopped dead in his tracks and looked down at her. She wasn't smiling.

"Have you asked Coach Hillier?" he said. "He could answer that better than I can."

Too wiseguy? he wondered. Still, it was the *right* answer—regardless of how she took it.

She put her hands on her hips, which was, to Alex, a very striking pose, even though she was wearing a backpack.

"Of course I asked him. He said, 'As editor of the newspaper, my answer is you should talk to people if you think there's a story there. As a football coach, I'll tell you that Matt Gordon is going to be an all-state quarterback this season and Alex Myers is a talented freshman.'"

Alex shrugged. "So there's your answer."

"I don't think it's that simple. I heard that Matt Gordon calls you Goldie because you have a golden arm."

He liked the fact that she was hearing these things, but he couldn't help but wonder *where* she was hearing them. Football practices were strictly closed to outsiders. He couldn't imagine anyone on the team telling her any of this. Maybe Jonas—trying to help him out?

"Do you know Jonas Ellington?" he asked.

"He's the wide receiver, right? Freshman? I hear he's *really* good."

"Where'd you hear that?"

She smiled. "From Coach Hillier."

"Have you met Jonas?"

"No, but I hope I will tomorrow night."

So. Not Jonas.

Her hands were back on her hips.

The bell rang, telling people that after-school meetings and clubs started in ten minutes. He had to get to practice.

"So?" she said.

"So what?" he answered.

"Are you better than Matt Gordon?"

He smiled.

"On the record or off the record?"

"On," she answered, sounding impatient.

"On the record, Matt Gordon's going to be an all-state quarterback this season," he answered. "I'm honored to be on the same team as him. He's a great guy and a terrific leader." He paused. "By the way, I mean every word of that."

Now she looked really upset.

"Okay," she said. "Off the record."

"Am I better than Matt?"

"Yes."

"Damn right I am," he said.

Then he smiled and walked away.

■ ■ ■

The opponent on Friday night was Mercer Academy, a prep school from the western part of the state. Chester Heights would play three nonconference games, all against prep schools. Then they would begin conference play the last Friday in September.

There were seven other schools in the South Philadelphia Athletic Conference. Although Alex did most of his reading on the Internet, he had picked up his father's habit of reading the sports section of the newspaper every morning. He had noticed that the *Philadelphia Inquirer* had made predictions for each of the local high school conferences in the area. Chester Heights was picked to win the SPAC—which people apparently referred to as the "S-pack." Crosstown rival Chester High School was known more for producing top basketball players—NBA players Jameer Nelson and Tyreke Evans had graduated from there, as had Wisconsin basketball coach Bo Ryan—but was picked second in the league. Apparently, the Chester Clippers had a senior quarterback named Todd Austin who was being pursued by quite a few Division I schools.

During the week, the coaches told the players constantly that Mercer was a "dangerous" team and that the game should not be taken lightly. After Coach Hillier had finished a quarterbacks meeting on Wednesday with a final warning about Mercer, Matt Gordon shot Alex and Jake a look but managed not to laugh until Coach Hillier had left the room.

"You might be in by halftime on Friday, Jake," he said. "These guys are never any good. They don't even recruit. The only prep schools that are good are the ones that recruit."

"Isn't it against the rules to recruit in high school?" Alex asked.

Gordon laughed again. "Ah, Goldie, still just a trusting freshman. Any prep team you see play on TV, anyone that's any good, recruits. They don't do it like colleges do; they just make sure good players are 'aware' of them. Might not be against the rules necessarily. My dad calls it coloring outside the lines a little bit."

"So these guys don't recruit."

"Nope. Maybe for basketball. Not for football. Trust me, if we aren't up 35–0 at halftime, my dad's going to be pissed. Heck, we'll win so easily, *you* might get in the game, Goldie."

"Get me in by halftime," Jake said, "and Goldie will get in the game."

"It's a plan," Matt said.

■ ■ ■

Even though he knew he wasn't likely to play much—if at all—Alex was excited by Friday afternoon. They'd all worn their jerseys to school and for the first time Alex felt a bit less invisible.

Last period was canceled for a pep rally in the auditorium. The players lined up outside the auditorium doors: freshmen first, then sophomores, and on up the line, except for junior Matt Gordon, who would go last as the offensive captain— and the star of the team.

"When you hear Coach Gordon call your name, remember, you jog out, you shake hands with him at the podium, then you jog up one aisle and circle back down the other, go up the steps on the other side of the stage," Coach Dixon said, "then go to the back of the stage and line up there until everyone's been introduced."

They had been prepped on this after practice twice already. They could hear the buzz inside the auditorium. Apparently, Mr. White was warming up the crowd for Coach Gordon.

Coach Dixon looked at Matt Gordon and Gerry Detwiler, the captains. "You two ready?" he asked. "You know what you're going to say?"

"Yeah," Gordon answered. "We're going to tell all the girls to come tonight and tell all the guys to stay home."

That got a laugh from the players.

Alex had wondered that first day of practice how Gordon and Detwiler were already the captains. Some coaches let the players vote. According to Bilney, Matt had asked his dad why he didn't and Coach Gordon had said, "Football teams aren't democracies. They're dictatorships."

The funny thing was that if Coach Gordon had allowed the players to vote, Alex was sure the results would have been the same: Detwiler was clearly the leader of the defense and everyone on the team looked up to Matt Gordon, even though he was a junior.

Alex heard wild cheering coming from inside, which meant Coach Gordon had been introduced. Coach Dixon opened the door so they could hear their names as they were called. Alex was right behind Jonas—third in line.

"We need you all out there tonight," he could hear Coach Gordon saying. "We have an outstanding football team, one that's going to make you proud. But there are *no* easy games. We need your spirit and your growls and your roars.

"Now, without further delay, let me introduce the 2014 Lions!"

Everyone in the room—or so it seemed to Alex—roared wildly. Alex could see that Coach Gordon had a stack of three-by-five cards—one, he assumed, for each player. He nudged Jonas.

"See the cards he's got?" he said.

Jonas nodded.

"I'll bet mine says, 'Will play over my dead body.' "

"Nah," Jonas said. "If Matt runs away from home and Bilney is crippled for life, he'll put you in."

When Coach Gordon got to Jonas he said, "Maybe the fastest player I've ever coached. You are all going to love him. He's a six two, 155-pound freshman, when he's soaking wet—let's welcome to Chester Heights number eighty-three, Jonas Ellington!"

Jonas jogged out to the stage as instructed and shook hands with his coach, who clapped him on the back, and then headed down the steps to the middle aisle, where kids were practically climbing over one another to high-five him or slap him on the back as he made his way toward the back of the auditorium.

Alex was next.

"A six one freshman quarterback, Alex Myers."

That didn't take long, Alex thought as he headed into the auditorium to near silence. He stopped at the podium to shake hands with Coach Gordon, who barely looked up at him. Apparently, Alex didn't move on quickly enough because Coach Myers turned his head away from the mike and said quietly, "Keep moving, Myers. Lot of players still left."

Alex jogged down the aisle and got a couple of high fives and an isolated roar here and there as he went. He could hear Coach Gordon's introduction of Stephen Harvey, the only defensive player among the four freshmen. "He's only a freshman, but he's going to be a terror at linebacker in the near future. . . ."

The enthusiasm was back in his voice. Alex couldn't help but laugh. But he wasn't at all sure what was funny.

10

Once Alex had taken his place onstage next to Jonas, the rest of Coach Gordon's introductions seemed to take forever. He couldn't help but notice that there was a one-liner of some kind about every player on the team. Even guys who played on special teams got some kind of complimentary mention: "He's always the first guy down the field on kickoffs. . . ."

The last two players introduced were the captains. Gerry Detwiler spoke briefly, telling the crowd, "We may get scored on this season, but it won't be often, and I *promise* they'll pay a price every time they do!"

The biggest roar was for Matt Gordon. His father's introduction was direct: "The quarterback who is going to lead *your* team to a state championship . . . MATT GORDON!"

Half the kids were on their feet as Matt jogged onto the stage. A lot of the girls whooped and shrieked.

"That's you two years from now," Jonas whispered as Gordon took the microphone from his beaming father.

"Maybe at another school," Alex answered.

Matt Gordon didn't talk for very long, but he hit all the right notes. "I just want to say that we are going to do everything in our power to win every single game we play this season. We believe we're good enough to do that, but we *can't* do it unless we come ready to play—and *you* come ready to play—against Mercer tonight."

Wild cheering and cries of "We're with you, Matt!" came from the crowd.

Finally Matt did a semi-turn so he could face the other players on the stage. "Gentlemen, Gerry and I are *honored* to be your captains. It will be the thrill of my life to lead all of you onto that field tonight. Let's GO!"

On cue, even though it hadn't been planned, he and Detwiler moved to the middle of the stage, hands in the air so that their teammates could join them. Everyone crowded around them, and Matt said, "On three—Lions all the way!"

Just as they did that, Alex heard a noise coming from the back of the room and looked up to see a swarm of cheerleaders tumbling and bouncing down both aisles. They were followed by the band, playing a marching-band version of "Welcome to the Jungle." The cheerleaders whipped up the crowd from in front of the stage and the band members filled the aisles, and the whole auditorium was in motion.

"Was it like this at your old school?" Alex whispered to Jonas, a little stunned.

"Nope." Jonas grinned.

When the song ended, Coach Gordon came back to the microphone.

"Everyone on their feet for the Chester Heights fight song!" he said.

Everyone *was* on their feet. Alex couldn't make out all the words, but there seemed to be a lot about snarling and clawing and *roar* was frequently rhymed with *score*. The fight song also came complete with hand motions that everyone clearly knew.

With a final roar still in the air, Coach Gordon declared the pep rally over and said he couldn't wait for tonight.

Neither could Alex. At least he'd have a good view of the game.

■ ■ ■

As Matt Gordon had predicted, the game was over before halftime. Mercer had no size, no speed, and little talent. On the other hand, they did have a really good band.

Alex had lots of time to evaluate both bands as he watched the game from the sideline. He also had time to stew over the fact that his father hadn't managed to come to the game. He tried really hard to focus. As a quarterback, he was given a headset so he could listen to Coach Hillier, who was sitting up in the press box, suggest plays to Coach Gordon on the sideline. Coach Gordon rotated wide receivers in and out of the game to get the plays in to Matt.

"No headset inside the QB's helmet?" Alex asked.

Jake shook his head. "Some states have gone to headsets in high school," he said. "Not here."

"Last year the running backs brought in the plays. I bet

he's using wide receivers now so he can play Jonas a lot without actually listing him as a one," Jake said.

Jonas was listed with the second team on the depth chart, but he was in for two of every three plays under the rotation system Coach Gordon was using.

By halftime, Chester Heights led 42–0 and Coach Gordon still had all the starters in the game.

Matt Gordon had run for four touchdowns and had thrown two touchdown passes—both to Jonas, one on an eighty-yard play right after a Mercer punt. It was already 21–0 at that point, and it was apparent that Matt could run the ball for at least eight to ten yards anytime he wanted. He took the shotgun snap and ran to his left, then—as the defense closed on him—he suddenly dropped back three steps and unloaded a pass downfield that went so high into the air that Alex thought it might bring rain.

Against a good team, the pass might have been intercepted or at least knocked down because the defenders would have had time to get back to where it came spiraling down. But there wasn't a Mercer player within ten yards of Jonas, who waited patiently for the ball and then sprinted, untouched, into the end zone.

"These guys are really bad," Jake said. "That ball could have been intercepted easily if they had anybody on the field with any speed."

"Except that Jonas would have outjumped them all," Alex said.

"True," Jake replied as they watched Matt and Jonas being mobbed as they came to the sideline. "He's our best asset."

Alex looked sideways at Jake to see if he was joking. He didn't appear to be.

"Well, the good news is, you'll get a lot of playing time tonight," Alex said. "You'll probably start the second half."

"Don't count on it," Jake said. "Coach Gordon isn't big on backing off. He wants to see our name in those USA *Today* rankings."

Every week, USA *Today* ranked the top twenty-five high school teams in the country. Alex wasn't quite sure how they could compare teams playing in a private-school league in California with a public-school team in Florida, but they did it anyway. Chester Heights had been listed that week under "others receiving votes," and Coach Gordon had mentioned that in his pregame talk.

"You want to be a ranked team?" he had asked. "You want to see our school's name in USA *Today* next week? You better go out and play like you deserve it tonight."

With a forty-two-point lead, Alex would have expected a fairly calm halftime locker room. He also would have expected the coaches to be talking to the twos about getting into the game soon.

He was wrong on both counts.

When the players assembled in the middle of the locker room and the doors were shut, Coach Gordon turned to Coach Gutekunst and said, "Coach, how many yards did we give up in the first half?"

"Eighty-four, Coach. Thirty-nine on one play."

Alex remembered the play. Mercer had faced a third and twelve from its own 8-yard line and the quarterback had managed to scramble free of the pass rush and find a receiver open for a first down at the 47-yard line. On the next play, a Mercer running back had fumbled, Chester Heights had recovered, and no harm had been done.

Until now.

"Thomason, was that your responsibility?" Coach Gordon said, looking at one of the starting cornerbacks.

"Yes sir."

"How did the receiver get so wide open?"

"I slipped."

"You *what*?"

"I slipped, sir. He made a cut and my feet went out from under me. I'm sorry."

"*Sorry?*" Coach Gordon roared. "You're *sorry*? When we're playing Chester for the league title and you slip, is that what you're going to tell your teammates—that you're sorry?"

Thomason hung his head. He was smart enough to know that there wasn't any answer that was going to get him off the hook.

Coach Gordon was pacing now.

"I know you twos are looking at the scoreboard and thinking you're about to get in the game." He shook his head. "Sorry. It isn't your fault the ones aren't performing. They're going to stay in until they get it right. If you're unhappy about that, talk to them."

He turned to walk away.

"Coaches."

The coaches followed him to a meeting room. Matt Gordon and Gerry Detwiler were on their feet as soon as he left.

The next few minutes were all about playing better and

playing harder and not making mistakes. Alex's head was spinning by the time the coaches walked back in.

"Did we walk into the wrong locker room?" he whispered to Jake Bilney. "Are we *losing* 42–0?"

Before Jake could answer, Alex heard Coach Gordon's voice cutting through the air—coming right at him like an incoming missile.

"Myers, did you have something to say to your teammates?" he said. "Perhaps you'd like to talk about all of your first-half contributions."

For a split second Alex considered saying, *Give me a chance to contribute, you jerk.* Instead, he settled for, "No sir. Sorry sir."

It was 63–0 by the end of the third quarter. Nobody slipped on defense—the poor Mercer kids were buried on just about every play. Finally, after Matt Gordon had scored his sixth touchdown of the night late in the third quarter, Coach Gordon began to empty his bench.

When the offense got the ball back early in the fourth quarter, Alex wasn't at all surprised when he heard Coach Hillier calling one running play after another with Bilney in the game at quarterback. But on the fifth play of the drive, with the ball at midfield, Bilney faked a handoff, dropped back, and hit a wide-open Andrew Feeley—the tight end—running straight down the middle for another easy touchdown. Pete Ross kicked his tenth extra point of the night to make it 70–0.

Alex noticed that the second-half touchdowns had been greeted by decidedly muted roars—actually, more like polite applause—from what had once been a fired-up crowd. Lions

Field had been packed for kickoff. Now the place was at least half empty.

"Did you audible that play?" Alex asked when Bilney came over and took off his helmet.

The long pass was not what he'd heard Hillier suggest from the press box. A quarterback could change the play sent in from the sideline if he spotted something in the defensive formation that made him believe a different play would work better.

Bilney shook his head. "No audible," he said.

That meant Coach Gordon had overruled Hillier's running play and called for the play-action pass.

"Gordon called it, not Hillier," Alex said.

"Figures," was all Bilney said in response.

The offense scored one more time to make it 77–0. By the time the clock wound under two minutes, every player in a Chester Heights uniform had gotten into the game—except for Alex. At one point, when the offense went back on the field with Bilney at quarterback, Alex saw Matt Gordon talking to his father and pointing in Alex's direction. Coach Gordon simply shook his head and walked away.

With fifty-six seconds left, Mercer had driven into Chester Heights territory against a defense now made up of all twos and threes. They had a fourth and four on the Chester Heights 33, when Coach Gordon suddenly called time-out. He waved all the twos and threes off the field and sent the starters back in after calling them into a circle around him.

"We do *not* let this team score," he said. "Get this stop right now and let's go home."

The defensive starters charged back onto the field. Coach

Klein called for an all-out blitz on the play, the linebackers pass-rushing along with the linemen. It was Gerry Detwiler who got to the quarterback and took him down before he had a chance to even think about getting off a pass. Detwiler jumped up and started pounding his chest as if he had saved the game, the season, and civilization.

Alex checked the scoreboard. Still 77–0.

Someone was calling his name. He looked up and saw Coach Gordon gesturing at him. He raced over.

"Go in and take a knee," he said. "Forty-seven seconds left so you'll have to do it twice. Think you can handle that?"

Again Alex managed to stifle his real answer. He put his helmet on and jogged out with the offense. It consisted not only of the other third-stringers but also of several players who had been cut after the tryouts. They had dressed for the game because they had already signed up to play on the junior varsity.

"Victory formation," Alex said, stepping into the huddle.

This was a football universal. When a team simply wanted to run out the clock by having the quarterback take the snap and kneel down, it was called "victory." Of course, Chester Heights could have played the whole second half in victory and won the game.

Alex took the snap, took one step back, and dropped to a knee. He flipped the ball to the referee.

"One more time, son," the ref said, glancing at the clock. There were forty seconds to play in the game.

Alex nodded, turned to his teammates in the huddle, and simply said, "Victory."

They lined up again. Alex started to drop to a knee with

the ball when—out of nowhere—he felt a shoulder collide with his helmet. He felt a stinging pain in the side of his head and in his ribs because he had been punched there at the same time. He went down on his back and saw someone looking at him through a face mask.

"You tell your —— coach that was for him!" was all he heard before someone pulled his attacker off him. Lying there, Alex could tell there was shouting and pushing and shoving going on all around. He knew he should get up so no one would step on him, but he was too stunned to move.

Then through the snarl of bodies above him, a Lion broke free and stood over him. "Wait for the trainer," Matt Gordon said. "I'll take care of you until he gets here."

"How's the head, Goldie?" Matt asked softly.

"I think I'm okay," he said.

Buddy Thomas, the trainer, was kneeling in front of him, a hand on his shoulder.

"I'm going to ask you a few questions, okay?"

Instinctively, Alex nodded, but that hurt, so he stopped.

Buddy must have seen him wince because he said to him, "Head's pretty sore, huh?"

"Yes," Alex said, remembering not to move his head this time.

"What's your name?" Buddy asked.

Alex almost laughed because he wasn't sure *Buddy* knew his name. There was a reasonable chance that Alex could answer the question wrong and Buddy wouldn't know.

"Alex Myers. But you call me 'rook.'" All the freshmen were "rook" in Buddy's training room.

Buddy smiled—the first time Alex had seen *that*—and Alex could hear some laughter from the players behind him.

"Very good."

"What day is it?"

"Friday."

"Do you remember who we were playing?"

"Mercer."

"What was the score when you came into the game?"

"Seventy-seven to nothing. We had the seventy-seven."

More laughter.

Buddy looked up at Coach Gordon, who Alex now noticed was standing off to his right.

The players from both teams were hovering around him quietly. He could see a number of security people in yellow jackets standing between the players from the two teams, just in case someone got angry again.

"I think he's going to need some Advil, but he doesn't have any concussion symptoms," Buddy said. "At least not right now."

"Good," Coach Gordon said. "Alex, do you feel like you can stand up?"

It was the first time Coach Gordon had called him by his first name.

"I think so," he said. "But my ribs are kind of sore."

"We'll take a look at that when we get inside," Buddy said as he reached down to help him up. "Gordon, do me a favor and get his other arm."

Matt Gordon took Alex by the left arm while Buddy Thomas got the right one, and together they got him on his feet. Alex felt some pain in both his head and his ribs, but nothing that made him want to scream. He looked around and saw that most of those still left in the stands were standing, and when he stood up, they started to clap. So did some of the players. One of the Mercer players walked up to him with his hand out.

"I'm really sorry, dude. I just lost it there for a second," he said. "You didn't do anything to deserve that."

Even though he was a defensive lineman, he wasn't a lot bigger than Alex. Which helped explain why the score had been 77–0. Alex shook his hand.

"It's okay," he said. "I understand."

Actually, he *did* sort of understand. Coach Gordon had run up the score. Unfortunately, *he* hadn't been in the game to take a knee on the final two plays. Alex had. So Alex was the one with the pounding head and the sore ribs.

"Come on, Myers," Buddy said. "Let's get a look at those ribs."

Alex smiled. He guessed by the time they made it inside, he'd be back to being "rook" again.

■ ■ ■

Buddy Thomas examined Alex's ribs thoroughly and told him he didn't think he had anything more than some bruises. "If they're still sore on Monday, we'll send you to get an MRI," he said. "But I suspect you're going to be fine. How's your head right now?"

The pounding had actually lessened by the time they got into the locker room, although Alex wouldn't have minded if someone had turned down the postgame music that was pulsing through the room.

"Not too bad," he said.

Buddy reached onto a shelf and pulled a bottle of Advil off it. "Take two now and two just before you go to bed," he said. "If you've got a headache in the morning, take a couple more. If it *still* hurts after that, call me and I'll get you in to see a doctor tomorrow. I suspect you're fine. Your memory was clear out on the field, which is a very good sign, and you didn't black out at all. Still, we have to be careful with any hit to the head.

"Got it?"

Alex nodded, and winced.

"All right, then. Go take a shower and get dressed. I'm going to go outside and talk to your mom."

"My mom? She's not here."

Molly had a soccer game that she was actually *playing* in, so Alex had told his mom to go to that game and not bother trying to catch some of his game afterward since he knew he wouldn't be playing. He was now especially grateful that she had agreed.

"No, she's here," Buddy said. "Coach Hillier called her. He didn't want her seeing anything on TV or the Internet about you being knocked out and panicking. He also thought she should come pick you up. She just texted me a couple minutes ago that she's outside with Ellington's mom waiting for you guys."

Alex nodded and was pleased to note that the pain wasn't as bad as it had been a few minutes earlier.

He got down from the training table. He was still wearing his uniform pants but had taken off his jersey and pads. Instinctively, he looked around for them.

"Don't worry about the uniform," Buddy said. "Taken care of. Mr. O's got it."

"Thanks," Alex said.

"Anytime, 'rook,'" Buddy said, smiling. "Next time you're out there to take a knee, remember to duck."

Alex laughed, which hurt a little. He walked into the locker room, which was already half empty. Some guys were still dressing, and he could hear the showers going. As he walked to his locker, several guys asked him how he was feeling or patted him gently on the back. Jonas was the only one left in the freshman area and he was putting his shoes on.

"So, you gonna survive?" he asked.

"Apparently, I'll live to kneel another day," Alex said, sitting down in front of his locker. He wondered if any football player in history had ever felt this tired after a game in which his role had been to kneel down twice.

"Coach Hillier called your mom," Jonas said. "She's outside with my mom right now."

"Yeah, I know."

"I'll go tell them you're coming soon—okay?"

"Yeah, good idea. I won't be that long."

Alex undressed slowly—he was still sore—and headed for the shower room, which had emptied out. He showered longer than he should have, but the hot water felt so good it was hard to get out. He walked to his locker, towel around his waist, and was pulling his clothes out when he heard a voice behind him.

"Alex, I'm really sorry. That was my fault."

He turned and saw Coach Hillier, dressed in what the players called his "civilian" clothes.

"How in the world could it be your fault?"

"Because I told Coach Gordon he had to get you on the

field. That it was unfair for you to be the one guy in uniform not to play. I'm not sure what I was thinking, since all you were going to do was kneel. Then . . . this happens. I'm sorry."

Alex thought about it for a moment. "Coach, you were trying to do something nice."

"Yeah, didn't turn out too well. Thank God you aren't seriously hurt."

Alex brightened. "Can you do something for me to make up for it?" he asked.

"Depends what it is," Coach Hillier said. "I don't think I can make you the starter."

Alex laughed. "I know *that*," he said. "But can I throw the ball down the field every once in a while in scrimmages?"

Coach Hillier hesitated. Then, slowly, he nodded. "Done," he said. "I'll deal with whatever comes with it. Get dressed and go see your mom."

"Did you talk to her?"

"Yes. And to your dad on the phone. She asked me to talk to him so he'd understand exactly what happened."

"What'd he say?"

Coach Hillier smiled again.

"That you should be starting."

■ ■ ■

Not surprisingly, Alex's mom was very concerned—even after she had spoken with Coach Hillier and Buddy Thomas. She was also full of questions.

Twice, in front of Jonas and Mrs. Ellington and with other parents coming by to express concern, Linda Myers asked her son exactly what had happened.

"I'll tell you later, Mom," he said both times. He knew it would take him a while to explain that he had gotten crushed because his coach had run up the score.

When they were finally in the car, he walked her through it. First he had to explain the concept of a kneel-down. Then he had to make her understand why he would be put in the game just to do that when he hadn't played all night. Then came telling her why his coach might run up the score on a weak team and why the players on that team might take offense.

"I don't blame them for being upset," she said. "That doesn't sound very nice or fair. But still, what that boy did to you was inexcusable."

Alex sighed. "He apologized. I'm sure he didn't really mean to hurt me; he just wanted to send me flying backward. And I'm fine."

Actually, his ribs were aching at the moment. But his head felt better by the minute. That was good. He had read enough about concussions to know that if he had one he could miss a lot of playing time. Then again, it wasn't like he was going to be starting—or playing at all—anytime soon.

"Still, shouldn't someone talk to his parents?"

Alex laughed—which hurt his ribs. "Mom, it's football. You don't talk to people's parents about a late hit or even a semi-dirty hit." He paused for a moment. "If they're still alive, it might be nice if someone talked to Coach Gordon's parents."

Even his mom smiled at that one.

From the backseat he suddenly heard Molly's voice. "Mom!" she cried. "McDonald's!"

Those were the sweetest words Alex had heard all night. His mom turned on her signal and pulled into the drive-through.

Alex felt much better after he had downed two double hamburgers, a large French fries, and a vanilla milk shake. If loss of appetite was a concussion symptom, there was no doubt he was fine.

He took a couple more Advil before he went to bed and, after tossing and turning to find a position that didn't affect his ribs, he fell sound asleep. He woke up only once, right around sunrise, after dreaming that Coach Gordon was trying to tackle him.

He quickly fell back asleep and awoke to his mother's voice coming from downstairs. He glanced at the clock next to his bed and saw that it was 10:08. He had been asleep for almost twelve hours.

"Alex, can you hear me?" he heard his mom say—no doubt for the second time.

"Yes!" he answered.

"There's a phone call down here," she said. "Should I take a message?"

Alex didn't have a lot of friends, especially these days, but the friends he did have would call him on his cell phone—which was sitting next to his bed.

"Who is it?" he called back.

"Don't know. It's a girl."

That got Alex's attention.

He rolled over onto his back and stared at the ceiling for a second to collect his thoughts. His head, he noticed, felt fine. His ribs were still a little sore, but that was all—a little sore. Who, he wondered, could possibly be calling. . . .

"Alex?"

"Coming!" he yelled back, and scrambled out of bed.

He padded down the steps, carefully sidestepping Papi, one of the two family cats. His dad had named him after David Ortiz because he was so big.

His mom was holding the phone in her hands when he came into the kitchen. "Someone named Christine?" she said softly, one hand over the receiver.

That got Alex's heart pumping a little faster.

"Hello?" he said.

"Alex, it's Christine Whitford. I hope I didn't wake you. How are you feeling?"

It *was* her. But why?

"No, I'm fine. I mean, I'm awake. . . ." He paused, telling himself to slow down. "It's okay," he finally added.

"I'm actually calling because the *Weekly Roar* assigned me to write a story about what happened to you last night. It's one of the sidebars."

Alex had no idea what a sidebar was, but he didn't want to embarrass himself by asking Christine to explain.

"So . . . you want to talk to me about last night?"

"Yes. The paper doesn't come out until Wednesday, but we need to turn in our stories by Monday."

"So . . . you want to talk to me *now*?"

Now it was her turn to pause. Or at least Alex thought there was a pause.

"I was thinking we might meet somewhere. Mr. Hillier assigned me the story. He said it would be better if I could describe how you look today . . . that I'd get better details in person than over the phone. . . ."

Her voice trailed off at that point. Alex didn't want to sound too eager. Even so, he answered quickly.

"Where could we meet?"

"How about Stark's? Do you know it? It's not too far from school."

Alex had no idea what Stark's was or where it was. That's why Google Maps existed. If it wasn't far from school, he could probably get there on his bike.

"I can find it," he said. "What time?"

"Noon?"

Alex looked at his mom, who was cracking eggs into a bowl and trying to look very busy. They had made a deal before the school year began: as soon as Alex finished his weekend homework, he was free to do pretty much whatever he wanted and she would try to drive him if he needed a ride. There was no way he was going to finish his homework by noon. But he suspected he could talk her into this one—especially if he showered right away and at least knocked off one subject before he had to leave the house.

"How about twelve-thirty?" he said, in part so as not to appear too fired up about having lunch with her but also to give himself a little more wiggle room with his mom.

"That's fine," she said. "Did my number come up on your phone? That's my cell in case you have any trouble finding it." Alex looked at the phone and saw a number with a 610 area code on it.

He nodded. "Yup, got it. Stark's at twelve-thirty."

He hung up and could feel his heart pounding. Excited—yes. Hungry—almost as much.

■ ■ ■

The negotiations with his mom went pretty well. Since he promised to get one subject of homework out of the way before he left, she was willing to make the deal. She did—naturally—want one thing in return: some information on Christine Whitford.

"She's a girl in my French class," Alex said. "And she works on the student newspaper. I guess Coach Hillier suggested she write something called a sidebar about me since I got hurt." He smiled. "I told you I'd take this town by storm."

She laughed. "Well, I'm glad to see your sense of humor is still intact." She put her hands on her hips, the move his dad always said made it impossible to say no to her. "So, tell me, is she pretty?"

Alex shrugged, hoping to sound casual. "Yeah, I guess so."

The look on his mom's face told him she wasn't buying the casual act.

"Alex . . ."

"Yeah," he said, finally. "She kind of looks like Emma Watson."

For a moment his mom looked confused. Then her face lit up. "Hermione?" she said. "Wow. She's *that* pretty?"

Alex thought for a moment. "Yeah," he said. "She's that pretty."

"You better shower," his mom said. "I'm assuming you feel okay, right?"

"Feel great," he semi-lied. His ribs were still a little sore. But everything else felt good right now.

■ ■ ■

Stark's was, according to Google, 3.7 miles from the Myers house. Alex raced through his shower, did most of his math, and was on his bike at 11:55. He didn't want to be late, but he didn't want to be early either.

He parked his bike at a rack that was around the corner from the big sign that said STARK'S—GREAT BURGERS SINCE 1964 and walked in the front door at exactly 12:32. Christine Whitford was sitting in a booth about halfway back and waved when he walked in. She got up to greet him and gave him a very businesslike handshake. She was wearing a white short-sleeved shirt, cutoff jeans, and flat, strappy sandals. Her long dark hair was tied back into a ponytail. She looked spectacular.

"Thanks for doing this," she said. "I hope it's not too big a pain. It's just that Mr. Hillier really thought the story would be better this way and it's only my second assignment."

Alex put up a hand as he slid into the booth opposite her. "It's fine," he said. "I have to eat anyway, don't I?"

She laughed.

"I talked to Mr. Thomas this morning and he said getting your appetite back would be a good sign. Do you feel hungry?"

"Actually, I'm starving," he said.

"Good," she said as a waitress approached. "Why don't we order right now and then get to work? I mean, you can look at the menu"—she glanced down at the closed menu sitting in front of Alex—"but if you've never been to Stark's before, you should definitely have a burger."

Alex nodded. "Sounds good to me."

■ ■ ■

They both ordered a hamburger, French fries, and a milk shake—his vanilla, hers chocolate. Alex noted that, like him, she didn't want cheese on her burger.

"You don't like cheese?" he asked.

"I like it on pizza," she said. "But not on a hamburger."

"Exactly," Alex said, laughing. "I guess we have something in common."

She actually blushed a little. "We also both like Mr. Hillier," she said.

She reached down and picked up a notebook. "Is it okay if we start?" she asked. "I told my mom I'd get home in time to finish my homework before dinner."

"Me too," he said. "Another thing we have in common—tough moms." He was happy to know he wasn't the only one.

She asked him about his background, how much football he had played in the past, and then why he had moved to Philadelphia. When he told her, she shook her head.

"Sorry," she said. "I know what that's like."

"You do?" he said.

She nodded. "But I was too young to really understand. I was only five. It was worse for my brothers. Seth was twelve and Danny was ten."

"Where are they now?"

"Both in college. Seth's a senior at Villanova; Danny's a sophomore at Princeton."

"Whoa, Princeton."

"Yeah, that's where my dad went. Seth got into Princeton too, but he got a full ride at Villanova. Plus, he knew my dad wanted him to pick Princeton."

Alex smiled. "Where do you think you'll go?"

She shrugged. "I have no idea. I'm just a freshman. I know I want to write. I love to write. . . . Can we go back to talking about you now?"

The answer turned out to be no because their burgers arrived. Alex understood after one bite why Stark's had been famous since 1964. The burger was big and juicy and delicious.

"Good call on the restaurant," he said as he reached for some French fries. "This place is great."

"Yeah, and the good thing is it's not too busy on Saturdays. It's packed on weekdays for lunch. Everyone who works in Chester comes here. At least that's what my mom says."

"What's she do?"

She smiled. "Back to talking about me again?" She took

a sip of her milk shake. "Paralegal in a law office. She started working again after the divorce. She was in law school when Seth was born and didn't finish. I think she'll go back and finish once I'm old enough that she doesn't have to drive me all over the place."

Alex knew his mom was hoping to take on some private tutoring work now that the middle schools were starting classes. She had been an English teacher before he was born and had always talked about going back to work again. Now she was planning to work part-time until he and Molly "got settled," and then she would look to get back into teaching.

Christine seemed to read his thoughts.

"Is your mom working?" she asked.

He told her and she nodded and asked what his dad did. "He works," Alex said. "All the time, he works." Then he realized that hadn't really been the question. "He's a lawyer," he added. "He travels a lot."

Christine didn't answer, just nodded again. Maybe she could tell by his tone that this was a delicate subject. There was, for just a second, he thought, a sympathetic look in her eyes. She looked down and then pushed her plate aside, as if to regroup mentally.

"Okay," she said, picking up the notebook and her pen again. "Tell me about last night."

■ ■ ■

Alex told her what he remembered about the game, including his surprise at being put in for two final kneel-downs and how stunned he had been, literally and figuratively, when the kid from Mercer had clocked him. Christine kept asking for details on what he remembered when he came to, and he said—honestly—that he wasn't ever really out. Finally she put her pen down and crossed her arms.

"Interview over?" he asked.

"Yes," she said. "But I do want to ask you one more question."

"I assume since you put your pen down that this is off the record," he said.

"Yes, it is. Because I want you to tell me the truth."

"Sure. As long as it won't get me in trouble."

"Did you mean what you said the other day, that you're better than Matt Gordon? Or was that just bravado?"

"If you tell me what bravado is, maybe I can tell you if I did it," he answered.

She laughed. "You really are kind of funny," she said, and her dark eyes lit up for a second in that way that made him feel slightly faint. "Bravado is when you say something to get someone's attention, to make it sound like you are very confident when perhaps you aren't."

He was shaking his head before she finished. "That wasn't bravado, then," he said. "Look, Matt Gordon's very good. He's a natural leader, and, seriously, he's a *really* good guy. His mom must be the greatest, because he sure doesn't get it from his dad."

"But?" she said.

"But Matt really should be a running back or a tight end. He's a little like Tim Tebow: Great athlete, strong, knocks people over all the time. But he doesn't throw the ball all that well. I don't think he can be a quarterback at a Division I college."

"Tebow was. He won the Heisman."

She *did* know her sports. "I said he was *like* Tebow," he said. "I didn't say he was as good as Tebow." He shrugged. "But maybe he will be. He's just a junior."

"And you *can* throw the ball," she said.

"I don't think Matt nicknamed me Goldie because I *can't* throw the ball."

"Can you run?" she asked.

"If I see someone coming, I run just fine," he said. "Kneeling down, going backward, I'm not nearly as good. If they ever give me a chance to do more than kneel down, you'll see."

She smiled again.

"I hope I get that chance," she said.

"Me too," he said. "Me too."

Alex was rounding the corner onto his street when his cell phone began to ring inside the pocket of his shorts. Thinking that maybe Christine had forgotten something—or maybe she just missed him?—he pulled over and took the phone out.

He was disappointed when he saw that the number had a 717 area code. Still curious, he answered anyway, pushing his helmet back on his head so he could get the phone to his ear.

"Is this Alex Myers?" a voice said.

"Yes," he said. "Who's this?"

"David Krenchek. I'm the guy who hit you last night. I was calling to tell you I'm sorry for what happened and I wanted to see how you're feeling."

"Wow. It's really nice of you to call," Alex said. "I'm curious, though, how'd you get my number?"

David laughed. "I told my coach I wanted to talk to you,

and he said he'd call one of your assistant coaches and ask for your number—because he really didn't want to talk to your coach ever again."

"He did run up the score," Alex said. "I'm sorry about that."

David laughed again. "Hey, man, you didn't do it. You just got clobbered *because* of it. I don't know what I was thinking. I was just so upset. We all were, actually. But that's no excuse."

"Forget it," Alex said. "I feel fine and I understand why you guys were upset. I don't think any of us felt great about it either."

"So, no aftereffects?"

"My ribs are still kind of sore, but the trainer said they're just bruised."

"I was worried," David said. "I've never done anything like that before. Of course, we never played anyone as good as you before. I don't know what Coach was thinking when he scheduled the game. I guess it was part of the deal to play you in basketball."

"We're playing you in basketball?"

"Yeah, pre-conference, just like in football. Difference is, we're good in basketball. Do you play?"

"Well, I'm just a freshman. I hope I'll play, but I don't know what the competition is like yet."

"Hey, you're on varsity football as a freshman—that's pretty good."

"Yeah. As a tackling dummy."

They both laughed at that one.

"Hey," David said. "Stay in touch, okay? You've got my number. Let me know how things go."

"You too," Alex said.

He hung up. Just like that, he felt like he'd made a friend. Maybe, he thought, he should talk to his parents about transferring to Mercer. He *knew* he would start there.

■ ■ ■

On Monday morning, for the first time since he had arrived at Chester Heights, Alex didn't feel invisible. Kids who had walked past him in the hall as if he weren't there were looking him in the eye and saying hello. Others paused to say, "How you feeling?" Some even stopped to ask if he was okay. In class, kids who had sat next to him without so much as nodding for two weeks all of a sudden wanted to talk.

If Alex hadn't known better, he might have thought he had thrown the winning touchdown pass, not just been knocked silly.

He was invited to no fewer than three postgame parties the next Friday night after the game against Cherry Hill Academy, a private school like Mercer but—according to the all-knowing Matt Gordon—a much better team.

The most impressive invite of all came from Hope Alexander. Hope was very tall, apparently a budding volleyball star, and had long blond hair. When she sat in the middle of the room for history class, it was as if there were a magnetic field around her desk, as boys, and girls too, scrambled to sit near her. Two weeks into school and *everyone* knew Hope.

As Alex and Jonas were walking out of history on Tuesday,

Alex felt a tap on his shoulder and turned to see Hope, who was looking him right in the eye. Alex wasn't used to girls being anywhere close to his height ever since he'd grown to six one, so he almost did a double take—in part because of that but also because she wanted to speak to *him*.

"Alex, you know about the party I'm having after the game, right?" she said, as if it were a given that he knew all about it but she was just double-checking.

"No, actually, I don't," he said.

Clearly prepared, she reached into the pocket of her shorts and brought out what looked like a three-by-five card. "Here's the address and the info."

She looked at Jonas. "Do you want to come too, Jonas?"

Alex was relieved and happy that she had managed to both notice and acknowledge Jonas.

"Probably not, but thanks," Jonas said. "I'll probably just hang out with my family like I did last week."

She nodded, put a hand on Alex's shoulder, and smiled. "Well, I hope I see *you* there."

Alex was semi-mesmerized as she walked away.

"Man, I scored two touchdowns in that game last week and you're a hero for getting clocked in the head," Jonas said, a big grin on his face. "Maybe I need to get carried off on a stretcher this week so I can get invited to some more parties."

"Not worth it," Alex said. "And I didn't get carried off on a stretcher. And you *are* invited *and* you're going."

"I am?"

"Oh yeah. I'm not going alone and I *am* going."

"You are?"

"Hope Alexander just invited me. Are you kidding—of course I'm going."

"You've got Christine," Jonas said. "Why don't you point out to Hope that I'm the star wide receiver?"

Jonas had a way of saying things that were obnoxious without actually sounding obnoxious. Alex knew he was kidding—or at least half kidding. Plus, he *was* well on his way to being the star wide receiver.

"I don't have Christine," he hissed, looking around the crowded hall in case anyone was listening. He was beginning to regret telling Jonas about the Saturday lunch/interview. Jonas had been on him about it for two days now.

"Come on, she decides to do a story on a guy for getting knocked out?" Jonas said. "She likes you. Even with your head on sideways you should see that."

"She said it was Coach Hillier's idea."

"Mm-hmm," Jonas said. "Why don't we ask Coach Hillier if that's true?"

Alex thought that wasn't a bad idea. "Let's see what the story says when it comes out tomorrow," he said. "Then maybe."

■ ■ ■

Alex hadn't gotten any scrimmage reps at all on Monday. According to Coach Hillier, this was because Buddy Thomas, after examining Alex prior to practice, had said he shouldn't throw a ball much more than ten yards until Wednesday as a precaution against stretching his ribs in a way that might be painful. Alex was tempted to grab a ball during warm-ups and hurl it as far as he could to show that he was fine, but he'd already done something like that once and that hadn't worked out so well.

Most of his teammates stopped at some point, either in the locker room or out on the practice field, to ask how he was feeling. So did the coaches—except for Coach Gordon. Apparently, whatever Buddy Thomas had told him was all the information he needed. The one noticeable change was in the training room: Buddy repeatedly called him either Myers or Alex, and instead of having one of the student assistants tape his ankles for practice, Buddy did it himself.

On Wednesday morning, Alex walked into school a few minutes early and saw stacks of the *Weekly Roar* next to the front door. Christine had told him the newspaper was printed late on Tuesday so it would be waiting when everyone arrived the next day.

He needed to find some privacy to read the story, so he headed for the one place it was guaranteed: the bathroom. The first bell was still fifteen minutes away, so it was empty. He locked himself in a stall and sat. The game got four pages of coverage in the eight-page paper, though two of the pages were filled with photos, including one of him being tended to by Buddy Thomas. The caption said, "Cheap shot."

The headline on Christine's sidebar was FRESHMAN QB CAN TAKE A HIT.

He was relieved that Christine had kept her word and hadn't used anything he had said off the record. He had worried that in his quest to impress, he might have trusted her too much. She had actually talked to a number of other people including Mercer's Coach Alan Hale and David Krenchek, the kid who hit him. Both had been very apologetic and had complimented him on how he had handled a difficult situation. Matt Gordon had confirmed that he had started calling Alex "Goldie" after first watching him throw a ball in practice. Only Coach Gordon was—surprise—less than gushy about him.

"He's a freshman and has a lot to learn," he said. "We're all glad he wasn't hurt seriously."

The last quote was from Alex and it was accurate. "The next time I get that kind of attention, I hope it's because of something I did rather than something someone else did to me."

He read the story a second time and breathed a sigh of relief. He couldn't see anything in it that would cause a problem. He sort of wished that Christine had written something that indicated he was a nice guy or that she liked him. She had mentioned they had talked while he "wolfed down a hamburger, proving that his appetite was unaffected." But that was about it.

The most interesting story about the game was in the sports editor's column by someone named Steve Garland. Mostly, Garland said it was hard to learn much from a 77–0 rout. But toward the end there was a paragraph that caught Alex's attention:

> It is difficult to question Coach Gordon's record on any level and there is every reason to believe this might be his best team. But he should consider himself fortunate that Alex Myers, the freshman quarterback who has already been labeled "Goldie" by his teammates because of his

"golden" throwing arm, wasn't seriously hurt on the game's last play. Coach Gordon's decision to keep trying to score in the fourth quarter was the obvious catalyst for what could have been a very ugly incident.

The rest was about Cherry Hill being a more significant test, although only league play would decide how great this season might be. What interested Alex wasn't so much that the sports editor would write a paragraph criticizing Coach Gordon but that the teacher who supervised the newspaper had allowed the paragraph to get into print.

That teacher was Coach Hillier. Now he had two questions to ask him at practice that afternoon.

Buddy Thomas officially cleared Alex to take part in all practice drills that afternoon. After looking his ribs over one more time, the trainer asked if he'd had any other symptoms since Friday: headache, nausea, lack of appetite. When Alex shook his head no, Buddy looked at him closely.

"You're sure?" he said. "I know you want to practice. But if there's anything at all, you need to tell me."

"Honestly, Buddy, I feel fine."

Buddy nodded. "Okay, Myers, I believe you. You're clear."

Alex jumped off the table with a big smile on his face. Buddy gave him a pat on the shoulder. "You're a tough kid, Alex," he said. "Hang in there."

Alex felt like he'd just been elected to the football Hall of Fame.

He spent most of practice at the defensive end of the field, mimicking the plays that Cherry Hill Academy was likely to run. He learned the third-string quarterback usually ran what was called the "scout team," meaning that he ran the plays the defensive coaches expected the upcoming opponent to run, based on scouting reports. The week before, in part because Mercer hadn't played a game but also—Alex suspected—because Mercer was so bad, there had been no scout team drills.

Alex loved running the scout team. He got a lot more playing time and Cherry Hill apparently had an offense that liked to throw the ball, so he got the chance to show off his arm on a few occasions—though none of the offensive coaches were watching. They were at the other end of the field running plays against the scout team defense.

After the scout drills were over, the team gathered at midfield to scrimmage, as it always did at the end of practice on Tuesdays and Wednesdays. Thursdays were usually reserved for special teams, although both Matt Gordon and Jake Bilney had told Alex that if Coach Gordon wasn't happy with what he saw on Tuesday and Wednesday, the offensive and defensive units might be on the field on Thursday too.

"The later it gets in the season, the less you want the extra reps on Thursday," Matt had said. "You're tired, you're sore. Though it's worse for the linemen than for us because we don't get hit."

As far as Alex was concerned, the more reps the team ran the better, because it meant he had a chance to play. Matt got, by Alex's count, eighteen plays, then Jake ran the next nine.

"Okay, Myers, you're in there," Coach Hillier said after Jake had badly underthrown a deep pass on his last snap.

A number of other third-teamers jogged into the huddle with him. The first play was a simple handoff. The second was a pitch play in which Alex had the option to run or pitch the ball as he turned upfield. He decided to pitch the ball, which led to a big run by third-string tailback Eddie Brackens.

"Nice job, Goldie," Brackens said as he jogged back into the huddle.

Coach Hillier was standing right next to Alex. "Okay, fellas, this is it, last play," he said. Alex tried not to show his disappointment. Three plays? When he heard the call, though, he perked up.

"X across, Z fly," Coach Hillier said. "On two."

As the players clapped hands and started toward the line, Coach Hillier put a hand on Alex's shoulder. "Don't force the Z if it's not there, Alex," he said. "Take what's there."

It was the first time he had called him Alex during practice. Did that mean something? He'd figure it out later.

The X receiver was Freddy Watts. He would go downfield about twenty yards and curl back into the middle. The Z was Darrell Winslow. He would run a straight fly pattern deep. Coach Hillier had read Alex's mind. Of course he wanted to throw the ball deep to Winslow.

Alex took the snap, made a quick play-action fake to Brackens, and dropped back, bouncing up and down on his toes to stay balanced as he watched his receivers. Brackens had drifted to the right as a safety valve if nothing was open.

The defense knew it was the last play of the day and clearly had a feeling that on his first day back, "Goldie" might be going deep. No one bought the play-action fake and Winslow had both a cornerback and a safety with him.

Alex thought he might be able to fit the ball in between them, but in the back of his mind he heard Coach Hillier's voice saying, Don't force the Z. . . .

Okay, Coach, he thought, we'll do it your way. Watts had single coverage and whoever was trying to stay with him simply couldn't. He was wide open. Alex stepped up in the pocket and fired a bullet that almost knocked Watts over as it hit him in the chest. Watts caught it, stumbled, and then fell backward onto the ground, clutching the ball.

"Nice throw," Alex heard Coach Hillier say softly from behind him. He walked up to where he was standing and added, "More important, smart throw."

The horn sounded, indicating the last period of practice was over. Everyone jogged to the middle of the field, where Coach Gordon was standing. As Alex started to take a knee, Matt Gordon put an arm around him.

"Goldie," he said. "You scare me."

Alex was glad he hadn't taken his helmet off. He wouldn't have wanted Matt or anyone else to see him grinning ear to ear.

■ ■ ■

As soon as Coach Gordon had given his brief post-practice talk about making sure to get enough rest and remembering that the easy games were now over—he'd said the same thing on Monday and Tuesday—Alex looked for Coach Hillier, who was talking to Eddie Brackens. He stood off to the side and waited. Clearly, Coach Hillier was demonstrating a technique of some kind to the running back.

When they were finished, Brackens jogged off to the locker room and Coach Hillier turned to Alex.

"That was a good decision on the last play," he said.

"Thanks, Coach," Alex said. "Do you have a minute?"

Coach Hillier looked around for a moment as if searching for someone. But then he said, "Sure, what's up?"

"I actually wanted to ask you a couple questions about the *Weekly Roar*."

"Uh-huh," Coach Hillier said.

Alex suddenly realized that both questions he had might be a little awkward for Coach Hillier to answer—the second one for sure.

"I was wondering," he said. "Was it your idea or Christine's to talk to me for that sidebar story she did?"

Coach Hillier smiled. "She's pretty, isn't she?" he said. "Also very smart. Well, this probably isn't the answer that you want to hear, but yes, it was my idea. I knew what happened to you was something people would be talking about, so I thought it made sense. I gave her your number."

He was still smiling. "I figured you wouldn't mind."

Alex smiled too. "No sir, I didn't."

"What was your other question?"

Alex paused, wondering if he should even ask. He'd come this far, though, so he plunged ahead.

"It's about Steve Garland's column."

Alex saw Coach Hillier's smile fade quickly.

"What about it?"

"He was kind of critical of Coach Gordon. You're in charge of the paper, so I was wondering . . ."

"Why I didn't make him take it out?"

"Yes."

Coach Hillier crossed his arms.

"That's a fair question," he said.

"And?"

"And you're not the first person to ask it today."

"So what's the answer?"

Coach Hillier looked at him for a moment, as if making a decision. "Okay," he said. "Okay. You're right, I do have the power to take something out of the paper if I think it's inaccurate or libelous or unfair. But ninety-nine percent of the time, I let the students make the decisions. That's how they learn. I try to be especially conscious of not censoring anything where the football team is concerned because there's an obvious conflict of interest for me as a coach."

"Who else asked you the question?"

"You should be a reporter," he said.

"I'm a quarterback," Alex said. "So who was it?"

Coach Hillier nodded in the direction of midfield, where Coach Gordon was talking to the two captains.

"Coach Gordon?" Alex said.

Another nod.

"The fact is, you got hurt because Coach Gordon kept trying to score in the fourth quarter. People have different opinions about the value of running up the score in a situation like that. I didn't question Coach Gordon about it at the time, and I'm the offensive coordinator, so I'm responsible too. What Steve wrote was a fair comment whether you agree with it or not. So I left it in."

"What did Coach Gordon say when you told him that?" Alex asked.

"Nothing," Coach Hillier said. "Which isn't good. It means he's angry."

"Does that mean something's going to happen?"

Coach Hillier shrugged. "I don't know. We'll see. But if you repeat what I just told you to anyone—including Jonas and especially anyone who works on the newspaper—something *will* happen to you and it won't be pleasant."

He smiled when he said it, so Alex smiled too.

"I hear you, Coach," Alex said. "Loud and clear."

■ ■ ■

On Friday, Alex found out that something had, in fact, happened in the wake of Steve Garland's column.

He had just sat down in his seat for French class, dreading the vocabulary test that was to come, when Christine Whitford came in and made a beeline for him.

"I have to talk to you after class," she whispered, looking very serious.

"Sure," he said, wondering what could possibly be so important.

Taking the vocab test would have been tough enough, but his mind kept wandering to what Christine could need to talk about and away from the verbs he was trying to conjugate. He finished just as the bell was sounding and handed the quiz to Mademoiselle Schiff, convinced he had gotten no more than half the questions right.

"Everything okay, Monsieur Myers?" she asked, surprising

him by speaking in English. She had been the only one of Alex's teachers who had not asked on Monday how he was feeling.

"What?" he asked, not really hearing the question at first. "No. I mean, everything's fine."

"You sure? You were looking around a lot during the quiz. Was it difficult for you today?"

"No, it was okay. . . . I mean, I hope it was okay. I'm just a little distracted."

She gave him a look that indicated she wasn't buying what he was telling her but wasn't going to pursue it. That was a relief because he could see Christine standing just outside the door looking impatient.

"*Au revoir, Monsieur Myers,*" Mademoiselle Schiff said, then added, "*Bonne chance ce soir.*"

It took Alex a split second to translate, but then he got it—or thought he did. She had said, "Good luck tonight." Did she mean with Christine?

"*Ce soir?*" he replied.

"*Oui,*" she said. "*La jeu de football, non?*"

"Oh—um, *oui,*" he said. "*Merci.*"

"*De rien,*" she replied.

Christine was practically tapping her foot by the time he got through the door.

"Sorry," he said. "Mademoiselle Schiff—"

"Forget it," she said, taking him by the arm. "Come on. We have to find a place to talk."

There was no pep rally that afternoon. According to the other guys on the team, Coach Gordon would play that card only three times during the regular season: the opener, the conference opener, and the finale against Chester. Christine walked briskly down the hall, poked her head into a break room—too crowded—and finally walked outside, where she found a spot under a tree that seemed to suit her.

"What's going on?" Alex said, truly baffled by now.

"Steve has been banned from tonight's game," she said in what would best be described as a screamed whisper.

"Steve?" Then he got it: Steve Garland, the sports editor. "Banned? What do you mean banned?"

"Coach Gordon told Mr. Hillier that Steve couldn't have a press pass for the game to sit in the press box or to talk to the players or coaches after the game. He said that if Steve wanted to act like a big-shot sportswriter he should get a job at the *Inquirer* or the *Daily News*."

"That sucks," he said. "But there's not much I can do about it. I'm the third-string quarterback."

"I know," she said. "But you *can* get some of the players to talk to Steve after the game."

"I thought he was banned?"

"From the *press box*," she said, sounding exasperated. "Coach Gordon can't keep him out of the stadium. Tell your friends on the team to talk to him."

Alex had seen several of the starters talking to reporters after practice, so he knew they were around, but he didn't really know how it all worked. No one wanted to talk to him. . . .

"So you want guys to talk to him outside the locker room, even though Coach Gordon has banned him?" he asked.

"Yes," she said. "Or maybe get me some of their cell numbers so Steve can call them over the weekend?"

"Do you know what kind of trouble guys will get in if they do that? Coach Gordon would kill them."

She put her hands on her hips, a move that instantly reminded Alex of his mom. He knew he was now officially a dead man.

"I *know* that," she said. "They can talk to him off the record. He won't use their names."

"How can they be sure of that?" he asked.

The hands were still on the hips. "If he uses their names, they can say they didn't know they weren't supposed to talk to him *and* they'll never speak to him again. He won't want that to happen."

Alex sighed. "I'll see what I can do. I don't know why, but I'll try."

She smiled at him. Which reminded him why he was willing to help.

15

The game that night was marginally more competitive than the Mercer game had been. Alex could see during warm-ups that Cherry Hill Academy had bigger players than Mercer, but their skill level, once the game began, wasn't that much better.

The score was 7–7 after one quarter, and Coach Gordon called the team around him at the quarter break to let all the players know how disappointed he was in their performance.

"If you expect to be a good football team," he said angrily, "you can't let a team like this think it can play with you!"

Whether it was their coach's angry words or just the inevitable fact that Cherry Hill didn't have enough players to compete with them, the Lions scored three second-quarter touchdowns. Matt Gordon ran for two and found Jonas wide open on a thirty-two-yard post pattern for a third.

That seemed to relax everyone a little bit, although Coach

Gordon rambled on at halftime about the need to not let up in the second thirty minutes. They didn't. The final score was 42–14, with the second-stringers giving up a late touchdown to make it that close. The fourth-quarter play-calling, especially once Jake Bilney came into the game at the end of the third, was much more conservative than it had been a week earlier—mostly straight handoffs. Bilney threw one pass, on a third and fifteen at midfield, and it was intercepted.

He trotted off the field to where Alex was standing next to Matt Gordon.

"I'm not sure why Dad called that play," Matt said. "That's not the kind of throw you're comfortable trying to make."

"You mean I'm not any good at it," Jake responded. "It's the kind of play I might have to make if you ever get hurt. Give your dad credit for knowing what he's doing. I just need to be better."

Matt Gordon said nothing in response. He just patted Bilney on the shoulder and said, "Don't be so tough on yourself, Jake."

Jake *was* tough on himself—frequently. Alex wondered how much of it had to do with feeling pressure from him as third string. Jake had already commented on that a couple of times.

But whatever Bilney's fears, Alex never saw the field all night. Bilney knelt down twice—without incident—after Cherry Hill's late touchdown and everyone shook hands when the clock hit zero.

Alex had already asked Jonas before the game if he would talk to Steve Garland over the weekend and Jonas had said yes, as long as Steve *promised* not to use his name.

Alex thought briefly about asking Matt Gordon but didn't: it wasn't fair to ask Matt to betray his father in any way. Matt might have been willing, but that didn't mean Alex should ask. Instead, he asked Stephen Harvey, who was getting enough playing time to make it worthwhile for Garland to talk to him.

Harvey gave him a look. "I saw that girl after the game last week," he said. "And I saw her story on you. She's pretty, but are you sure you want to take this kind of risk to impress her?"

He was speaking very softly. They were standing in the freshman corner of the locker room while everyone else undressed to shower after Coach Gordon's brief postgame talk.

"I'm not trying to impress her," Alex said.

"Really?" Harvey said. "What are you trying to do?"

Alex hadn't really thought about that.

"Okay, maybe I am trying to impress her," he admitted. "Will you help?"

Harvey thought about it for a moment. "Sure. Why not? But if the guy uses my name, I'm gonna get mad at *you*, not him."

"Understood," Alex said, still not sure why he was doing this. Actually, he was sure but suspected it wasn't a great idea.

Bilney, already dressed, walked over. "Matt and I are going to Hope's party," he said. "I heard you were invited too. You going?"

"I think so," Alex said. "Any reason not to?"

"None at all," Bilney said. "You're not the one who can't complete a pass."

"Come on," Alex said. "Third and fifteen, they were waiting for you to throw."

"Yeah, well, maybe that shouldn't have been the play call at 42–7. But you know, I know, Matt knows, and even his father knows that you could have made that play work. You can throw left-handed better than I can throw right-handed."

He wasn't even smiling a little bit when he said it.

∎ ∎ ∎

Alex's mom dropped off Alex and Jonas at Hope Alexander's house, which was definitely in the McMansion part of town. The house had to be twice as big as any house Alex had ever been in.

"Why don't they just move the school here?" Jonas murmured as they got out of the car on the circular drive. It was ten-thirty and Jonas's mom, who was doing the pickup, had said she would be there about midnight. Alex had mixed emotions about that: part of him wanted to stay late; part of him wondered if anyone would talk to them. He was glad to have Jonas riding shotgun.

The place was packed. Much to his surprise, Hope Alexander came over to greet them when they walked in.

"I'm *so* glad you guys made it," she said. "Jonas, great playing tonight!"

"Thanks," Jonas said, clearly pleased she had noticed.

"There's food and drinks all over the place," she said. She leaned in close for a moment. "No alcohol—my parents are here."

Alex was kind of relieved to hear that. He'd told his mom there wouldn't be drinking, but he kind of thought there might be. The last thing he wanted was someone asking him if he wanted a drink. He had enough on his plate without dealing with that question—much less the answer, whatever it would be.

They walked into what Alex assumed was the living room—it was massive—and heard thumping music. There was a DJ, and furniture had been moved aside to open up a dance floor. A lot of kids smiled or waved at them, a few shouting over the noise, "Nice game, Jonas!"

"Let's go outside!" Jonas yelled in his ear, pointing at some open doors in the back. There were clearly plenty of people out there too. "Can't hear anything in here."

Alex nodded and they walked outside. There was a table piled high with food and drinks. The two of them made a beeline for the food. Alex had just picked up a plate and was setting his sights on a tray filled with buffalo chicken wings when he spotted Jake Bilney standing under a tree.

With Christine Whitford.

They were just talking, each holding a drink. But it was the *way* they were talking that brought Alex up short: Jake was leaning forward just a little and down so he could hear Christine better. Christine was looking up at him as she talked, with that magnetic smile turned up to full wattage.

Jonas noticed Alex staring.

"Easy, big fella," he said.

"What?" Alex said, starting to put some wings on his plate.

"You don't like Bilney talking up your girl. I get it."

"She's not *my* girl," Alex said.

"You'd like her to be your girl," Jonas said. "And if you tell me that's not true, I'll tell you you're a liar or crazy or both."

"Look—celery sticks," Alex said, pointing at the bowl in front of them.

"Yeah, right," Jonas said. "*That's* what you're focused on right now."

■ ■ ■

They left shortly after midnight. Alex wished it could have been sooner. The food was good and they found a place to sit and eat, but other than the occasional hello or wave or "Nice game, Jonas," no one came near them.

They got up and mingled and, at Jonas's urging, Alex finally went over to say hello to Christine. Jake had wandered off and Alex had breathed a sigh of relief. She was standing in the same spot, brushing her hair back with her hand, when he walked over.

"Hey, do you need something to drink?" he asked.

"Oh, no thanks," she said. "Jake just went to get me another Coke."

Alex's heart sank. Jake hadn't left. He'd just gone back for more drinks.

"I didn't know you two were friends," he said, realizing how dorky that sounded as soon as he said it.

She smiled. "We're not. I never met him before tonight. He seems like a nice guy."

"Great guy," Alex said—too enthusiastically. "He just gets down on himself a lot for not being as good a player as he'd like to be."

That was a mean thing to say. If Christine thought so, she didn't say anything.

"I guess Matt got the talent and he got the looks," she said.

Ouch. Alex was still trying to think of a response to that remark when Jake walked up behind him.

"Goldie, you made it," he said.

He handed Christine a Coke.

"I was just telling Christine how tough it is to watch you unleash those rockets every day in practice."

"And I was telling Jake he should talk to Steve Garland," she said, giving Jake what Alex *knew* was a flirty smile.

"And I told Christine the *only* reporter I wanted to talk to was her," Jake said, smiling back at her. "And the subject will *not* be the football team."

"I better go find Jonas," Alex mumbled, wishing the ground would open up and swallow him whole.

They both looked at him as if they'd just remembered he was there.

"Yeah, sure," Jake said. "See you at practice on Monday, Goldie."

"Bye, Alex," Christine said. "I'm glad you're feeling okay."

Alex walked away dazed. This made two Fridays in a row that he'd been blindsided.

■　■　■

The last nonconference game of the season would be the team's first road trip. The game was at Main Line Prep, which wasn't that far from Villanova University. He remembered going to a basketball game at Villanova two years earlier with his dad and his uncle when the family had spent Thanksgiving in Philadelphia.

Alex had great memories of that afternoon. It had been just the three of them and Villanova had played La Salle, one of its local rivals. Now it felt like a lot more than two years had passed. His dad still hadn't found time to come and visit them, although he had promised to come "sometime in September." The Main Line game was on September 19 so, Alex guessed, his dad still had two weeks left to make good on that promise.

School was now in its fourth week and Alex was starting to feel more comfortable. At the very least, he now had a routine and a small handful of friends. He ate lunch every day with Jonas, Stephen, and Tim Matte, who was Stephen's best friend and played on the basketball team. Occasionally Matt and Jake joined them. The subject of Christine Whitford had not come up since the party.

Tim was the only person, as far as Alex knew, who was aware that Alex had enlisted Jonas and Stephen to talk to Steve Garland after the Cherry Hill game.

"I'll be very curious to read what the guy writes tomorrow," Jonas said quietly during lunch on Tuesday. Matt and Jake were not there, so it was okay to talk. "Based on what happened and what he asked, I don't think Coach is going to be too happy when he reads it."

Stephen laughed. "Ya think? If someone writes that the only coach on the planet who is better than Coach Gordon is Bill Belichick, Coach would be mad because he was ranked second. I promise you he's gonna go nuts."

"You think we might get in trouble?" Jonas asked.

"I don't know how he'd know it was us—Garland promised he wouldn't use my name."

"Me too," Jonas said. "But I'm still nervous."

"You should be," Tim said. "I think you're both crazy to have talked to him."

All eyes turned to Alex.

"Hey, I didn't force you guys to do it," he said defensively. "And anyway, nothing's going to happen. Coach will be pissed but not at any of us. What's he going to do, ban the guy again?"

"I hope you're right," Jonas said.

"Me too," Stephen added.

"I'm right," Alex said. "Don't worry. I'm right."

■ ■ ■

He was wrong.

Alex first suspected trouble when he picked up the *Weekly Roar* the next morning. He went through the same routine as the previous week—arriving early and taking the newspaper to the bathroom for privacy.

The headline on Steve Garland's column was direct: BANNED.

The column explained how he had been told by his editor, who also happened to be an assistant football coach, that he would not be allowed to sit in the press box or to talk to any players because he had accused Coach Gordon of running up the score against Mercer.

Garland wrote:

> *Gee, I wonder how anyone could possibly think someone was running up the score in a game that ended 77–0.*

It's a good thing none of the Mercer players or coaches wanted to sit in the press box last Friday, because they would have been banned too, based on the fact that they tried to kill poor Alex Myers on the last play of the game.

Ouch, Alex thought—remembering the play and thinking how Coach Gordon would react to reading that sentence.

Then came the quotes. From one player: "We all knew we were running up the score, but we also know Coach has very high expectations for this team. We all do. The fact that we need to pay attention all the time should be obvious to all of us after the first quarter against Cherry Hill."

That was clearly Jonas: honest, but careful. And, Alex thought, not too bad.

The next quote wasn't as careful. "If I'd been from Mercer, I'd have been mad too. I think Coach knew he almost got Myers hurt by running up the score, and that's why we backed off on Cherry Hill late in the game. I know I felt better about it."

That was Stephen. He had expressed similar sentiments to Alex. He had talked about how much he loved to watch college football and about seeing Notre Dame throw a late touchdown pass the year before against Navy to make the final score 50–6 and how much that bothered him. To him, this was even worse.

Garland closed his column with one final shot:

This is clearly a very talented and deep team. No one questions Coach Gordon's knowledge of the game or his ability to get the most from a team. If they stay healthy,

the Lions should go deep into the state playoffs come
November.

But that's still not an excuse for lacking compassion
for an overmatched opponent. That's what I was saying
last week, and even if I'm banned from the entire state of
Pennsylvania, I'm not going to apologize. It was true then
and it's true now.

Whoo boy, Alex thought, he *might* be banned from the
entire state of Pennsylvania.

By lunchtime, everyone had read the column.

"You still think no one's going to get in trouble for this?"
Stephen asked as he munched on a grilled-cheese sandwich.

"Steve Garland," Alex said. "Who else is he going to get
mad at? He didn't use your names, just like he promised."

Alex looked up to see Christine Whitford walking toward
their table. She did not look happy.

"Did you guys hear what happened?" she asked.

Jonas's head was on a swivel, clearly afraid someone would
notice her talking to them.

"What?" Alex asked. "Did Garland get banned again?"

She was shaking her head even before he finished the
question.

"No, that's not it. I mean, probably he is. Coach Gordon
fired Mr. Hillier as an assistant coach."

"WHAT?" they all said at once.

Instinctively, they looked around—Christine included—
to make sure no one was paying any attention to them. It was
late in lunch hour and the room was half empty. Alex noted
with some relief that the table where Matt Gordon and Jake

Bilney and most of the football team's upperclassmen often sat was already empty.

"He just told us," she said. "We always meet in the newspaper office at lunch on Wednesday to plan the next edition of the paper. He told us that, as of this morning, he is no longer a football coach. He said Coach Gordon gave him a choice: the paper or the team, and he chose the paper."

"So he didn't actually get *fired* as a coach, then," Jonas said.

"Technically no, I guess," Christine said. "But he did say Coach Gordon accused him of being disloyal for letting Steve's column run."

Remembering his conversation with Coach Hillier about Garland's first column, Alex understood. Coach Gordon had, for all intents and purposes, ordered Coach Hillier to control Garland a week earlier. Coach Hillier had stuck to his principle of letting the students run the newspaper as long as they weren't inaccurate or unfair. It had cost him his job.

Alex couldn't help but feel partly responsible. Maybe if he hadn't convinced Jonas and Stephen to talk to Garland, this wouldn't have happened. Then again, Garland was going to rip Coach Gordon for banning him, with or without quotes from the team.

"I should go talk to Coach Hillier," Alex said.

"He's still in the newspaper office right now," Christine said.

"Does he know who talked to Garland?" Stephen asked.

He didn't sound scared so much as curious. Alex was convinced that very few things scared Harvey. He had a linebacker's mentality: kill or be killed.

"I honestly don't know," Christine said. "I don't know if he asked Steve or if Steve told him. He didn't ask me, I know that."

"We should all go talk to him," Jonas said. "There's still fifteen minutes until fifth period starts.

"Where's the newspaper office?" Stephen asked.

"Basement. It's at the very end of the hall on the right, across from the yearbook office."

They all stood up and, without another word to Christine, headed for the door.

Coach Hillier—now Mr. Hillier, apparently—was sitting behind the one desk in the small office that said THE WEEKLY ROAR on the door.

If he was surprised to see Alex, Jonas, and Stephen, he didn't show it.

"What can I do for you guys?" he asked when they walked in.

"We just heard," Stephen said, taking the lead as the oldest in the group. "We can't believe it."

"Have a seat," Mr. Hillier said, indicating chairs scattered around the room. They each grabbed one and sat in front of his desk.

"Look, fellas, here's the deal," he said. "I think Coach Gordon is right about this. I know none of the three of you are interested in journalism, at least not at the moment, but one thing you learn—and one thing I try to teach—is that journalists and the people they cover shouldn't be friends. They can like one another and respect one another, but there are times when they are on opposite sides.

"Coach Gordon said I was trying to work for opposing sides, and he was right."

"Even on a high school paper?" Alex asked. "I mean, Steve Garland is a student at Chester Heights High School, just like we are."

"True," Mr. Hillier said. "And I'm a teacher at Chester Heights High School, so we'd all like to see our teams do well. But Steve wants to be a real reporter someday and I think he's got the talent to do that. There are others on the paper like him. My job, as the faculty advisor to the paper, is to ask them to do what a real reporter—one who gets paid to do it for a living—would do in any given situation.

"Steve's criticism of Coach Gordon was, in my mind, fair. He talked to people about it and formed an opinion. He didn't write that Coach Gordon was a despicable human being for doing it; he wrote that he thought Coach Gordon made a mistake and that mistake almost led to a serious injury to one of his players.

"I told Coach Gordon I thought Steve had a valid point and that trying to ban him because he disagreed was petty. In fact, I told him I admired Steve for figuring out a way to get players"—he nodded at Stephen and Jonas—"to talk to him. That was good reporting on his part."

"So you knew it was us?" Jonas said.

"Sure. Steve told me, and he told me exactly how it happened, how Christine talked to you, Alex, and you talked to these guys. *That* is how a newspaper works."

Seeing the looks on the boys' faces, he laughed. "Don't worry. I didn't tell *Coach Gordon* any of you were involved. That's another thing journalists do—protect their sources. Coach Gordon didn't even ask me who it was because he knew I wouldn't tell him."

"Won't you miss coaching?" Alex said.

"Sure I will. Of course! But I'd miss working with the newspaper kids too.

"Coach Gordon gave me a choice this morning, but really I made my choice when I ran Steve's column this week.

"Don't worry, guys." He smiled. "You'll be in good hands with Coach Brotman running the offense. He knows what he's doing."

Alex still felt queasy about the whole thing. He liked Coach Brotman, who coached the offensive line, but he felt a special bond with Coach Hillier . . . Mr. Hillier.

"Coach, do you think Coach Gordon will try to find out who talked?" Alex asked.

"Absolutely," Mr. Hillier said, just as the five-minute warning bell prior to fifth period rang. "Absolutely."

■ ■ ■

Mr. Hillier was absolutely correct.

The locker room was buzzing as everyone got dressed for practice. Everyone knew that Coach Hillier was gone and why. Clearly, Coach Gordon was angry. No one knew what awaited them when they got on the practice field.

When the whistle blew and they all gathered at midfield, Coach Gordon was wearing sunglasses under his cap, so it was hard to read his face as they all took a knee. They found out what he was thinking quickly enough.

"A football team is a family," he said, his voice measured and even. "Families are loyal to one another. Families know there is *us* and there is *them* and no one outside the family can possibly be *us*."

His voice was rising. "There are at least two members of this team who forgot that over the last few days. Coach Hillier also forgot that, which is why he's not here." He paused. "He's not here, you should all know, by choice. I told him he could be part of this family or he could supervise the student newspaper but he couldn't do both.

"He understood. He made a choice. We'll miss him because he's a fine football coach, but we have all we need to be successful this season right here on this field right now."

Another pause. He looked around at his players. Most, Alex noticed, were not looking at him. They were staring at the ground.

"Now, for those of us who are still here, who still want to win a state championship, I think we all understand that this sort of thing can't go on. So we're going to do two things. First, no one is to speak to anyone in the media—not just the student paper, *anyone*—without my approval or the approval of Mr. Hardy."

Frank Hardy was the athletic director. The joke around the team was that the most important thing he did every day was to make sure Coach Gordon always had hot coffee waiting for him.

"Someone from the staff—either Mr. Hardy or one of the

coaches—will be present for all interviews," Coach Gordon continued. "If someone asks to talk to you after a game, you tell them they have to check with Mr. Hardy or with me. If they say they've done that, tell them to find a coach who can supervise the interview.

"No exceptions. No saying, 'Coach, I didn't know.' You've been told very clearly."

Alex wondered if this meant he could no longer talk to Christine Whitford after French class. The answer was probably that he couldn't.

"One other thing. I expect those of you who spoke to this reporter, Garland or whatever his name is, to come and tell me. I'd also like to know *why*. Your confession will remain private and you won't be punished beyond me telling you that you made a mistake and that you had better not make it again.

"Today and tomorrow are amnesty days. No discipline of any kind, because we've got a game to play on Friday and that is priority one. But if no one has come forward by the time we get off the bus back here after the game Friday night, everyone on the team will be in here to run on Saturday morning. And every morning after that, until whoever did it comes forward.

"I want you to understand I'm not upset with what you said. I'm upset that you said anything at all to someone who you knew had been banned from talking to members of this team. Family. Loyalty. Us versus them. Remember that—*all* of you.

"Okay, let's report to the position coaches and get started."

As they all stood up, Alex felt as if Stephen and Jonas were boring holes through his head with their eyes. He wondered if any of the other players could sense the tension coming off him.

Someone was calling his name—specifically, his nickname.

"Goldie, over here." It was Matt Gordon, waving at him. Oh God, Alex thought, does Matt know?

He jogged over to where Matt was standing with Jake Bilney.

"Coach Brotman still has to work with the O-line during drill periods," Matt said. "My dad says he'll get someone in here to work with us on our drills by Monday. He'll probably come over to help us himself, but for now we're on our own.

"We know what we're supposed to do anyway," he added, "so it's no big deal. Let's get started."

Alex could feel himself exhale. He thought he could feel Bilney doing the same thing. He was willing to bet Matt had noticed Jake talking to Christine at the party and that might make him a suspect in "Garland-gate." The three of them lined up alongside one another and began tossing warm-up passes to the receivers stationed about twelve yards away. After five throws, the receivers would move back about two yards.

They were about halfway through their warm-ups and Alex was starting to breathe more easily and get into the rhythm of throwing when Matt, who was no more than five feet away from him, started to talk to him softly.

"Did you go to see Coach Hillier today?" he asked.

Alex was tempted to lie but decided that was a bad idea. "Yeah, I did. At the end of lunch hour, when I heard."

Matt stepped into a throw and kept talking without ever turning his head. The only other person who could possibly hear him was Jake since Matt was in the middle, with Jake and Alex flanking him.

"I went to see him too. Personally, I think my dad is making a big mistake. We need him. He's helped me a lot with my fundamentals. Even you need him."

One thing about Matt, Alex thought, he was anything but predictable.

"He told *me* he understood your dad's position. That he could be on one side or the other but not both."

"Yeah, I know," Matt said. "But really, who cares? It's the student newspaper. Guy said Dad ran up the score. Well, guess what? He did. We all know it and Dad knows it. Sometimes he gets carried away with the whole 'head coach is king' thing. I told him that."

"And?"

The receivers were now standing about twenty-five yards away and they were making their last five throws.

"And he told me I was the quarterback and he was the coach. End of story. I talked to Garland—we've got a history class together. He's not a bad guy. But this isn't over. And if Dad goes on with this witch hunt, it will be bad for all of us."

The whistle blew. They all jogged to the next set of drills. Alex's arm felt warm and loose. His mind was spinning.

■ ■ ■

"So what did Christine tell you?"

Alex and Jonas were standing in front of their lockers the next morning. They had a few minutes before the bell for first period rang.

"She said we shouldn't confess," Alex said, speaking in

a hushed voice and glancing around in case anyone got too close to them. "She talked to Coach—Mr. Hillier—about it. He told her Coach Gordon won't necessarily punish us directly, but he'll make sure everyone on the team knows it was us and we'll be ostracized."

"Ostra-what?" Jonas asked.

Alex smiled. That was almost exactly what he'd said when Christine had used the word on the phone the previous night.

"It means we'll be treated like traitors," Alex said. "Don't worry. I had to look it up even after Christine explained it to me."

Jonas said nothing for a moment. "But if we don't confess, the whole team will be running every morning. *And* Jake knows you got a thing for Christine. He might tell Matt or even Coach that you were involved."

"He doesn't know I have a crush on Christine," Alex said, feeling his face flush.

"Alex, *everyone* knows you have a crush on Christine. You *should* have a crush on Christine."

"Yeah, well, I think *she's* got a crush on Jake."

"She'll get over it."

Alex didn't answer that. He was thinking about what Christine had said about the whole team having to run. "Mr. Hillier told Christine that Coach Gordon will give up the running thing quickly because in the end it will hurt the team. She says we have to just stay cool and ride this out."

"Easy for her to say," Jonas said.

17

The trip to Main Line Prep on Friday proved difficult in more ways than one.

To begin with—rain. It was one of those steady, dreary, all-day rains that started soon after Alex woke up and showed no sign of letting up throughout the morning and afternoon.

And then—traffic. They thought they had planned for traffic. They left school at four o'clock. Maybe fifty rain-soaked students were standing outside to cheer them on as they boarded the buses: one for the offense and offensive coaches, another for the defense, and another still for the band and the cheerleaders.

The plan was to arrive at about five, relax inside for about thirty minutes, and then go out for initial warm-ups at five-thirty. Everyone was taped and in uniform—except for pads and helmets—since the visitors' locker room at Main Line

Prep was, according to Buddy Thomas, "too small to fit fifty goldfish, much less fifty football players."

They were in trouble right from the start. The rain had caused a number of accidents and they sat on I-95 for an hour, unable to move. It was 6:05 by the time they got off the bus. Mr. Hardy had called ahead to see if kickoff could be pushed back to seven-thirty. The answer had apparently been a firm no.

Since the players sat front to back based on class, Alex and Jonas were in the back row and couldn't hear what Mr. Hardy was telling Coach Gordon. But the word drifted back pretty quickly that Main Line didn't want to delay the start because it didn't want fans sitting in the rain for an extra thirty minutes.

"I wouldn't want to sit out there any more than I had to either," Jonas said.

"Why don't you go tell Coach Gordon that?" Alex said.

Jonas didn't even bother responding.

The game didn't go a whole lot better—at least at the start. Even though Coach Gordon had told them to shake off the weather and the long bus trip and focus, there was a sense of dread on the sideline early. The only touchdown of the first half came when Matt, trying to roll out, slipped and underthrew the ball so badly that one of Main Line's cornerbacks intercepted it easily and practically jogged into the end zone from thirty yards out to make the score 7–0 after the extra point.

There was also a play-calling issue. Coach Brotman always worked the game from the sideline so he could be in direct contact with his linemen. Coach Hillier had called plays from the press box, where you had a better view of the entire field. Now Brotman was trying to call plays, but after Matt threw the interception, Coach Gordon told him to just worry about the O-line and he would do the play-calling. Alex was standing a few yards away and it looked to him like Coach Brotman was relieved.

Alex also heard Matt, who had taken off his helmet as he came off the field after the poor pass. "It isn't Coach Brotman's fault," he said to his father. "I slipped and made a bad throw."

Coach Gordon said nothing. He just stared out at the field, hands on hips, the rain pouring down the Bill Belichick–style hoodie he had put on because of the weather.

Halftime began with lots of shouting and profanity—most of it from the coaches. They broke into offense and defense, but the locker room was so small that the coaches had to keep their voices down. Then the room suddenly got deathly quiet.

"Any thoughts?" Coach Gordon asked the other offensive coaches.

Silence.

"I've got one," Matt Gordon said.

Everyone in the room looked at him. It was usually a given that only the coaches talked at halftime. The players were expected to listen and nod. Then again, Matt wasn't just any player.

"What is it, Gordon?" his father said.

"We need to get out of the spread option," Matt said. "For one thing, Will and I are having a terrible time with the snap because the ball's so wet. For another, it's very hard to make cuts and get to the outside on this field. If we were at home on field turf, it would be different. But this is regular grass and it's a mess and it's going to get worse. We'd be better off playing straight power football. Run the I-formation. Move one of the tight ends to fullback for an extra blocker and go straight at 'em. I know the guys on the line can do it. If they're blocking straight ahead, they're bigger and stronger than Main Line's defense."

Silence. Matt had basically told his father to scrap the offense he was so proud of—the offense that put his son in position to be a star.

Finally Coach Gordon blinked. The silence had probably lasted thirty seconds. It felt more like thirty minutes to Alex.

"Okay, we'll try it for two series. But that's all. Crenshaw, you're the fullback, just like in goal line," he said, turning to backup tight end Mike Crenshaw, who usually came in to block for the tailback when the team had the ball inside the 5-yard line. "You okay with that?"

"Yes sir."

"Okay," Coach Gordon said. "Let's go find out what you boys are made of."

Alex couldn't help but note that it was the *boys*—not the coaches or the head coach—whose manhood was apparently at stake.

■ ■ ■

Matt Gordon turned out to be a brilliant offensive coordinator. His idea that running straight at the Main Line defense would get the Chester Heights offense moving was a hundred percent correct. The Lions were helped immeasurably by the fact that Main Line's tailback fumbled on the first play of the half. Gerry Detwiler jumped on the ball at Main Line's 29-yard line and the game turned quickly after that.

Matt handed the ball to starting tailback Craig Josephs on six straight plays. Josephs ran off right tackle or left tackle each time, with Crenshaw leading him into the hole. Crenshaw was a senior who didn't play more often because he was a little too small at six three, 230 to be an offensive lineman and didn't have good enough hands to be a consistent tight end. Blocking straight ahead was the best thing he did, especially given the extra step that starting from the fullback position gave him. He absolutely bludgeoned Main Line's defensive tackles, opening up wide gaps in the line. Josephs scored from the 4-yard line and Pete Ross, the placekicker, somehow dug the ball out of the mud to make the extra point and tie the game at 7–7.

The atmosphere on the Chester Heights sideline changed completely. Even though Matt had done little more than turn and hand the ball to Josephs, everyone knew he had been responsible for the sudden change in their fortune.

"Best coach on this sideline named Gordon might not be the one who everyone calls 'Coach,'" Jonas said to Alex as Ross prepared to kick off. "Something as simple as that and none of the coaches thought of it."

"Or were afraid to say anything," Alex said.

"Hey, the fact that Coach was smart enough to listen should count for something, don't you think?" said Jake, who had been standing nearby. "A lot of coaches wouldn't let a player even *make* a suggestion like that, much less follow it."

Alex supposed that was true, but he also found it kind of ironic that Jake Bilney seemed to be more of a true believer in Matthew Gordon Senior than Matthew Gordon Junior was.

As had been the case the entire first half, Chester Heights shut down the Main Line offense on the next series. When the Lions got the ball back, the new offense was still working. Once, for variety, Matt stuck the ball into Crenshaw's stomach and no one from Main Line even noticed he had the ball until he was twelve yards downfield. This time, Matt scored on a quarterback sneak from the 1-yard line. The Lions led 14–7.

On the next series, with time running out in the third quarter, Main Line moved their defensive backs almost onto the line of scrimmage to stop the straight-ahead runs. On a third and three at Main Line's 48, Matt suddenly began shouting instructions at the line, clearly changing the play. Or, Alex thought, pretending to change the play. He had done that before.

Alex knew that Matt had been calling the plays himself. On almost every play, Coach Gordon was sending one of the receivers in with the instruction "Check with Matt." That meant Matt was free to call what he wanted, although the understanding was that most of the calls were going to be simple running plays. Matt had mixed in Crenshaw's one run and one counter play. His only carry had been on the quarterback sneak for the touchdown.

Now Matt ducked under center, took the snap, and began to run to the right with the ball. Alex could hear the panicked cries of the Main Line defenders, "QB sweep! QB sweep!" as they scrambled to get to Matt before he could round the corner and turn upfield.

But he never did turn upfield. Instead, just before he got to the corner, he stuck the ball in Jonas's stomach going in the other direction. A reverse!

The entire Main Line defense was heading in the wrong direction—pursuing Matt—when Jonas got the ball in his hands. He was around the corner in a split second, racing straight down the field with no one from Main Line even close to him.

If Main Line had any life left in it at that point, it drained away as soon as Jonas crossed the goal line and flipped the ball to the referee as if nothing dramatic had happened.

The fourth quarter opened with another hold by the defense, and the Lions once again took the ball the length of the field, eating up seven minutes off the clock. It was Crenshaw who scored the touchdown this time, diving in from the 2. Alex figured Matt engineered the TD for Crenshaw since his blocking had been so critical throughout the second half.

The final was 28–7. Jake came in to run the offense on the last series and got knocked down on one handoff, which meant that Alex was the only player on the Chester Heights sideline who didn't have mud on his uniform when the teams met at midfield for the postgame handshakes. Alex noticed the Main Line coach, Bobby Chesbro, pointing a finger at Coach Gordon as they approached one another. Wondering if something was up, he wandered close enough so he could hear what was said as the coaches shook hands.

"That was a great adjustment you made at halftime, Coach," he heard Coach Chesbro say. "Taught me a lesson."

"Thanks," Coach Gordon said. "Good luck the rest of the way."

Alex almost laughed. He wanted to say something to Jake, but he was a few yards away talking to a couple of Main Line players. Matt was also talking to several Main Line players. He was so covered in mud you could barely read the 12 on his back.

Alex noticed that Matt, Jonas, Gerry Detwiler, and Craig Josephs were all being followed by camera crews. Clearly, there were a lot of media people covering the game, which wasn't that surprising since both teams had been ranked in the *USA Today* top twenty-five that week: Chester Heights at number twenty, and Main Line at number twenty-two. He also noticed that the assistant coaches were making sure that none of the players stopped to talk to any of the media types.

"Locker room, fellas," he heard Coach Brotman say. "Let's get out of the rain. Guys, give these kids a break. They're all soaked."

That was for sure, Alex thought, but that wasn't why Coach Brotman—and the other coaches—were pulling everyone away from the TV cameras and the writers with their notebooks and tape recorders.

They all trooped into the tiny locker room and waited for the doors to close.

"Great win, fellas," Coach Gordon said when everyone was quiet. "You showed what kind of team you are in that second half.

"We're gonna give game balls to all you guys on the O-line for the way you blocked, and we're gonna give one to you too, Crenshaw, because there are Main Line guys still lying on their backs out there from some of the blocks you threw."

They all cheered for the O-line and Crenshaw. Alex waited for Coach Gordon to go on, because clearly no one deserved a game ball more than Matt.

He continued. "And you know what? We're gonna give game balls to everyone on defense too. You guys didn't allow a single point all night. You kept us in the game until we figured things out offensively."

More cheers. Alex, in the back of the room, looked at Jonas.

"We?" he mouthed.

Jonas shrugged.

"Two more things," Coach Gordon said. "One, no one talks to the media tonight. There will be a lot of requests. Just say, 'Sorry, I have to get on the bus.' I will do the talking for the team tonight.

"Second, you have the weekend off. The players who were involved in the incident with the student newspaper this week have come forward. So the matter's closed. We'll see you all at the usual time Monday."

Alex was standing between Jonas and Stephen when Coach Gordon announced that the Steve Garland matter was closed. He glanced at them, but neither one looked back at him.

He realized this was not the time or place to even exchange glances.

Coach Gordon had left the locker room, presumably to talk to the media, while everyone got dressed. No one showered—there were only four showers in the entire locker room—so everyone just changed into dry clothes for the bus ride home.

As soon as they walked through the door, Alex felt the TV lights on them and he heard several voices shouting Matt's name.

"Matt, give us a minute!"

"One question, Matt!"

"I feel like the president," Matt said to Alex and Jake without cracking a smile.

Alex noticed Christine Whitford and Steve Garland standing with a clump of other media people who were separated from the players by yellow-jacketed security guards.

On the bus, Alex sat next to Jonas and they both pointedly said nothing. The bus was quieter than Alex expected after a win. He suspected everyone was exhausted—and relieved that Garland-gate was apparently over. He was dying to ask Jonas or Stephen if they had changed their minds and talked to Coach Gordon, but couldn't do it.

Finally, just before the bus turned into the school parking lot, Alex's phone buzzed. Cell phone calls weren't allowed on the bus, but—on the way home—texts were allowed. Alex figured it was his mom telling him she was waiting for him. The rain had finally stopped.

Alex looked at his phone and saw the text wasn't from his mother but from Stephen.

It said, *Stark's—11:30 tomorrow?*

Jonas was looking at his phone too.

"You get this too?" he said, showing Alex his phone.

Alex nodded, just as his phone buzzed again.

NO Christine, the second message said.

"Okay?" he asked Jonas.

"Fine," Jonas said, and they both sent their answers to Stephen as the bus pulled up in front of the locker room.

■ ■ ■

By now, phone calls from Christine didn't surprise Alex anymore.

She texted him early on Saturday morning, asking him to call her. He debated whether to ignore her, text back, or call.

He finally opted for calling—knowing it was probably a mistake.

"Can we meet for lunch today?" she asked.

"No," Alex answered too quickly. "I mean, why?"

"You saw what happened after the game," she said. "No one was allowed to talk to anyone on the team."

"I know. But after what happened last week, it's just too risky for any of us to talk. If *anyone* is quoted, even anonymously, Coach Gordon will go nuts."

"I know. I'm just curious how you all reacted when Coach Gordon decided to give up on the spread option and go to the I-formation at halftime."

"Coach Gordon?" he blurted. "Who said it was Coach Gordon's idea?"

"He did," she said. "You mean it wasn't him? Was it Coach Brotman?"

Alex caught himself. If Coach Gordon had decided to take credit for the change in offense, *he* wasn't going to be the one to contradict him.

"Sure, it was him."

"Come on, Alex."

"I really don't know who it was," he said, not happy that he was lying but not feeling like he had a choice. "The coaches go off into a corner for a while and we can't hear what they're saying."

"So you just don't want to give him credit for being smart, then."

"What!"

Now *she* was defending Coach Gordon? Who would she get *that* from? Oh God—it had to be Jake.

She was talking and he was half listening.

"You know I'll find out the truth one way or the other," she was saying. "So will Steve. The assistant coaches still talk to him."

"Find out from them, then. They should know."

She sighed, clearly exasperated. Alex realized that he did a lot better not giving in to her on the phone than he did in person.

"How about if we meet at Stark's for lunch to talk about all this?"

"Can't," he said. "Have plans."

"With who?" she asked, almost sounding indignant.

"Don't sound so shocked—I do have friends."

"I know," she said. "I just thought we were . . . friends too."

He started to say something like, *That's funny, we weren't friends until I got knocked silly and you got a story out of it.* Or, *Seems to me like you're a lot friendlier with Jake than you are with me.* He caught himself, though—neither comment was a good idea.

"We are," he said. "But I can't talk to you right now. I'm the third-string quarterback and if I get caught doing something that upsets Coach Gordon, he'll cut me altogether. Look what he did to Coach Hillier, and that could have cost us the game last night."

"What do you mean?"

"Nothing," he said. Geez, if he stayed on the phone much longer he was going to say something he shouldn't. "I gotta go," he said. "My mother's calling me to breakfast."

"No, she's not," Christine said. "You're just afraid to talk to me."

She really was too smart for her own good—or his.

"You're right," he said. "Which is why I have to go now."

He hung up feeling guilty, but letting her join them at Stark's would be a disaster on every possible level.

■ ■ ■

"Well, who was it, then?" Jonas asked.

They were sitting at a back table inside Stark's. Much to Alex's relief, there were no familiar faces around when he walked in the door and found both Stephen and Jonas waiting for him, even though he was two minutes early.

They hadn't wasted any time getting to the point: Jonas said he hadn't spoken to Coach Gordon and Stephen said the same thing. Alex figured it went without saying that he hadn't confessed, but he confirmed that for the two of them nevertheless.

Which led to Jonas's question. Who?

Alex had been wondering all night and had a theory. "What if no one said anything . . . ? Is it possible that Coach Hillier had it right, that Coach Gordon didn't want the entire team running for days and so he just *said* people had turned themselves in so it would look like he got what he wanted, even though he really didn't?"

They both stared at him for a second.

"So he bluffed?" Jonas said. "Waited until the last possible minute and then decided running everyone would hurt the team, so he backed off without admitting he backed off?"

"I wouldn't put that past him," Stephen said.

A waitress came to take their orders. The place had been virtually empty when Alex walked in, but now people were starting to fill the tables. Still, no one from school. He was sitting with his back to the wall, facing the front of the restaurant, so he could see everyone who walked in.

"Actually, it's pretty ingenious," Alex said. "He's got everyone scared to talk to anyone in the media, especially to anyone on the *Weekly Roar*, and the rest of the team probably believes a couple of guys turned themselves in. We only know he's lying because we're guilty, and we're sure not going to tell anyone else that."

They were both nodding in agreement.

"You know he didn't give Matt any credit for changing the offense last night when he talked to the reporters," Stephen said. "Took all the bows himself."

"How do you know that?" Jonas asked.

Stephen reached down to the empty chair next to him and picked up a copy of the sports section of the *Inquirer*.

"Page four," he said. "Right at the top. Read the first quote."

Jonas took the paper and opened it so Alex could look over his shoulder. The headline, CHESTER HEIGHTS MUDDLES THROUGH MUD AND MAIN LINE, was stretched across the top of the page, making it the number one high school story of the day.

Jonas read the quote from Coach Gordon aloud: "'What we were doing in the spread option wasn't working because of the conditions. Sometimes you have to adjust on the fly. It wasn't a hard decision to make. I thought the kids did a really good job of running an offense we don't practice very often because we usually only use it in our goal-line package.'"

Alex grunted. "Pretty carefully worded. He doesn't actually *say* it was his idea. . . ."

"But he makes you think it was," Jonas said, finishing his sentence.

"I wonder how Matt feels about that," Alex said.

Stephen shrugged. "I think Matt gets who his father is. He's always turned it into a joke when someone brings up his father. I remember once he said, 'My mom always says we need two houses: one for us and one for my dad and his ego.'"

"His mom might not have been joking," Jonas said.

Their hamburgers arrived. Alex was savoring his first bite when he looked up and saw something that almost made him choke on his food.

Christine Whitford.

"Oh boy," he managed to say as his food went down too quickly. "Trouble."

Stephen and Jonas looked up as Christine, after a quick pause to look around the room, started walking toward their table.

"Did you invite her?" Stephen asked, clearly not pleased.

"Swear to God, no," Alex said.

"Good," Stephen said. "Then you can tell her to leave."

■ ■ ■

"So I guessed right," Christine said as she reached the table.

"You guessed wrong if you thought you were welcome here," Stephen said in a tone he usually reserved for the locker room.

"Lighten up, Harvey. I'm not here to get anyone in trouble," she answered. Alex figured Christine was about five four and weighed 110 pounds. Stephen Harvey was six three and a rock-hard 220 or so. Clearly, though, there was no backdown in Christine.

Alex guessed she had biked over because her long dark hair looked windblown—and yet still somehow perfect. Stephen's tone bothered Alex, but he didn't say anything. He understood why Stephen was upset.

"You've already gotten us in trouble," Stephen said. "You got the whole team in trouble by getting Alex to talk Jonas and me into talking to your boy Garland. Can't you just leave it alone?"

"He's not 'my boy,'" she said defensively. "He's the sports editor, and all three of you know he hasn't written a word that isn't true."

"That's not the point, Christine," Alex broke in. "Maybe it is from your point of view, but not from ours. We're *on* the team—at least at the moment. We still have to answer to Coach Gordon every day. *You* don't. Garland doesn't. Coach Gordon's actually right: we're us and you're them. The three of us and all the other guys and Coach Gordon are on the same team. You're not."

"We're not supposed to be," Christine said.

"That's fine," Alex said. "But right now we're having a team-only lunch. And you aren't on the team."

The look on her face was tough for Alex to take because she was clearly hurt. Or angry. Or both.

"You know this isn't going to go away," she said. "All those other people bought Coach Gordon's story that none of you were going to talk to the media because everyone was so wet and tired from the game. We know better. We're going to write about it this week. And we also know it was Matt's idea, not his father's, to change the offense at halftime. We're going to write that too."

"How did you find all that out?" Jonas said.

Her smile returned—if only for a moment. "I told you, Steve's a good reporter. So is Kim Gagne. And, even though I'm not as experienced as they are, so am I."

Alex knew that Kim Gagne was a senior, like Garland, and that he wrote the game stories each week.

"Well, good for you, then," Stephen said. "But if you write that, Coach Gordon won't be happy at all. And he'll take it out on us."

She shrugged. "That's not really our problem, is it?" she said. "We're not on the same team. Right, Alex?"

She turned and walked away.

Alex looked at his hamburger. Suddenly he wasn't very hungry anymore.

Steve Garland's story the following Wednesday was everything that Alex had feared it would be. Not only did it mention the gag order that Coach Gordon had imposed on the entire team, it also noted that he had taken credit for the change in the offense that had been suggested by his son.

Garland wrote:

> *We all know that our very talented coach is insatiable when it comes to feeding his ego, but this is way over the line. The irony is that Coach Gordon always preaches loyalty to his team. Everything is about us versus them. And yet, when it comes down to it, it seems to be about him.*

Those words had to sting—regardless of whether they were true or not.

Garland's story wasn't the worst of it, though. Someone—maybe Garland?—had told Comcast SportsNet–Philadelphia and the *Philadelphia Daily News* about Coach Gordon taking credit for changing the game plan. On Wednesday, the entire school was buzzing about an interview Coach Gordon had done with Michael Barkann on Comcast about what Barkann called "the allegations."

Alex, Stephen, and Jonas huddled over Stephen's computer at lunchtime, watching the interview.

"Trust me, Michael, no one wants to give credit to Matt more than I do," Coach Gordon said, lighting up the screen with a smile when Barkann asked him the question. "In fact, Matt and I had discussed the possibility of *starting* the game in an I-formation because of the conditions. Matt asked for a half to try to run our normal spread option and I thought that was the right way to go.

"I think he felt, since I had gone along with his wishes as the captain and the quarterback in the first half, that he should be the one to bring up making the switch—which he did—at halftime. I was very proud of him."

Barkann followed up with the question that Alex would have asked.

"Last week, we're told, your players were only allowed to talk to the media if a coach was present. You told me before we started this interview that none of your players are available to talk at all—including Matt. Why is that?"

Another big smile from Coach Gordon.

"Michael, as much as I like you and quite a few media members, my first and only job is to do what's best for our football team. We're starting league play this week against a very good team—and that's not coach-speak, they're three and oh, just like we are—from King of Prussia High. Unfortunately, we've had one youngster on our school paper who doesn't really understand the ethics of journalism—at least not yet. That's created some issues for us to deal with and the last thing we need right now are issues off the field."

Alex wondered if somewhere in there was an answer to Barkann's question. Apparently, so did Barkann.

"I'm not sure I understand what a problem with the student newspaper has to do with keeping your players from talking to me or anyone else in the media," he said.

One last smile from Coach Gordon. "Well, Michael, the good news for me is that you don't need to understand. Thanks for coming out."

Coach Gordon faded from the screen and was replaced by a shot of Barkann standing just outside the stadium in front of the sign that said WELCOME TO THE LIONS' DEN, which fans passed under as they entered.

"It's tough to question Matthew Gordon based on his coaching record," Barkann said. "And it's almost a certainty that if we had talked to Matt Gordon Junior he would have backed up his father's story. But there's clearly something amiss inside what is a very good Chester Heights team when the coach is letting stories in the student newspaper affect his team. We've learned that offensive coordinator Tom Hillier, who is also the faculty supervisor of the student newspaper, abruptly resigned last week because of the dispute between Coach Gordon and the paper.

"From Chester Heights High School, I'm Michael Barkann."

Harvey shut the computer and shook his head. "Boy, not good when Michael Barkann is questioning you. He's like the nicest guy in Philadelphia."

"What's the *Daily News* story say?" Jonas asked. Stephen had a copy of the paper with him.

"Same thing only more direct: Questions about whether Coach took credit for Matt's idea; gag order for the team; Coach Hillier resigning; Coach being paranoid. There's a great line from Garland. He says he didn't realize how many friends he had on the football team until all the players were ordered not to speak to him."

"Oh boy," Alex said. "I'll bet that played well in the football offices."

■ ■ ■

There was no talk of Steve Garland or gag orders or anyone in the media that afternoon at practice. King of Prussia *was* a good team—just watching tape of them was enough to make that clear—and there was a heightened sense of anticipation for this first in-league game. That's what would decide whether they had a chance to play for the state championship.

"They're fast," Matt Gordon said to Alex and Jake as they warmed up. "Last year we beat them only because they had three fumbles. Otherwise, they beat us. I'll have to be a lot better than I was last year if we're going to win."

Alex was dying to ask Matt about whether he and his dad had really had any discussion about the offense before the Main Line game. He knew that was a bad idea—in fact, it was unfair to Matt to ask. As Jake had said when Alex brought it up, "You don't ask anyone to say their father's a liar—even if he might be."

That was the closest Jake had ever come to saying anything that indicated he might doubt Coach Gordon.

Alex had never thought of his father as a liar, but he was hurt that he still hadn't found time to make it to Philadelphia. On three different occasions his dad had said he was "hoping" to make it down for a weekend. All three times he had called back to say that something had come up.

At one point his dad had suggested that he and Molly come up for a weekend, but Alex had games every Friday and Molly had soccer games on Saturdays. They could maybe get there by train late on a Saturday, but it'd be about ten hours of train time for about six hours of visiting time. His mom had said they could go to Boston for Thanksgiving but not before then. If his dad really wanted to see his children, he'd have to make the effort.

"Dave, get real," Alex heard her say on the phone one night. "It's up to *you* to come see your kids; it's not up to *them* to come see you."

Alex didn't question his father's love for him, but as each week slipped past, he felt like he and Molly were slipping in his dad's pecking order of priorities. He kept telling them they were number one—but he had a strange way of showing it.

■ ■ ■

There was another pep rally on Friday afternoon. It wasn't much different from the first one, although Coach Gordon insisted that "*never* have we needed your support more than we need it tonight. This is about *us versus them*! Remember that!"

Alex wondered exactly who *them* was. It appeared to be a lot of people *not* wearing opposing uniforms. Coach Gordon introduced him a little bit differently. "He's proven he can take a hit—Chester Heights' quarterback of the future . . . Alex Myers!"

Alex guessed that was an improvement. Jonas didn't. "Does he think it was funny that he almost got you killed?" he whispered when Alex joined him onstage.

"I'm not sure he thinks anything is funny," Alex answered.

"*That* you've got right," Jonas said. He wasn't smiling.

■ ■ ■

Even though he knew he wasn't going to play—even to take a knee, since that had apparently now become Jake's job—Alex couldn't help but feel a rush of adrenaline when his mom dropped him off at school a couple of hours after the pep rally. He had gone home long enough to get something to eat and knock out some French vocabulary. He was carrying something between a B and a C in French and he badly wanted to improve. Getting the toughest part of his homework out of the way early on the weekend seemed like a good idea.

It was the first cool night of the fall, the heat of summer having finally faded. There was a comfortable, humidity-free breeze blowing as he walked from the car to the locker room. As he was about to walk under the WELCOME TO THE LIONS' DEN sign, he heard a voice calling his name.

He turned and saw Christine approaching. Oh no, he

thought, not here. Other players were bound to be walking past since it was four-fifty-five and they were due in the locker room at five.

"Christine, I can't talk. I'm going to be late," he said.

"I know, I know," she said. "Five o'clock, right? I just wanted to say good luck and to tell you I'm sorry if everything that's gone on has caused you any trouble. You haven't done anything to deserve it."

He was puzzled. If she didn't want to cause trouble, why was she telling him this *now* and why *here?*

"Thanks," he said. "I gotta go."

"Maybe we can talk this weekend," she said as he started to walk away.

Her hair was hanging loose and blowing in the breeze, and she was giving him that smile. Why did she have to be so pretty?

He looked around. No one in sight.

"Okay," he said. "We'll see."

He knew he was crazy to even think about spending time with her. Even though Coach Gordon had said nothing about the Barkann piece or the *Philadelphia Daily News,* Jake had ventured a quiet question in practice while the quarterbacks were warming up, but Matt had just shaken his head and said, "Someday I'll tell you everything, Jakey. But not now. It's too raw."

Alex didn't doubt it. As jealous as he was of Matt's stardom, he certainly wasn't jealous of his life. Dealing with Coach Gordon every day at practice wasn't exactly a barrel of laughs. He couldn't imagine what it was like to then go home with him every night. Still, at least Matt had a day-today relationship with his father, Alex thought. And maybe their relationship was different away from school. Then again, maybe not.

Alex walked into the locker room and realized the reason he hadn't seen anyone else outside was that just about everyone was already there. The tension in the room was entirely different than it had been the three previous weeks. Even though they had expected a tough game at Main Line, they all knew the outcome wouldn't have any real bearing on their season. Sure, they wanted to go undefeated, but the goals were to make the playoffs *and* win the state title. Losing to Main Line would not have affected their chances of achieving those goals. Losing the league opener to King of Prussia would absolutely affect their chances.

That was the theme of Coach Gordon's pregame speech. "The season begins tonight, men," he said. "The first three games were meant to prepare us for tonight and they did. All of you who were on the team last season know how good King of Prussia is. You've seen them on tape. There's nothing for me to say right now except that this kind of game is why you all play football. It's what all the work and effort is about. Go out and make sure all the work pays off."

The stadium was packed. Jake had told Alex that tickets had been sold to people to sit or stand on the grassy knoll behind the far goalpost. That meant a stadium that seated about eight thousand would probably have about twelve thousand people in it. The King of Prussia side of the field was just about as full as the Chester Heights side. It was easy to pick out the Cougar fans because they were all dressed in bright yellow.

When the players ran onto the field through a cordon of cheerleaders with the band playing the school fight song, Alex felt a chill run through him. The student section was roaring repeatedly as the band marched up the field to get into position to play the national anthem.

"What are they supposed to be?" Jonas asked, pointing at the King of Prussia fans as they stood on the sideline while the captains went out for the coin flip.

"McDonald's French fries?" Alex answered, suddenly feeling hungry. He had only eaten a small bowl of pasta and some broccoli because he didn't want to feel full. Why it mattered, since he was only going to be watching, he wasn't sure.

Matt and Gerry won the toss and, as always, elected to defer—King of Prussia would get the ball to start the game. Alex looked around as the Lions' kickoff team lined up. Everyone in the stadium was standing. The roars were still coming at them in waves. It was fun to be part of this.

Or, at least, sort of part of this.

It took just three plays for Alex to understand that King of Prussia was every bit as good as advertised.

It wasn't so much that they were big—in fact, their linemen probably weren't as big as Main Line's. But they were *fast*. After two quick pitches had picked up thirteen yards and a first down at the King of Prussia 44, quarterback Hal Spears took the shotgun snap and began running left, straight at the spot—or so it seemed—where Alex, Matt, and Jake were standing on the sideline.

Just when Alex was about to backpedal to get out of his way, Spears planted his left foot so hard that two Chester Heights defenders went flying past him as he came to what looked like a full stop. He cut straight up the field and was gone—fifty-six yards, untouched, into the end zone.

"Wow," Jake said. "That little guy is going to be hard to catch."

"He was last year too," Matt said. "He's probably going to Michigan or Texas, from what I've read."

"As a quarterback?" Alex said. "He can't be more than five nine."

"As a tailback or a wide receiver," Matt said. "He can't throw a lick."

"He may not need to," said Jonas, who had been standing directly behind them, putting on his helmet as the offense got ready to go on the field. The extra point had been good and the Lions were down 7–0 in under two minutes.

"Go get us even," Alex said to Matt and Jonas.

They tried. Jonas made a circus catch on a third-and-eight throw from Matt to keep the opening drive alive, but Chester Heights sputtered after crossing midfield. On another third and eight, Matt was sacked for a six-yard loss and out came the punt team.

This time, the defense managed to stop King of Prussia, helped by one of the KOP slotbacks, who dropped a pitch from Spears and had to fall on it for a five-yard loss.

It was still 7–0 at the end of the first quarter. Another Chester Heights drive ended when Matt overthrew Jonas on one play and then was intercepted trying to find Craig Josephs running a curl pattern over the middle. One of the King of Prussia linebackers read the play perfectly, dropped in coverage, and intercepted the pass at the 29-yard line.

Matt came to the sideline, clearly angry with himself. He grabbed Jonas by the shoulder. "That's on me, I'm sorry," he said. "I should have looked Craig off and gone deep to you. Just as I released the ball I saw you break open, but it was too late. I wasn't patient enough."

"Don't worry," Jonas said, tapping Matt's helmet. "We'll get 'em the next time."

Just as Matt was nodding in agreement, Coach Gordon came over.

"Matt, you've got to wait on your receivers. Stop panicking in the pocket. You had time!"

"I know, Coach. I'm sorry—"

"Don't be sorry—*perform*," his father said, and stomped away.

Matt said nothing, just took off his helmet and walked to the bench to get some water.

"You really think you'd want to be him?" Jonas asked.

"Not in a million years," Alex said.

King of Prussia was driving again. Spears had thrown one pass all night—a screen on a third and long that had been diagnosed perfectly for a seven-yard loss. But he was so quick and elusive, the defenders had to respect him whenever he began to run. That allowed him to find his backs and slots on pitch plays that consistently picked up big chunks of yardage.

The Cougars moved the ball steadily to the Lions' 12-yard line. There, on first down, Spears began to run right, then suddenly pulled up and lofted a pass into the end zone. With the entire Chester Heights defense packed in tight to stop the run, there was no one near the receiver. The pass wobbled a bit, but it didn't matter because the receiver could have caught the ball and eaten a sandwich before anyone from Chester Heights got near him.

Alex looked at the clock. There was 10:14 left in the half and it was now 14–0.

"We're in trouble," he said to Jonas and Jake.

"Keen football analysis there," Jake said. "You should be on television."

He wasn't smiling when he said it; there was nothing to laugh about.

Once again, the offense was able to move the ball. Matt made a great fake on a pitch and cut up the left side for twenty-seven yards to get into King of Prussia territory. Then he ran a reverse, flipping the ball to Jonas, who picked up twenty-four to the KOP 22-yard line. The sideline was alive. A quick-answer touchdown was just what the Lions needed.

Matt handed the ball to Josephs on a counter and he picked up five to the 17. Matt tried to run the same play the other way, but this time it was only good for a yard.

Third and four. Alex was certain that Coach Gordon was going to call an option left. He would want the ball in Matt's hands, and the left side of the O-line was usually more reliable at opening a hole when Matt ran wide than the right side.

Sure enough, he was correct. Unfortunately, it appeared that the King of Prussia coaches had scouted at least as well as Alex had, because it looked like all eleven defenders were pursuing Matt as soon as he took the snap. With no chance to make a pitch, he bravely tried to turn upfield and fight through the entire defense to pick up yardage.

He made it back to the line of scrimmage—which was a victory in itself—and even lunged forward a yard to the 15. That would set up fourth and three. Alex glanced at the clock, which was down to 6:09.

"So do we go for it or take a field goal?" he asked Jake.

Jake didn't answer. He was staring in the direction of the

play, where everyone was picking themselves off the ground—except for one player, who was lying flat on his back.

It was Matt Gordon.

A chorus of voices began calling for Buddy Thomas, who was working on wrapping someone's ankle. Buddy looked up, realized something was wrong, and went straight to Coach Gordon, who was standing at the 25-yard line—the players and coaches had to stay between the 25's by rule—with his arms crossed.

When Buddy got there, Coach Gordon put his arm across his chest to stop him from going on the field.

"Wait. Give him a minute to get up," he said.

Alex understood. If Buddy went onto the field, Matt would *have* to come out of the game, even if he was just shaken up a little. With fourth and three coming up, Coach Gordon wanted to wait as long as he possibly could before being forced to take his quarterback out.

A couple of the Lions had knelt down next to Matt to check on him. Just as Coach Gordon stopped Buddy, they began waving toward the sideline, indicating that help was needed.

"Go," Coach Gordon said to Buddy, who sprinted in Matt's direction as soon as he got the order.

Everyone waited and watched.

Alex was about to say something to Jake when he heard Coach Gordon calling him. "Bilney," he barked. "Get over here."

Jake looked like he'd seen a ghost. It had just occurred to him—as it had just occurred to Alex—that he was going into the game.

Jake was pulling his helmet on as he reached Coach Gordon.

"Run pitch ninety-four," Coach Gordon said.

Even with a helmet on, Alex could see terror in Jake's eyes.

"Coach, it's fourth down," Jake said.

"I KNOW THE DOWN AND DISTANCE, BILNEY! THIS IS WHY YOU'RE ON THE TEAM! GO!"

"Coach, should I wait until they get Matt up—"

"*No!* Get in the huddle with your teammates and let them know we're going to get this first down."

Alex realized Coach Gordon was right about that. At this moment, they needed to see Jake in the huddle displaying some confidence. That was what they needed. He suspected that wasn't what they were going to get.

■ ■ ■

Buddy Thomas stood up and pointed a finger at two of the backup linemen on the sideline, indicating he needed them to help get Matt off the field. That was actually a relief: if Matt was seriously hurt, Buddy would have asked for a stretcher. Two of the backup defensive linemen raced onto the field and helped Matt to his feet.

He was holding his right leg in the air, clearly not wanting to put weight on it. Buddy had taken his shoe and his sock off. His helmet was off too and Alex could see that his face was masked in pain. As he was slowly helped to the sideline, the crowd on both sides of the field stood to applaud him.

Buddy walked with him, pointing to the cart that sat behind the bench and in front of the stands. It was used, most of the time, to transport equipment. "Get him on the back of the cart. Is Doc here . . . ?"

"Right here," Alex heard someone say behind him.

He looked up and saw Dr. Joe Vassallo, who was the team doctor—unofficially, of course, since he didn't get paid, according to what Alex had been told. His son had played at Chester Heights and was now on the team at Virginia.

"Good," Buddy said. "It's his ankle."

"What do you think?" Dr. Vassallo said as they helped get Matt situated as comfortably as possible on the back of the cart.

"Hard to tell. At best, it's a sprain; at worst, he broke something."

"I'll take a look. We'll want an MRI tomorrow to be sure."

The entire team was standing in a semicircle, listening to Buddy and the doctor. They were blasted out of their trance by the sound of the whistle. Alex looked back to the field and saw his teammates breaking the huddle.

Oh yeah, he thought, the game is still going on.

Jake stood behind center in the shotgun formation, calling signals. Alex knew that pitch ninety-four, the play Coach Gordon had called, was a simple sprint to the right—the even number, four, indicated that the play was going right. And the nine meant Jake would be running wide, meaning the linemen should try to force the defenders to the inside so he could run outside. Josephs, the tailback, would trail him for a possible pitch.

Jake took the snap and went right. Alex could see that the entire defense was within two yards of the line, knowing a cold quarterback coming into the game wasn't likely to throw. Just like Matt on the play before, Jake was surrounded before he could take two steps. In desperation he tried to pitch the ball back to Josephs. But his arm was hit as he pitched and the ball ended up at Josephs's feet. He was swarmed as everyone went after the football.

It didn't really matter who fell on it because it was fourth down and the ball was going over to the Cougars regardless.

"Should have kicked the field goal," Alex said—to no one. Jake and Jonas were both on the field and no one was standing near him.

He heard a voice calling his name and turned around. Matt was on the cart with Dr. Vassallo sitting next to him. He was holding up a hand to indicate to the driver not to leave yet.

"Goldie, come here a second," Matt said once he had Alex's attention.

Alex jogged over. Several players were standing nearby trying to encourage Matt or telling him he was going to be okay. Alex noticed that Dr. Vassallo had already put a wrap around Matt's ankle.

"Hey, fellas, give me a second with Goldie," Matt said.

Alex now had his back turned to the field and he could hear the coaches trying to encourage the defense as it headed out.

"Need a stop, guys, need a stop!" he heard everyone saying.

"What's up, Matt?" Alex said. "How's the ankle?"

He knew that was a dumb question. Matt had no idea how the ankle was.

"The ankle hurts," Matt said, forcing a smile.

"Matt, we need to go," he heard Dr. Vassallo say.

"Give me one sec," Matt said.

He put his hand around Alex's neck so he could pull him close.

"Listen to me, Goldie, you're the QB now," he said softly. "You're going to have to pull this game out in the second half. It's got to be your team now. I *know* you can do it."

Alex looked up to see if he was joking. Unless the tears glistening in his eyes were because he thought this was funny, he wasn't.

"Matt, Jake's the QB until you get back. . . ."

"No, he's not—and he knows it better than anyone. I may not be here at halftime, but one of these damn coaches had better stand up and tell my dad to put you in the game."

"Coach Hillier . . ."

"Isn't here," Matt finished. "Don't worry, Goldie. My dad's stubborn and he can be a jerk, but he hates to lose. So get ready. You're going to have to save us tonight."

"Gotta go, Matt," Dr. Vassallo said again.

"You got me?" Matt said, pulling Alex so close they were almost nose to nose.

"I got you," Alex said.

Matt let him go.

"Okay, then," he said. And the cart pulled away.

They managed to get to halftime still down only 14–0. The only noise in the stadium as the teams jogged to the locker rooms was coming from the King of Prussia side. French Fries could get very loud.

Unlike a week earlier, Coach Gordon didn't shout. He seemed to understand that he was now coaching a team that needed a different kind of motivation.

"Fellas, I have complete confidence in Jake," he said. "He ran our offense on almost every snap for five JV games last season and he's playing with much better players around him right now. We just have to take a deep breath and stay patient. We aren't going to score three touchdowns on our first possession. One at a time. Defense, just keep doing what you're doing. If you keep hitting Spears, he's going to cough up the ball, so be ready—make it happen. Okay, let's split up."

He had made no mention of his son or his injury, except

for saying he had confidence in Jake playing quarterback. If the thought of putting Alex into the game had crossed his mind, he certainly didn't mention it.

The locker room had two meeting rooms in it, one for the offense and one for the defense. Alex followed the other offensive players down the hall. He was about to walk into the offensive room when he felt a tap on his shoulder. He turned and saw Coach Brotman standing behind him.

Before he could say anything, Coach Brotman signaled to follow him, which he did—down the hall to the empty shower room.

When they got there, Coach Brotman, after a quick look around, as if he thought someone might be taking a halftime shower, said quietly, "You're going to have to play in the second half. I want to be sure you understand that."

"Did Coach Gordon say—"

Coach Brotman put a finger on his lips to indicate Alex needed to be quiet. "*No,*" he said in an emphatic whisper. "But all of us know you can throw the ball in ways Jake can't begin to touch. We're down 14–0. If Matt couldn't get us going on the ground, how in the world is Jake going to do it?"

Alex started to answer, then realized it hadn't really been a question.

"He's *not,*" Coach Brotman said. "We'll give it our best shot coming out here to start the half, but you make sure you get your arm loose when we get back out there."

"But if Coach Gordon doesn't want—"

"That's *my* job. Your job is to be ready to play. Now get back in the meeting room."

It was too late. Everyone was filing back out by the time

Alex got there. Jake walked by him without a word. He looked almost as if he were in a trance.

When they went back on the field, Alex found Jonas and asked if they could play catch so he could warm up a little.

"You going in?" Jonas asked.

"No," Alex said. "At least not yet."

It was Chester Heights' ball to start the second half. The Lions were able to pick up a quick first down after the kickoff. But on second and six from the 44, Coach Gordon called the same play that had failed so miserably on the fourth down in the first half, except he ordered Jake to run left instead of right.

Jake did as he was told, took about two steps, and slipped. The ball went flying out of his hands and one of the King of Prussia linemen was on it in a split second. The Chester Heights side of the stadium went completely silent while the King of Prussia side celebrated. Alex saw Jake, on his knees, pound his fist into the ground in frustration.

When Jake came to the sideline, Alex greeted him with the clichéd "Keep your head up, lot of game to play" line of encouragement.

Jake just looked at him and, again, said nothing.

One more time, the defense came through—although it needed some help. The Cougars moved the ball quickly to the 13-yard line and had third and three from there. Spears faked as if to run and dropped back quickly. He had a receiver open in the end zone, but somehow he overthrew the ball. It was now his turn to pound the turf in frustration.

KOP sent in their field-goal unit. A thirty-yard kick was not usually a sure thing for a high school kicker, but this one was good and the Cougars were up 17–0 with 10:58 left in the third quarter. The band gamely played on, but the silence from the Chester Heights fans was deafening. Even more deafening than the roars.

The kickoff return team was taking the field—again—when Alex heard a cheer behind him. Surprised, he turned and saw the equipment cart rolling down the running track in the direction of the sideline. Sitting in the front passenger seat with a pair of crutches on his lap was Matt Gordon.

A couple of guys raced over to help him out of the cart. He quickly hobbled over to where Alex and Jake were standing. The crowd was still cheering, in part because Matt deserved it, in part because there was nothing else to cheer about.

As the kickoff sailed through the air, Alex asked the inevitable question.

"How bad is it?"

"Bad sprain, no break," Matt said. "They took me down the street to the hospital for an X-ray. They might still do an MRI tomorrow, but the doc is pretty sure it's just sprained. He said three to four weeks. I say two."

He turned to Jake. "What do you think, Jakey?"

"I think Goldie plays or we lose."

Jake was clearly upset with himself—more so with the situation. He waited for Matt to say something encouraging, but Matt simply tapped him on the helmet as Jake pulled it on and said, "Hang tough."

Jake didn't say anything but sprinted over to Coach Gordon to get the first play as Monte Johnston, the kick returner, was pulled down at the Chester Heights 30.

Matt turned to Alex. "Get your helmet on. And be ready to run 24 post, no matter what my dad calls."

"Whaaa?"

"Just do what I tell you, Goldie—trust me."

He hobbled away at that point, leaving Alex totally baffled. Jake was bringing the team out of the huddle. The first play call—predictably—was a quick pitch to Josephs, who managed to cut up the edge to pick up seven yards. Alex was still watching Josephs when he heard someone yell, "Hey, Buddy—it's Jake!"

Alex saw Jake sitting on the ground, holding his right knee. Buddy glanced at Coach Gordon for instructions. Coach Gordon had a stunned look on his face. *Both* his quarterbacks injured? Before he could say anything, a couple of the linemen began waving for Buddy just as they had done for Matt.

Alex saw Coach Gordon visibly sigh. "Go," he said to Buddy.

He then looked around as if he expected another quarterback to appear by magic. Or maybe he thought Matt was going to throw away his crutches and go back into the game in street clothes.

Alex was watching the scene as an interested spectator when it suddenly occurred to him that everyone on the sideline was staring at him.

"Myers!" Coach Gordon barked.

Alex knew now why Matt had told him to put his helmet on—which he hadn't. He was pulling it over his ears—which always hurt at least a little bit—as he jogged over to Coach Gordon. He could see that Buddy was helping Jake to his feet.

Alex's mind was going in ten different directions. He was

wondering how in the world Matt and Jake had concocted a plan for Jake to fake an injury. He *was* faking—Alex was convinced of that. Somewhere in the distance, even though he was standing a foot away from him, he heard Coach Gordon talking to him.

"Nothing fancy, Myers," he said. "We've got second and three. Run 25 toss sweep to Josephs and let's pick up a first down. Bilney may be ready in a play or two—we'll see. Let's just hang on to the ball right now."

"Yes sir."

"You understand me?"

Alex heard his instructions. He also heard Matt's voice in his head. *No matter what my dad tells you, run 24 post.* That was the same play Coach Gordon had just called except for two things: the running back—Josephs—would be cutting to his right instead of left on the snap, and Alex would *not* toss him the ball. Instead, he would fake the toss, drop back, and throw the ball as far down the field as he could to the wide receiver lined up to the left, who, he noticed, just happened to be Jonas.

Alex honestly wasn't sure who he was more afraid of disobeying at that moment: Matthew Gordon Senior or Junior. Jake was almost off the field.

"What's he got, Buddy?" Coach Gordon asked as they approached.

"Said he heard something pop in his knee," Buddy said. "I can't feel anything. Probably needs an MRI to figure it out. I'll get Doc down here."

"Work on him on the bench for a while," Coach Gordon said.

He turned to Alex. "Go!" he said.

Right, Alex thought, I'm in the game. Now, what the hell do I do next?

■ ■ ■

When he got to the huddle, everyone was standing around as if deciding whether to keep playing the game. They were all looking at him, clearly thinking, *What are you doing here?*

That was exactly what Alex needed to see. He was here because Matt and Coach Brotman and, he guessed, Jake thought he was their best hope. He knew he could throw 24 post, especially with Jonas there to run under it.

"Okay, guys, come on. Let's huddle up," he said, trying to speak with authority but without sounding arrogant about it. He and Jonas were the only freshmen in the huddle. Four of the O-linemen were seniors. He needed them on *his* side.

The response was what he wanted. Before he could call a play, Will Allison, the center, who was the unofficial captain of the O-line, spoke up. "Listen up, guys," he said. "Goldie knows what to do. We all know he can throw it better than anyone we've got. He's in charge now."

Allison's confidence made it easy for him to decide what to call.

"Okay," he said. "24 post, on one. Break!"

He said it firmly because he knew the call would surprise his teammates. No one flinched or said anything. They just clapped their hands in unison on the word *break* and turned to the line of scrimmage. The play clock was under ten because of the hesitation when he had arrived in the huddle, which was why Alex had thought to go with a quick snap.

He lined up in the shotgun behind Allison and called out, "Gold!" which meant nothing except it was the first sound everyone heard and meant Allison was to snap the ball.

Which he did, perfectly, to Alex, who turned as if to pitch to Josephs—who was running to the right as if he were going to get the ball. Alex made the fake, then drifted back to pass.

As soon as the snap had hit his hands, instinct had taken over. He wasn't thinking about the score or all the eyes on him or the fact that he had called a play that contradicted a direct order from his coach. All he could see was Jonas, who was racing behind the King of Prussia cornerback and coming open just as Alex stepped up in the pocket and released the ball.

Once the ball came off his fingertips, he knew he had thrown it just the way he wanted to. His momentum carried him in the direction of the line of scrimmage and he watched as Jonas, running full speed, raced under the ball at the KOP 25 yard line, gathered it into his arms, and cruised into the end zone.

Alex's arms went into the air and he could feel his teammates pummeling him as they all ran downfield to congratulate Jonas.

"*That's* the way to throw it, Goldie," he heard Allison say, a phrase repeated by several others as they all high-fived their way down the field. The Chester Heights sideline had exploded, stunned by the suddenness of the touchdown—and by the quarterback who had thrown the pass. Alex knew he still had a silly grin on his face as everyone trotted to the sideline while the kicking team went in for the extra point.

Matt was waiting. He took his right hand off his crutches to give Alex a high five.

"I knew you could do it, Goldie," he said. "I just knew it."

Coach Gordon was right behind him.

"Was that an audible, Myers? It didn't look like one from here."

"No sir. I called it in the huddle."

"Was that what I told you to call?"

"No sir," Alex said, offering no excuse and waiting for the hammer to come down on his head.

"I called it," Matt said. "I called it because I knew Alex could make the throw and we needed a quick score to change the momentum."

Coach Gordon stared at his son, then at Alex as another roar went up from the Chester Heights sideline as the extra point went through, making it 17–7.

"We'll discuss it after the game," he said finally, turning and walking away.

The biggest advantage Alex had was that King of Prussia knew nothing about him. If they had heard his name at all, it was as the kid who had gotten clocked on the last play of the Mercer game, leading to a near brawl. The assumption among the coaches would be that he was a runner first and a passer second—like Matt Gordon and Jake Bilney—since that was the style Coach Gordon liked in his spread-option offense.

But seeing Alex throw the ball fifty yards in the air to Jonas had to confuse them. They had no idea what to expect when Alex trotted back onto the field to start Chester Heights' next offensive series. The third quarter was almost over. King of Prussia had moved the ball into Chester Heights territory but had stalled at the 39 and opted to punt. Their punter had kicked the ball out of bounds at the 11-yard line, meaning the Lions were eighty-nine yards from the goal line with a little under sixteen minutes to play, trailing by ten points.

Alex hadn't had time to feel nervous when he'd gone into the game for Jake—who was now sitting on the bench with his knee wrapped. Buddy Thomas had told Coach Gordon that Jake could go back in "if there was an emergency," since there were no other quarterbacks in uniform.

Completing the pass to Jonas was a massive boost for Alex's confidence. He knew the call had caught the KOP defense completely off guard and that helped, but he'd put the ball exactly where he needed to put it and his arm felt as loose as he could possibly hope for it to be.

"That was one great throw," Jonas had said to him when they had hugged on the sideline after the touchdown.

"If I'd thrown it ten yards farther I think you'd have gotten to it anyway," Alex said.

"You're right," Jonas said with a grin. "Throw it up there and I'll go get it."

Coach Gordon was calling the plays, using the normal shuttle of wide receivers to bring the plays in, but Matt was standing next to him, leaning on his crutches. Whether he was there to make suggestions or just to give Alex confidence, he wasn't sure.

With the Lions deep in their own territory, it made sense not to try anything dangerous. Twice, Alex handed the ball to Josephs on simple "blast" plays up the middle—the O-line blasting off the line, going straight ahead to try to create a hole. Josephs picked up nine yards to the 20, setting up third and one.

Max Plesac brought in the play. Mike Crenshaw, the second tight end, who came in on short yardage situations, was with him. "Dive 25, set, B circle," he said. Alex looked at him for a second to be sure he was hearing correctly. Plesac understood and repeated the call. "Dive 25, set, B circle," he said a second time.

This time Alex just nodded, stepped into the huddle, and made the call.

The play was for Crenshaw—who almost never did anything other than block. Alex was to fake a handoff to Josephs, then throw a pass over the middle to Crenshaw, whose job was to fake a run block, then circle into the defensive backfield to catch the pass. The play was risky because the throw had to get there quickly and accurately and because Crenshaw did not have the world's best hands. His nickname among his teammates was "Clank" for a reason.

Still, the element of surprise would be decidedly in their favor. Alex moved under center to take Allison's snap, then turned and stuck the ball into Josephs's stomach. But he never let go of it, and Josephs never completely wrapped his hands around the ball. Alex pulled the ball back, stood up, and looked for Crenshaw.

There he was, his hand up to make sure Alex saw him. It was impossible *not* to see him because he was ten yards behind the line of scrimmage and no one on the King of Prussia defense was anywhere near him. They had all gone for the fake to Josephs, who was buried under a half dozen white jerseys.

Alex flicked the ball with his wrist, relying on the muscle memory of all the drills in practice, where the quarterbacks repeatedly threw ten-, twelve-, fourteen-yard passes over and over. The ball hit Crenshaw right in the chest. Alex could see him bobble it briefly, and for a split second he thought he might drop it.

But he didn't. He was a good five yards behind everyone when he caught the ball at the 30 and turned to run. If he had been Jonas or one of the other wide receivers, the play would have been a cinch touchdown. But Crenshaw was six three, 230 pounds and ran like the lineman he usually was.

Two defenders ran him down at the King of Prussia 45. Crenshaw was so strong that he carried them on his back for a few extra yards, finally being brought down at the 38.

There were lots of "Way to go, Goldie"s in the huddle as Jonas brought in the next play. Alex wasn't listening. He was remembering something he had read in a magazine story about Mike Krzyzewski, the great basketball coach.

"Next play," Krzyzewski had said. "Make a good play—forget it, next play. Make a bad one, same thing—next play."

"Okay, guys," Alex said. "*Next* play. We still have to score."

They were all looking right at him as he called it. He felt completely comfortable, as if he'd been doing this all his life, as if this was where he was born to be.

■ ■ ■

Six plays after the pass to Crenshaw, Josephs scored on a simple counter play from the 4-yard line. Alex started to sprint right but then handed to Josephs, who—with the defense pursuing Alex—had a huge hole and could practically walk into the end zone.

The extra point made it 17–14, with 10:26 still left in the game.

Unfortunately, Hal Spears wasn't done yet. He took King of Prussia down the field in a long, clock-eating drive. Every play seemed to pick up four, five, or six yards. Three times King of Prussia had a third down, but it was always short yardage and they picked up the first down—usually on a Spears keeper of some kind.

"The defense has got to get off the field," said Matt, who had come over to counsel Alex whenever King of Prussia had the ball. Jake, his knee wrapped, was also standing there. Alex didn't ask him about his "injury." This wasn't the time.

King of Prussia picked up another first down at the Chester Heights 20. The clock was now under five minutes. A touchdown would pretty much put the game away.

Spears ran an option to the left and picked up five yards to the 15. He ran the same play to the right, but this time the defense, led by Detwiler, buried him for no gain. It was third and five.

"Do or die right here," Jake said.

Spears took the snap and started right again. This time, though, he pitched the ball to his tailback, who had some open space. Alan Fitzgerald came up from his safety spot and tackled him solidly right around the ten-yard line.

"Did he get it?" Alex asked.

"Can't tell from here," Matt said. "Too close."

The officials were waving for a measurement. Players on both sides were pointing in opposite directions—the King of Prussia players signaling first down, the Chester Heights players contradicting them. Alex saw the referee get down on one knee to spot the chain. He stood up and held his hands about a foot apart. The Chester Heights fans cheered lustily.

"They'll go for it," Matt said. "If they get it, they can almost run out the clock. Even if they don't, we've gotta go ninety yards to score."

The King of Prussia coaches had called time-out to make a decision. Alex noticed that the clock was at 3:12. Either way, the offense wouldn't have much time to go the length of the field to even get within field goal range to try to tie the game.

Not surprisingly, Matt was right. Spears jogged back onto the field when the time-out was over, then called a play and brought his team to the line of scrimmage.

"Be ready, Goldie," Matt said. "If we hold them, the game's in your hands."

"And if we don't?" Jake asked.

"Game's over," Matt said.

Spears lined up in the shotgun, took the snap, and ran straight ahead—a quarterback sneak disguised by the shotgun. At least that was the intent. Gerry Detwiler had the play figured out the instant Spears started forward. He knifed through a blocker, then grabbed Spears by a leg and wrestled him to the ground as Spears tried to dive forward.

"He's *short!*" Matt screamed as all twenty-two players—or so it appeared—dove on the pile to try to move it in one direction or the other.

Alex had no idea how Matt could tell if Spears had made

it or not, but he started to put his helmet on as soon as he said it. The officials pulled everyone off the pile, took a look at where Spears and the ball were, and signaled Chester Heights' ball right away. Spears had actually lost half a yard, thanks to Detwiler.

As the defense came off the field celebrating, Alex started on but was stopped by Matt grabbing his shoulder.

"It's your game, Goldie," he said. "Go be a hero."

■ ■ ■

The clock was at 2:59 when Alex stepped into the huddle. Coach Gordon had reminded him as he started onto the field that the Lions had all three of their time-outs left.

"Try to save at least one in case we need a field goal," he said.

Alex nodded. He was hoping they would at least get into field goal range.

Not surprisingly, King of Prussia was in a prevent defense—dropping all four defensive backs and their line-backers deep to "prevent" a long pass. When Alex walked behind the O-line to take the first snap, he could almost hear his father's voice in his head while watching the Patriots go into a prevent defense.

"You know why they call this a prevent defense?" David Myers would say without fail. "Because it *prevents* victory."

Now Alex hoped it would allow him to *create* victory. Or at least a tie and overtime.

Jonas had brought two plays with him from the sideline because they would go no-huddle when they had to—on plays when the clock didn't stop. The first one was a simple turn-in route to Alan Fitzgerald, an extra receiver who was in instead of a tight end to add speed and a better pair of hands.

Fitzgerald caught the quick pass at the 18 and dived to the 19 for a nine-yard gain. Alex rushed everyone to the line and ran the exact same play—as called—but to Jonas on the other side. Jonas eluded a tackler and scrambled to the 33 for a first down.

Fitzgerald, who had gone out after the first play, raced back in with two more calls. Alex called them both as fast as he could and glanced at the clock as they lined up: 2:12 and counting.

He threw a quick out pass to Josephs, who was just as surrounded by defenders and dragged down trying to get out of bounds after a six-yard gain. They were at the 39. In the back of his mind, Alex figured they had to get to at least the King of Prussia 20 to give Pete Ross a realistic shot at a tying field goal.

The second call was a pass to Tom Revere, another of the wide receivers. But just as Alex was about to release the pass, he noticed one of the safeties coming up on Revere. He *should* have just thrown the ball out of bounds and stopped the clock. Instead, he pulled it back down and took off. He picked up five yards and a first down to the 44, but the clock was running, down to 1:31.

They had to use a time-out.

Alex jogged to the sideline.

"You can't scramble at this point," Coach Gordon said, his voice remarkably calm given the situation. "No one's open, throw it away."

"Yes sir."

To Alex's surprise, Coach Gordon looked at Matt, who was standing off his right shoulder.

"What do you think, Matt?"

"There's time, Coach. No need to throw deep yet."

Coach Gordon nodded and called two more short passes.

The first one, a pass over the middle to Revere, worked in large part because Alex whizzed it in between two defenders. Even he was a little surprised that the ball got through all four hands to reach Revere, who caught it while going down at the KOP 43 for a pickup of thirteen. Alex rushed everyone to the line and tried a quick sideline-out to Fitzgerald. But the corners were playing a little tighter now and were naturally trying to deny the pass near the sidelines. Alex led Fitzgerald a tad too much and the ball slid off his fingertips.

The clock was at 1:06.

The incomplete pass stopped the clock and gave them the chance to huddle. Jonas came back in with two more plays and an instruction: "Anything inside the 30 with the clock running, we call time," he said.

Everyone nodded. The huddle was very much all business, no phony "Let's go get 'em, guys" talk. Everyone was locked in. Speed mattered.

They came to the line, and with all four receivers taking off on deep routes, Alex found Josephs running a little circle route just behind the line and in front of the linebackers. The tailback picked up twelve to the 31 and then jumped up and called time. Alex could see Coach Gordon throw his head back on the sideline. He hadn't wanted to use the time-out so soon. There were still fifty-one seconds to go.

Still, this was no time for second-guessing. As he jogged to the sideline again, Alex could see that everyone in the stadium was on their feet.

Coach Gordon wanted to run a quick square-out to Jonas, whose speed forced the corners to play off him, and then run a draw to Josephs. "Spike the ball after the draw—unless it's third down," Coach Gordon said. "If it's third down, we'll have to use the last time-out and then spike the ball before the field goal."

Alex nodded. He noticed that his stomach was in a knot, but it was a feeling he liked.

Coach Gordon was right in thinking Jonas would have some space: Alex found him for eight yards to the 23. They lined up again, and as the clock rolled to thirty-five seconds, Alex stuck the ball in Josephs's stomach and he picked up eight more to the 15. They were in field goal range now. The clock was at twenty seconds and counting. Everyone on the sideline was screaming at Alex to get to the line, take the snap, and spike the ball to stop the clock.

Alex grabbed Jonas by the shoulder as everyone was scrambling to line up.

"Take off for the end zone!" he screamed so he could be heard over the din.

"WHAT?"

"You heard me. When Allison snaps the ball, take off!"

Jonas gave him a terrified look but said nothing.

The clock was at fifteen seconds as Alex put his hands under center. Allison snapped the ball and he took one step back, looked at the ground, and made a motion as if to spike the ball straight down.

Except he never let go of the ball. Everyone in the stadium was expecting the spike and both teams had stopped playing when Alex began his spike motion.

Except for Jonas. As instructed, he had run straight to the end zone. Alex straightened quickly and lofted the easiest pass he had ever thrown in his life over everyone to where Jonas was standing, wide open, in the end zone. He caught the ball and threw his arms into the air. More important, so did the official, signaling touchdown.

The clock was at nine seconds.

For a split second, time seemed to stop because everyone was so stunned. Then the Chester Heights sideline and stands exploded. Alex and Jonas were both pummeled by their teammates as the sideline emptied to celebrate.

When Alex finally got to the sideline, Coach Gordon had his hands on his hips. Alex prepared for a tirade.

"Myers, I should want to kill you," he said, almost smiling. "But that was brilliant. Even if you throw an incomplete there, you still stop the clock and we get the field goal team on."

Alex couldn't help but grin. "Yes sir," he said. "That's what I figured."

"Of course, if you'd fumbled or been intercepted, you'd have been running every morning until Thanksgiving."

"Yes sir. I know."

Before Coach Gordon could say another word, Matt grabbed him around the neck.

"I told you, Goldie!" he screamed. "I told you! Your game! Welcome to being a star, pal. Welcome to being a star."

Matt Gordon wasn't joking about Alex becoming a star.

As soon as King of Prussia's attempts to keep the kickoff return alive by lateraling the ball over the field had failed—the ball finally came loose at the KOP 42-yard line and was swarmed by a half dozen players as the clock ran to zero—the field was flooded with celebrating fans and with media.

A number of TV cameras raced in his direction, and Alex had no idea what to do. As if by magic, Mr. Hardy, the athletic director, appeared at his side.

"Stand right here and do them all at once," he said.

"But, Coach Gordon—"

"Said it's okay. Everyone can talk tonight." He nodded in the direction of Matt, who was leaning on his crutches and talking to several reporters.

Apparently, the miracle victory had wiped out all the bad feelings of the past few weeks—at least for the moment.

Alex did as he was told, stopping where he was as the cameras rushed toward him. Two yellow-jacketed security guards, apparently on orders from Mr. Hardy, stood to each side of him, saying, "Folks, please don't get too close. Give the young man some room."

They did—more or less.

"Alex, tell us about the last play," said a very tall blond-haired woman who was practically standing on top of him.

Alex shrugged. "Everyone in the stadium knew we were going to spike the ball to set up the field goal," he said. "Jonas happened to be right next to me as we were going to line up, so I just told him to take off for the end zone. I figured if he wasn't open, I'd throw the ball away and that would stop the clock anyway."

"Did Coach Gordon know you were going to do that?"

Alex couldn't see the questioner because of all the lights shining in his face.

"No," he answered. "It was a spur-of-the-moment thing."

"What'd he say about you ignoring a play call?"

Alex was tempted to tell them about the *first* time he'd ignored a play call on his first snap, but didn't. "He said he thought it was okay because there was really no gamble in it." He paused. "Unless I fumbled or threw an interception. Then I suspect I'd have been in big trouble."

It went on like that for several minutes until Mr. Hardy stepped in.

The question that caused Mr. Hardy to end the informal press conference came from someone with a notebook, not a camera. "Do you think you'll be the starter when Matt Gordon's healthy?"

Mr. Hardy literally stepped in front of Alex as soon as the question came out of the reporter's mouth, but not before Alex said, "Absolutely not."

"Need to get Alex to a shower, folks," he said. "Thanks."

There were some protests, but they weren't going to do anybody any good because there were now *four* yellow jackets surrounding Alex to clear a path for him to the locker room. Alex could see that Jonas had also been talking to reporters and was also now being escorted to the locker room.

They were both hustled through the door. Matt was being dropped off by the equipment cart at the same moment, and they saw that the celebration had already begun.

When Alex and Jonas walked through the door, Gerry Detwiler, who was standing a few feet away, said, "How about these two rookies!"

The entire room broke into cheers and applause and Alex and Jonas were mobbed. In the midst of it he heard Coach Gordon's voice saying, "Okay, fellas, listen up for a second—listen up!"

They settled down. Normally, Coach Gordon stood in front of the room, but now he was standing on a chair. He held up his hand for quiet.

"To say that was a great win is an understatement . . . ," he said. They started to whoop but he put his hand up again and they stopped.

"You overcame a 17–0 deficit, remarkable under any circumstances, especially against a very good team. You did it after *two* quarterbacks got hurt. Defense, what an amazing job you guys did shutting their offense down when it mattered most—especially on that fourth down play. Gerry, no one's a bigger hero than you tonight—no matter what anyone outside this locker room says."

They cheered lustily for Detwiler. Alex agreed with what Coach Gordon had said: the final drive couldn't have happened if Detwiler hadn't tackled Spears short of the first down marker on King of Prussia's final offensive play.

Coach Gordon turned in the direction of Buddy Thomas, who flipped a football to him. "Every one of you deserves a game ball tonight—I mean that. For right now, though, we're going to give three." He tossed the ball to Detwiler.

"That first one is for you, Gerry, and everyone in here knows why."

More cheers. Detwiler smiled and held the ball over his head for a moment.

Buddy tossed Coach Gordon a second ball. "This second one is for Ellington, if only because he's dumb enough to listen to what a freshman quarterback tells him to do with the game on the line!"

More cheers as Coach Gordon flipped the ball to Jonas. He just grinned happily.

Buddy tossed one more ball to Coach Gordon.

"And the last one . . ." He paused for dramatic effect. "I'm not sure who to give the last one to."

Everyone began hooting and a chant began—somewhere in the back of the room. "Goldie, Goldie, Goldie!"

"Yeah, I guess so," Coach Gordon said. "Myers, I swear that was the dumbest, smartest, bravest call I've ever seen.

I'm honestly not sure right now whether I want to cut you or kiss you. For now, I'll settle for this."

He tossed the ball to Alex, who caught it and then was buried as the "Goldie, Goldie" chant began again.

Once the celebrating abated, everyone showered and dressed quickly. It was Friday night. The older guys would probably be going out. Most of the younger ones had family waiting for them outside. Alex had looked at his cell phone as he started to take off his uniform and it was filled with texts. The only one he read was from his mom.

WOW! it said. *We're waiting outside. How soon do you think?*

He quickly wrote back, *15 minutes*, and headed for the shower.

It was closer to twenty-five by the time everyone had come up one more time to tell him how great he had been. When he walked outside, there were still several reporters who wanted to talk to him. Coach Brotman had warned him and told him it was up to him whether he talked more or not.

"Can you give me a minute to go see my mom and sister?" he asked.

They all seemed okay with that.

Even forty-five minutes after the game had ended, there were people everywhere. Finally he heard his mom's voice somewhere in the crowd, calling, "Alex, we're here."

At first he saw only a hand waving, but as he walked in the direction of the voice, people parted—all backslapping him as he went—to let him through. There was his mom and there was Molly. And standing a few steps away was someone else: his dad.

He hugged his mom and Molly and then stared at his father.

"When did you get here?" he asked as his father shook his hand. They had never hugged very much in the past, so Alex didn't think to hug him now.

"Believe it or not, at halftime," his dad said, smiling. "I guess I brought you luck."

"Luck had nothing to do with it," Alex heard a voice say.

He turned and there, leaning on his crutches, was Matt Gordon.

"Glad you could make it, Mr. Myers," he said, putting his hand out. "We were all beginning to think you were a figment of Alex's imagination."

Alex wasn't sure who was more stunned by Matt's crack—Alex, his mom, or his dad. Only Molly seemed oblivious.

"Nice to meet you too," Alex's dad said. "I hope you're not too badly hurt."

"I'll be fine, thanks," Matt said. "Couple weeks. As long as Goldie's healthy, we'll be fine."

"Goldie?" his dad said.

"They call him Goldie for his golden arm," his mom explained, and Alex gaped at her—stunned that she knew.

Matt put his hand out to Alex. "I'm proud of you," he said. "I knew you were going to be good, but honestly, I never dreamed you'd be this good this fast."

"Thanks," Alex said. And then, gingerly, because he wanted to, he hugged Matt.

Matt waved goodbye and limped off to talk to some friends.

"Well, I guess this calls for a celebration," Dave Myers said. "I know it's late. . . ."

"It's okay, we've got the whole weekend."

"Actually, we don't," his dad said sheepishly. "I have to be in Washington tomorrow for some meetings. I'm sorry. I just thought driving through to see the game and get a few hours with you and Molly was worth the effort."

Effort? Alex wondered about that. Driving to DC with a stop in Philadelphia on the way wasn't exactly a major effort.

"Dave, why don't you take the kids to eat," Alex's mom said. "Maybe you can go someplace where you can sit and talk for a while."

"Good idea," Alex's dad said. "Okay?" He looked at Molly.

"Yeah, it's fine," she said. But the look on her face told Alex that she hadn't known it was a drive-by visit.

"Great, then," his dad said. "My rental car's a few blocks away because I got here late. Maybe Mom can drop us off there."

"Rental car?" said Alex.

"Yeah, I rented a car because I'm flying back from DC on Sunday.

"Oh. So it *didn't* seem worth the effort to stop and see your kids on the way home."

The words came out of Alex's mouth before he could stop them. And a silence opened up between them because no one really knew *what* to say. . . .

Meanwhile, a steady stream of people were patting Alex on the back, saying, "Way to go" and "Great game" and "Have a great weekend."

Then Jonas came over, laughing and full of the excitement for the win. "There you are, Alex!" he said. "The whole team's going to this party. We gotta go—we're the heroes of the hour! Jake can give us a ride if you come right now. . . ."

Alex looked from his father to Jonas and back again. Hero of the party or dinner with a drive-by dad? No contest.

"I'll see you later, Dad."

As it turned out, there were four people in Jake's car for the ride over to the party: Jake, Alex, Jonas, and Christine Whitford.

"You get all your work done?" Jake asked Christine.

"It was easy tonight," Christine said. "Everyone was very willing to talk."

Christine offered Alex the front seat, but he turned it down. When they got to the party, Jake didn't even ask Christine what she wanted to drink. He just said, "I'll get us drinks," and disappeared.

Before Alex could decide whether to ask Christine if they were dating, he and Jonas were swallowed by admirers. Alex spent most of the evening sitting on a couch re-creating the final drive while people hung on his every word. At one point he noticed that Hope Alexander was sitting right next to him while April Lowenthal, who wasn't nearly as tall as Hope but at least as pretty, was on the other side. Jonas looked to be getting the same kind of attention.

He knew he had come a long way from the day when Mr. O wouldn't even look up at him while shoving the number 23 practice jersey at him. Still, he wondered what his dad was doing. And he hoped Molly had gone out to eat with him.

■ ■ ■

When Alex got home, it was well after midnight. His mom was still up, clearly waiting for him. She asked if he wanted to talk.

"Maybe later," he said.

"You sure?"

"Completely sure," he answered. "I'm really tired, and I don't *know* what I think about what's going on with Dad."

She nodded. "To be fair to your father, I'm not sure he understands what's going on right now either."

That actually sounded right. . . .

"Yeah," he said. "I think. Good night."

He turned to walk upstairs. "Hey, Goldie," she said.

He stopped and saw her grinning.

"Congratulations," she said. "You got to show everyone what you can do tonight."

He smiled back at her. "Night, Mom."

He walked upstairs and fell into bed a few minutes later. In spite of the confusing thoughts about his father and the adrenaline still pumping from the game, he was asleep in no time.

Moments later, he heard his cell phone buzzing and rolled over in bed. He was stunned when he looked at the clock on the night table and saw that it was nine-fifteen. He'd been asleep for more than eight hours!

He picked up the phone and at the top of the lengthy list of texts saw one from a familiar number: Christine Whitford's.

Stark's 11:30? was all it said.

It occurred to him that in all the commotion at the party he hadn't seen Christine or Jake again. Jonas's mom had come and picked them up, so he had no idea if they had still been there when he left.

He sat up in bed and thought about it for a moment: Coach Gordon had lifted the media ban the night before, so talking to her now was almost certainly okay. He wondered if he should call someone to be sure.

He decided against it. He remembered something he had read once: sometimes it's better to ask for forgiveness rather than permission. The fact was, he wanted to see her.

He texted back: *OK.*

He started to add a sentence but decided against it. No need to appear overeager. Or overly curious about her relationship with Jake.

His mom had taken Molly to her soccer game, so he made himself a bowl of cereal and then read the *Philadelphia Inquirer* that his mom had left on the kitchen table so he couldn't miss it. Below the fold of the front page of the sports section was a picture of Matt, on his crutches, hugging Alex on the field after the game. The caption said, "Injured Chester Heights quarterback Matt Gordon celebrates with backup Alex Myers after the Lions' stunning comeback win over King of Prussia Friday night. Details: D-4."

Alex turned quickly to D-4 and there, at the top of the

high school page, was the headline: FRESHMAN QB SHOCKS KING OF PRUSSIA IN FINAL SECONDS. Below the headline was another photo, this one of Jonas catching the final touchdown pass. The story was written by Andrew Bogusch.

Before Friday night, Chester Heights freshman quarterback Alex Myers was a third-string quarterback who had taken two snaps all season—the second one leading to a brawl as he kneeled down to run out the clock in the season opener against Mercer.

Now he's a star.

With all-city quarterback Matt Gordon and backup Jake Bilney both injured, Myers came into the Lions' conference opener against King of Prussia with his team down 17–0 and their dreams of a state title about to go up in smoke before the leaves had even turned.

All Myers did from that point on was lead Chester Heights to a stunning 21–17 victory, capped by a touchdown pass to fellow freshman Jonas Ellington with nine seconds to go—a play set up by Myers faking a spike when everyone in the stadium thought the Lions (1–0, 4–0) were trying to set up for a tying field goal.

"That was the plan," Lions Coach Matthew Gordon said. "We were going to spike the ball, kick the field goal, and try to win in OT. Myers had a last-minute idea and sent Ellington to the end zone." Gordon smiled. "I told him if he'd fumbled or been intercepted, he'd have been running steps from now until Thanksgiving—or longer."

Instead, Myers will probably be running from media demands, lovesick girls, and—quite possibly—a

*quarterback controversy in two to four weeks, when Matt
Gordon's sprained ankle heals.*

Alex had been smiling until he got to the words *quarterback controversy*. That was the last thing in the world he
wanted—which was a strange realization. He'd come here
wanting to prove he should be the starter. Now it was all
more complicated.

He went back to the story. It went through the play-by-
play of the game and ended with a quote from Alex: "Matt's
our quarterback and our leader," the quote read. "I'm really,
really happy we pulled this off tonight. I expect him back
soon. In the meantime, this is a thrill I'll never forget."

He nodded as he read the quote, as if agreeing with himself.

He couldn't resist the urge to go online to find some of the
TV interviews he'd done and to read a couple of other sto-
ries on the game. Unfortunately, the common threads were,
"Wow, what a comeback" and "quarterback controversy."
In one story on the *Philadelphia Daily News* website, Coach
Gordon was asked if there would be an issue when Matt was
healthy.

"You're kidding, right?" Coach Gordon was quoted as saying. "We're talking about an all-city player who might be the
best quarterback in the state. My guess is Myers would be
the first one to tell you that Matt's the starter. Actually, he'd
be the second one: I'm the first."

That wasn't a bad answer, but Alex wondered if being
asked the question would somehow make Coach Gordon
cranky when they got back to practice on Monday.

He decided not to worry about it—until Monday.

. . .

It was a spectacular fall day, the humidity and heat of the summer having finally broken. Christine Whitford was sitting in a back booth waiting when Alex walked in. To Alex's surprise, he was stopped three times en route to the booth by people who recognized him and wanted to congratulate him.

"Better get used to that, Goldie," she said as he slid into the booth.

"Can we just keep it at Alex?" he asked, smiling nonetheless.

She shrugged. "I doubt it. Everyone knows it now."

"I'd prefer it if *you'd* call me Alex."

"Okay, Alex. So whose idea was it for Jake to fake the injury?"

Whoa. This girl didn't mess around. Blindsided yet again . . .

"I should be asking you that," he finally said. "I didn't spend any time with him after the game except when we were all in the car. If he'd talk to anyone, I think it'd be you."

She looked at him sharply for a moment. "He wouldn't even admit to me that he wasn't really hurt," she said finally.

"Then why do you think he was faking?" Alex asked.

"Someone else told me."

"Then ask whoever it was whose idea it was."

"I did. He said it was Jake's."

"And you don't believe him?"

"I'm not saying that. But I'm not sure. Jake wouldn't talk about it at all, and I can't write that he faked it unless someone else confirms it."

"You mean besides Matt."

"What makes you say my source was Matt?"

"If it's not Jake and it's not me, it had to be Matt."

She looked away for a moment and Alex knew he was right. He wondered *why* Matt would tell her.

"Regardless of who it was, I can't write it based on one source unless Jake confirms it, and he won't."

"Well, I *can't* confirm it because I don't know." Alex wasn't sure he'd tell her even if he did know, but he didn't feel the need to tell her that. He paused, then plunged forward. "I can't believe you can't get Jake to tell you something."

He thought she reddened a little. "What's that mean?"

"You are dating, aren't you?"

More redness.

"We haven't been on a date. We've just kind of hung out at parties."

"But you think he's good-looking."

"He *is* good-looking," she said. "That isn't always the reason you go out with someone—unless you're a guy."

He decided not to pursue this any further. The fact that she had said she hadn't actually been on a date with Jake was a little bit of good news. It was also, he suspected, the last bit of news he was going to get on that front.

"So why won't he tell you?" Alex said.

"I think he's embarrassed," she said. "How would you feel if the best way to help your team win was to fake an injury?"

She had a point. Which actually made Alex a little angry. Jake had done a very brave thing—whether it was his idea or Matt's. He shouldn't be humiliated in the newspaper for it.

"Why can't you just let it go?" he said. "Why do you guys

have to make trouble every week? We just had an amazing win and you're going to write that Jake faked an injury?"

"For the good of the team. I'm not going to attack him for doing it. Neither is Steve. Jake knew we were going to lose unless you got in the game, and Coach Gordon wasn't going to put you in."

"How do you know that?"

"*Everyone* knows that!"

She was probably right. But still. "Even if that's true, how does it help the team to say so now? I don't see how humiliating Jake and calling out Coach for something you only *think* he would have done is 'for the good of the team.'"

He leaned back in the booth as the waitress came to take their order. She appeared bored while Christine ordered, but when she turned to Alex, her eyes went wide.

"Hey, you're the kid I saw on television last night! The quarterback!"

"Um, yeah," Alex said. "Can I have a medium-rare burger with French fries and a Coke?"

"Sure you can!" the waitress said, now bubbling over with enthusiasm. Alex guessed she was about his mom's age.

She turned to Christine. "Bet you're proud of your boyfriend, aren't you, sweetheart?"

"He's not my boyfriend," Christine said, now clearly blushing. "I'm just doing a story for the school newspaper."

The waitress leaned down and playfully batted Christine on the head. "Well he *should* be your boyfriend, hon! Just look at him!" With that, she walked away.

Christine looked as if she wanted to run from the room screaming.

Alex couldn't resist. "You heard her," he said. "Just look at me!"

She let out a deep breath. "Had you pegged right from the beginning. Big-ego football player."

"Come on," he said. "I was joking."

She leaned forward.

"Okay, then, prove you're different. Tell me the truth about Jake."

Alex sighed. "I honestly don't know whose idea it was."

"Whose idea do you *think* it was?" she asked, her eyes wide open with anticipation.

He looked around the way you're supposed to when you are about to reveal something you shouldn't.

"You can't quote me on this because I don't know. But I suspect it was Matt," he said.

"That's what I thought," she said. "I knew he was holding out on me."

"So Matt *is* your source."

"I didn't say that," she said, suddenly a little flustered.

"Why did he tell you it was Jake?" Alex said, ignoring the non-denial denial.

She gave up the charade. "Because he figured I knew the truth, and he wanted Jake to come off as the hero of the story. Heck, everyone at the party knew he wasn't hurt. Jake was *dancing* before the end of the night."

"With you?"

"Doesn't matter," she said.

It mattered to Alex. And he knew the answer was yes.

Jake Bilney was officially listed as "questionable" for the next Friday's game at Lansdowne with a "slightly sprained knee." He wore a light wrap on it to practice and didn't take part in any of the drills that involved running, although he did take part in all the passing drills.

Emmet Foley, whose older brother Conor was a starting safety, was called up from the JV team to back up Alex at quarterback in case of an emergency and to take all the snaps Alex didn't take when the team scrimmaged. Jake was held out of the scrimmages.

"I'm fine if they need me," he told Alex. "But you better stay healthy so they *don't* need me."

Actually, no one was terribly worried about the next few games. Having survived the King of Prussia game, Chester Heights was now entering what was expected to be the easiest part of the schedule: Lansdowne, Haverford Station, and

Bryn Mawr Tech were traditionally the three weakest teams in the league. In fact, the three of them had one win total—Bryn Mawr's win over Haverford Station the previous Friday.

"If I had to get hurt, this was the time to do it," Matt said as they warmed up on Monday. He was still on crutches, but the doctors had told him he would be in a walking boot by the end of the week. He wouldn't play the next two weeks but expected to be back for the Bryn Mawr game. "Honestly, no offense, Jakey, but we could win the next three with you at quarterback playing left-handed. With Goldie, we're golden."

Alex had warned Jake on Monday about Christine's story. Jake didn't seem too concerned. "She told me she was going to write it," he said. "I can't stop her, but no one can prove it. I did hurt my knee, just maybe not as bad as it seemed at the time."

"But Coach may get upset again. . . ."

"Nah, we bailed him out," Jake said. "Matt was right all along. You had to play. The results prove it. I bet Coach doesn't say a word about it."

So Alex let it drop, and Jake turned out to be right.

The *Weekly Roar* came out on Wednesday with extra coverage of the game, including a column by Steve Garland on how remarkable Alex's performance had been.

"The only problem with Myers's Miracle," he wrote, "is that now Coach Gordon will have to decide in a few weeks if he plays his best quarterback or his favorite quarterback. They may not be the same person."

Ouch, Alex thought.

Then there was Christine's story, saying that "several of

the upperclassmen, along with backup quarterback Jake Bilney, had talked among themselves at halftime about the fact that Alex Myers had to take over behind center if the Lions were to win the game."

She never actually said Jake faked the injury, but she did write, "Jake Bilney may have saved the season by going down and staying down when the Lions most needed to get Alex Myers up—and in the game."

Ouch. Again.

And yet, not a word from Coach Gordon that day at practice. He was as cheerful as he had been all season—which didn't exactly make him cheerful, but at least bearable. Matt was acting as an unofficial quarterback coach. Coach Gordon hadn't replaced Coach Hillier—Alex figured it was tough to do midseason. So when the QBs went off to drill, Coach Brotman focused on the O-line because everyone believed that Alex and Jake and Emmet were in good hands with Matt.

Alex couldn't resist asking the question when he had a chance.

"Your dad say anything about the stories in the *Weekly Roar* today?" he asked.

Matt shook his head. "I think he's finally figured out that getting upset about what's in the student paper doesn't do anybody any good." He smiled. "Besides, Jakey's girlfriend had the story right. We all knew you had to play. My dad knows that."

"She's Jake's girlfriend?"

He thought he knew the answer but wanted to see how Matt would answer.

Matt stood up to balance himself and pointed a crutch directly at him. "She should be *your* girlfriend, Goldie," he said. "You gotta quit acting like you're a third-string guy. You're not—not any more than you were a third-string quarterback."

Alex didn't say another word.

■ ■ ■

The next two weeks could hardly have gone better for Alex—and for the team.

Lansdowne and Haverford Station were as bad as advertised. Alex came out of the Lansdowne game with Chester Heights leading 42–0. Jake was in uniform, but Emmet Foley came in and simply handed the ball off for the rest of the night. The final was 42–7. A week later at Haverford Station it was 44–0 when Alex came out and Jake took his place. Jake did the same thing that Foley had done—kept handing the ball off to several backup tailbacks—until Foley came in to do the same on the final series of the game. This time the final was 44–7.

Alex was hardly spectacular in either game, but he didn't need to be. Coach Gordon's game plan was simple—run the ball most of the time, mixing in an occasional pass to keep the defense honest. Alex only threw the ball deep once, and that was on an audible—where he changed the play at the line—because he noticed that *no one* from Haverford Station was anywhere close to Max Plesac. He faked a handoff to Craig Josephs, took a couple steps back, and lofted a pass to Plesac, who could have walked backward into the end zone.

Other than that, it was an option play here, a pitch there,

and putting the ball into Josephs's stomach a lot. The tail-back rushed for 294 yards in the two games, largely because Chester Heights' offensive line completely dominated both opponents.

Matt was off the crutches for the Lansdowne game and had started throwing again on Tuesday prior to the Haverford Station game. There hadn't been any discussion about who the starting quarterback would be for the game at Bryn Mawr. Alex assumed that was because there wasn't any doubt it would be Matt.

On Sunday night, Alex received an email from Coach Brotman saying that he and Coach Gordon would like to meet with all three quarterbacks in the football offices Monday lunchtime. "I'm designated to bring lunch," he wrote. "Matt's a McDonald's guy. Jake likes Burger King. You get the deciding vote. Tell me what you want."

Alex laughed. He liked Coach Brotman. He certainly wasn't nearly as involved with the QBs as Coach Hillier had been. In fact, if Chester Heights had a quarterback coach, it was Matt Gordon.

He wrote back that he preferred McDonald's and told Coach Brotman what he wanted to eat. He wasn't looking forward to the meeting all that much since he figured he knew what it was about. Still, the thought of not eating the cafeteria food was appealing, even if he would miss all the attention he was now receiving. Not only did people practically line up to sit with him and Jonas and Stephen, but he also had no fewer than twelve invitations to the holiday dance. Alex had told all twelve girls he couldn't make a commitment, in part because the dance was the Saturday after

Thanksgiving and he wasn't sure he'd be home, but more importantly because it was the night after the state finals. He hoped they'd be having a big team celebration.

There was another reason he was noncommittal: if he *did* go, the only girl he really wanted to go with was Christine Whitford. He had no idea if she would go with him, but he had decided to follow Matt Gordon's advice and at least ask her. If she was going with Jake, fine, but he'd give it his best shot.

■ ■ ■

"I think all three of you guys know why I asked you here, but just in case you don't, it's about who's going to start on Friday against Bryn Mawr."

Coach Gordon had been sitting behind his desk, but now he stood up and walked in front of the whiteboard in the corner of the room, which listed all the players on the football team's roster.

Matt, Jake, and Alex were sitting on chairs in front of the desk. Coach Brotman was standing near the door. All three quarterbacks were gobbling French fries at that moment.

"Honestly, Myers, this is more for your benefit than anyone else," Coach Gordon continued, arms crossed. He actually appeared to be a little uncomfortable—which surprised Alex. "You did a great job bringing us back in the King of Prussia game and you've done everything we asked you to do the last two weeks. I have every confidence that anytime you're in a game we have a chance to win."

He paused. Alex looked at Matt, who had his head down. Jake was sipping a Coke.

"I think, though, as we move ahead, the most experienced guy needs to be our starter. I'm not a coach who says you can't lose your job because you get injured, because—to be honest—if someone comes in and is better, he's playing.

"I talked to Matt about this last night," he continued. "You know Matt's your biggest supporter around here." He paused. "When I told him he was starting against Bryn Mawr, he asked me straight out, would he be the starter if he wasn't my son."

Coach Gordon paced back and forth for a brief moment. "I told him he was the starter in spite of being my son. And that's the truth."

He stopped talking. Everyone was looking at Alex. Apparently, he was expected to respond.

"Coach, if you had said anything different, I would have argued with you," Alex said, realizing as the words came out of his mouth that he was telling the truth. "Matt's the leader of this team. I couldn't possibly have played as well as I did against King of Prussia if not for Matt."

"You wouldn't have played at all if not for Jake," Matt, who had been uncharacteristically quiet, added with a smile. Everyone laughed—even Coach Gordon.

Alex thought for a moment before answering. In August, he probably would have said something like, *Coach, it's your call, you're the boss*, and left it at that, because back then he was convinced he was the team's best quarterback. Now, even knowing he had the best arm and had played well in Matt's absence, he realized he was not—*yet*—the best quarterback or even close to being the team's leader.

"Matt's our quarterback, Coach," he said finally—

meaning it. "You didn't need to explain that to me. But I appreciate it."

"Alex, you are a remarkably mature young man," Coach Gordon said, surprising Alex by calling him by his first name. "I want you to understand, you're still going to play. We'll work you in for a series here and there to keep the defenses off balance. You are a perfect counterpart for Matt with the way you throw the ball. Plus, knowing you might play will make it tougher for teams to prepare for us.

"So get ready every week as if you're still the starter, because you are going to play."

"I'll do that, Coach. Don't worry."

"I know you will," he said. "I'll see you all at practice."

He sat down at his desk. The meeting was over.

As the three of them walked out, Matt put his arm around Alex. "I knew the first time I saw you that you could play football," he said. "I didn't know what a good guy you were. Thanks for making that easy on everyone. You could have complained if you wanted to and it would have been legit. You played great."

"You *are* the leader of this team, Matt," Alex said. "We're better when you're out there."

"I hope so," Matt said softly. "I hope so."

26

With Matt back at practice, Alex's role changed once again. Matt took about seventy-five percent of the snaps with the first team and Alex took the rest. Alex and Jake split the second- and third-team snaps, which meant Alex was still on the field a lot while the team was scrimmaging.

Matt was held back a little bit in practice that week. The bolder play calls—the options designed to get to the corners and the play-action passes—were called almost exclusively when Alex was on the field. Every once in a while Alex caught Matt grimacing after he'd made a cut, but his movement looked fine to him.

Not surprisingly, the Wednesday edition of the *Weekly Roar* was filled with speculation about who would start at quarterback. Coach Gordon had said only, "We don't know if Matt will be ready next week. If he's one hundred percent, I expect he'll be the starter."

Steve Garland had written a column—a fair one, Alex thought—wondering if Coach Gordon would be affected in either direction by the nepotism issue: would he favor Matt because he was his son or be tougher on him?

> Most players on the team believe that Coach Gordon holds Matt to a higher standard than any other player. It is one reason why Matt is so highly thought of by his teammates. And yet, one wonders, when crunch time really comes around, does Matthew Gordon think like a coach or like a father?
>
> With luck, we'll never need to learn the answer to that question.

Bryn Mawr Tech was not as bad as the Lions' two previous opponents, but they were still no match for Chester Heights, which was 6–0 coming into the game and now ranked number fourteen in the USA Today national poll. The Chargers led 7–0 after Craig Josephs dropped a simple pitch midway through the first quarter that gave them a short field to work with. But the Lions came back quickly: Josephs went fifty-nine yards on a perfect option pitch from Matt Gordon, and then they killed a lot of clock with a twelve-play, seventy-one-yard drive that put them up 14–7. When Bryn Mawr punted with 2:38 left in the half and Chester Heights took over on its own 29, Coach Gordon sent Alex in to run the two-minute offense.

"Nothing heroic," he said as he sent him onto the field. "Take what's there. If that's nothing, throw the ball away. No turnovers!"

What was there, not surprisingly, were a lot of short passes allowed by a backpedaling defense. The Lions moved to midfield with 1:09 left and one time-out remaining. On first down, Alex play-faked and then wound up as if he were going deep to Max Plesac. He then stepped up and spotted Jonas, who had also started to run a deep route but had pulled up and come back toward the ball. Alex found Jonas wide open at the 30, and Jonas made it all the way to the 18 before being wrestled out of bounds with fifty-two seconds to go.

On the next play, Alex handed the ball to Josephs, running a straight draw up the middle, and he bulled to the five. Alex ran up to the line and spiked the ball with twenty-two seconds left, the plan being to save the time-out to get the field goal team on the field.

Plesac raced into the huddle, delivering Z wide right. That play was a quick toss in the right corner to Jonas. Alex could see that the defense was rotating in whatever direction Jonas lined up. He nodded at Plesac, stepped into the huddle, and called, "22 draw, look—Y middle."

Plesac raised an eyebrow but said nothing. The play was a fake draw to Josephs with Mike Crenshaw, the second tight end—known as the Y for play-calling purposes—faking a block and then running to the goal line. With luck, the linebacker he was blocking would take the run fake and Crenshaw would be open.

They came to the line and Alex took some extra time since the clock wasn't running after the spike. The play clock was down to two seconds when he took the snap, turned, and stuck the ball into Josephs's stomach. Sure enough, the linebacker had bitten on the run fake, and there was Crenshaw wide open at the goal line.

Except he wasn't wide open. Alex saw the safety coming up on him just as he released the ball, but it was too late. The safety stepped in front of Crenshaw and, before anyone in a Chester Heights uniform realized what had happened, the ball was in his arms and he was gone, racing down the sideline. Alex turned to chase but knew right away it was futile.

Touchdown, Bryn Mawr Tech.

Alex felt sick. He had overruled the coach's call and had turned what should have been *at worst* a 17–7 lead into a 14–14 tie at halftime. Coach Gordon's call, he realized, was the smart call: even if Jonas was covered in the corner, the pass would be likely to fall incomplete and the field goal team would have come on the field. And even if, by some chance, Alex threw a poor pass and it was intercepted, then the defender would have been leaping and diving in a corner of the end zone to make the play. There couldn't have been a return. Alex's call—a pass over the middle—put the possibility of a return into play, and worst of all, that was what had happened.

He jogged to the sideline. Coach Gordon and Matt both met him as he arrived.

"Was that an audible?" Coach Gordon asked.

"No sir."

"So you just overruled my call in the huddle."

"I thought I saw something—"

"Apparently, you didn't."

The extra point sailed through to tie the game. The clock

read 00:00. The teams started for the locker rooms with the Bryn Mawr crowd going nuts. Coach Gordon put a hand on Alex's shoulder—not gently.

"If both Matt and Jake get hurt in the second half, you're not going in," he said, not raising his voice but with razors in it. "You understand?"

"Yes sir."

"And Coach Brotman will meet you at school at six o'clock tomorrow morning. Once was okay, especially because you were right. Twice is unacceptable. I'm still the coach."

Alex had his head down.

"Do you understand me, Myers?"

"Yes sir."

The worst part of it, Alex thought as he followed his teammates to the locker room, was that poor Coach Brotman had to wake up at five o'clock on a Saturday morning. He hadn't done anything to deserve that.

Alex had.

■ ■ ■

Matt Gordon took control of the game in the second half, leading two long drives and one short one that was set up by a Gerry Detwiler interception. The two captains got the game balls after the 35–21 victory and they were both deserved.

Alex felt no joy in victory. Matt and Jake both told him it was okay, that this too would pass, but it didn't feel that way. When he came out of the locker room, Steve Garland was waiting for him. He could see Christine talking to Detwiler.

"Did you get benched in the second half?" Garland asked him.

"If I did, I deserved it after the interception," Alex said, not mentioning that he had changed the play. "It was a dumb play on my part."

"Aren't you being a little hard on yourself?" Garland asked.

"Probably not hard enough," Alex said, excusing himself because he saw his mom and Molly standing nearby. They had driven to the game even though it was away from home.

Although his mom didn't really get football, she knew enough to know that Alex had messed up. He had told her—and his dad, on the phone—about the new plan for him to play a series or two each half.

"You okay?" she asked.

"I'm fine. Can we go home, please?"

She nodded. Even Molly looked sad. "No party tonight?" his mom asked. "You did win the game. . . ."

Alex had the usual array of Friday-night party invites on his phone.

"Mom, I have to be at school at six o'clock tomorrow morning," he said.

"Why?" she asked.

"I'll tell you in the car."

When he explained, she was silent for a moment.

"Is he wrong to be angry?" she asked finally. "I don't really understand."

"He's completely right," he said. "I got cocky and I paid for it."

He looked at his watch. It was almost eleven o'clock. He'd have about six hours to sleep.

· · ·

Coach Brotman was waiting for him when he pulled up on his bicycle the next morning.

"Coach said five trips up and down," he said. "If you go hard, you can stop after four."

"Is that from you or Coach Gordon?" Alex asked.

"From me. You messed up, Alex, and I think you know it. The important thing isn't that you be punished but that you understand what you did wrong."

"I do understand," Alex said. "I got carried away with myself."

"You get it, then," Coach Brotman said. "By the way, you aren't the first freshman to get a little bit of a big head."

Alex worked the steps hard. The sun wasn't up yet since it was mid-October and almost time to set the clocks back. It was cool, very cool, and as he ran, he could see his breath. The workout actually felt good.

"Okay, Alex, that's enough," Coach Brotman said after his fourth trip up and down the thirty-five rows of steps. "Locker room's open. Go take a shower and get some rest. I'm going home."

"Thanks, Coach. I'm sorry you had to get up early because of me."

Coach Brotman waved him off. "I've got a fourteen-month-old," he said. "I'm usually up by now anyway."

He tossed Alex a towel and walked in the direction of his car.

Alex took a long shower, actually reveling in having the shower room to himself. Some of Mr. O's guys were in early cleaning uniforms, but the locker room was otherwise empty.

The sun was just starting to come up when he pushed the locker room door open. He was glancing east, enjoying the sight of the rising sun, when he heard a voice say, "I'll bet you could use some breakfast."

He turned and saw Christine Whitford standing there. He smiled.

"You know, for some reason, I'm not surprised you're here."

"I heard what happened."

"Of course you did."

She smiled. "What does that mean?"

"It means you know more about what happens on this team than most of the players."

She was still smiling the mesmerizing smile.

"Isn't that what a reporter is supposed to do?"

She was wearing blue jeans and a blue-and-white Villanova sweatshirt. The sun was starting to warm the morning air, but it was still cool.

"I don't know what a reporter is supposed to do," he said. "I'm not a reporter."

"I know," she said. "You're a football player." She paused for a second before adding, "With a pretty good French accent."

That made him laugh. "You didn't get up this early and come down here to compliment my accent."

"No, I didn't. In fact, my story for Wednesday is about Craig Josephs and Gerry Detwiler and their chances to make all-state."

"Should be pretty good. We're seven and oh and Gerry

makes big plays in every game. Craig's already rushed for almost a thousand yards.

"Nine hundred seventy-nine," she said.

"Sorry, Hermione," he said. "I should have known you'd have the exact number."

"Hermione?"

"Harry Potter?"

He thought she blushed for a split second. "Are you saying I'm a know-it-all or that I look like Emma Watson?"

"Both."

"Hmm. Come on, let's go to breakfast."

"Where? Why?"

"Pat and Steve's. We should talk."

"I've never heard of Pat and Steve's."

"Just get on your bike and follow me."

He was tempted to ask her what she wanted to talk about, but he knew he wasn't going to turn her down, so he just shrugged and followed her to the bike rack.

Christine was aware—naturally—of what he had said to Steve Garland about the interception after the game. In fact, she had his quotes written down word for word in a notebook she took out once they were seated.

Pat and Steve's looked like something out of the old TV show *Murder, She Wrote*, which Alex had grown up watching in reruns with his grandmother. She never called the show by its actual name. She would simply stand up at the end of Sunday dinner and say, "Time to watch Jessica"—Jessica Fletcher being the name of the woman who solved murder mysteries every week on the show.

The restaurant had a counter just inside the door, tables in the middle of the room, and booths lining the wall that looked out on a grove of trees, making it feel a lot more like Cabot Cove, Maine, than Philadelphia, Pennsylvania. Alex was certain that Angela Lansbury, the star of the show, was going to walk through the door at any moment.

Alex had realized on the bike ride over that he was starving. He ordered French toast, bacon, and orange juice. Christine asked for an omelet and tomato juice.

As usual, she came right to the point. "So did you get benched in the second half last night?"

"Very subtle first question. I read *All the President's Men* this summer. . . ."

"I read it in seventh grade."

"Yes, Hermione, I'm sure you did."

"Actually, my dad insisted I read it."

"Why?"

"He's an editor at the *Daily News* and that was the book that inspired him to become a journalist. It is pretty inspiring, didn't you think? Two reporters actually changed the world. . . ."

"So it *is* in your blood. I should have guessed."

She didn't answer, just smiled. He plowed on.

"Anyway, one of the things I noticed in the book was that Woodward and Bernstein never started with the hard questions. They started with the easy ones."

"How's your orange juice?" she said, grinning.

"If I did get benched, I deserved it," he said, figuring he'd made his point.

"Why?" she asked. "Everyone makes a bad throw now and then."

"Are you going to quote me on this?"

"Depends on what you say."

He shook his head.

"Not good enough. You can't quote me because if Coach wants to tell you or anyone he benched me, he can. But it's not my place to do it."

She sighed. "Fine. I won't quote you."

"I didn't get benched for throwing the interception. I got benched for changing the play in the huddle." He stopped for a second. "Actually, I'm surprised you didn't know that. You know everything else."

She took a sip of her tomato juice.

"No one told me that," she said. "I'm guessing they thought it was up to you whether you wanted to tell someone that."

He had to admit he would not have told anyone other than Christine that. He just couldn't seem to keep his mouth shut when talking to her. Then again, he doubted any of his teammates would blame him. It was pretty apparent that he and Jake weren't the only ones who talked to her. Matt had been the one who told her about Jake faking his knee injury.

"Do you think you'll play against Lincoln next week?"

"I have no idea. I'm hoping running steps this morning was the end of it. I'll probably be able to tell Monday at practice."

"The worst part of this is that you gave Coach Gordon an excuse not to play you," she said.

"He doesn't need an excuse not to play me. Matt's the starter."

"You're better than Matt."

He shook his head as their food arrived and waited as the waitress put the plates down, asked them if they needed anything else, and then moved away. He wondered if Christine had said that as a ploy to get him to talk more or if she really meant it.

"*No*, I'm not," he said. "Look, you're about the smartest person I know, but you do *not* understand football. Not only is Matt a really good quarterback—different than I am, but really good—he is the leader of our team. That's very, very important."

"You led the team back in the King of Prussia game."

"One game, and KOP had never seen me before."

She took a bite of her omelet and pointed her fork at him for a moment.

"You're wrong," she said. "I *do* know football. And when you get to the playoffs—*if* you beat Chester and get there—you're going to need a quarterback who can throw. That's *you*, not Matt."

Alex focused on his French toast for a while. Then, without really thinking it through, he blurted, "Will you go to the holiday dance with me?"

She looked surprised for a split second and then smiled.

"Maybe," she said.

"Maybe?" he said, stunned because that was the *only* answer he hadn't considered as a possibility. "Are you waiting for Jake to ask you?"

"No," she said firmly. "I think Jake's a good guy, but he's always mad at me for not being on Coach Gordon's bandwagon." She paused. "And for saying you're better than Matt."

"So why maybe?"

"It *is* the night after the state championship game."

"And?"

"How about if you guys win, I'll go with you."

"So you'll only go with me if we're state champions? That's ridiculous!"

"I was kidding," she said, laughing at his outrage. "Sure, I'll go with you." She paused to watch his face light up. "But only if you admit you're better than Matt. You said you were back in September. And now I'm convinced."

"Matt would never have made the dumb play I made last night. I've learned a lot from watching him. You can't say that I'm better than he is. We have different strengths."

"I can say it, and I do," she answered. "But I'll go to the dance with you anyway. I like loyalty."

■ ■ ■

Alex did play, for one series, in the Lincoln game, and he got one series in the game against Thomas Jefferson the week after that. (Matt Gordon called it the "presidents portion" of the schedule.)

In both games he got in for the second offensive series of the third quarter. The Lions were leading comfortably in both cases: 21–0 against Lincoln and 24–7 against Jefferson. He followed the play calls to a tee, not even bothering to consider an audible. He threw four passes total.

They won both games so easily it was almost dull.

There was the usual congratulatory text from his dad after the Jefferson game with a promise to be at the next one and *if not, then the playoffs!* Always there was a hedge in the promises. Alex had intentionally stopped thinking about how much he missed his dad. It just hurt too much.

Coach Gordon hadn't said anything to him about the changed call and the benching after his stint running the steps. He was now back to splitting scrimmage reps with Jake behind Matt, although he was still listed second on the depth chart. He also alternated with Jake running the scout team offense again—which really hurt because he wasn't even practicing plays his team would be running in the game.

Naturally, the person who tried hardest to keep his spirits up was Matt Gordon.

"Just learn from your mistake," Matt counseled. "I know you felt awful when it happened, but long run it was probably good for you. And it didn't hurt the team, so just let it go."

"It didn't hurt us because you won the game in the second half."

"And you bailed us out in the King of Prussia game. I don't see you going around bragging about that. So don't beat yourself up for one mistake."

Matt was right, and Alex knew it. Still, it bothered him that his playing time had been cut back as the season was wrapping up.

They would finish the regular season at home against their archrival, Chester. The Clippers were 8–1, having lost their season opener to a school in Texas in a game televised on ESPN. Like Chester Heights, they had a 6–0 conference record, meaning the winner would advance to the state playoffs. The loser would go home.

■ ■ ■

On Monday, there was very little of the usual joking or teasing during pre-practice stretching. Even Matt was a little tight.

"The nine wins will mean nothing if we lose this game," he said as the quarterbacks warmed up. "We'll be remembered as a team that had a lot of potential but couldn't get it done when we had to get it done."

"How good are they?" Jake said. "Do you know?"

"We beat them pretty easily last year, but they have some transfers and a lot of returning starters. They throw the ball a lot—I checked their stats. I think their quarterback, Todd Austin, is being recruited by some midlevel D1 schools. I've seen some film of him and he's pretty good—better than last year."

He smiled. "His arm's almost as strong as yours, Goldie."

Everyone chuckled at that and things felt a little more normal. But there was no doubting the pressure everyone was feeling. All the coaches were a little more short-tempered than normal when mistakes were made. During Wednesday's practice, Josephs fumbled a pitch on one play, and then Matt overthrew Jonas on a pass over the middle a play later. Coach Gordon's whistle blew.

"Everyone to midfield," he said. "Right now."

It was after five o'clock and the sun was already starting to set. It occurred to Alex that at this hour next week it would be dark because the clocks would be set back on Saturday night. It was chilly now; it would no doubt be cold then. He hoped they would get the chance to be cold.

"Listen, fellas," Coach Gordon said. "We're about to play our tenth game. I know you're all feeling some pressure because of what's at stake. But you have *got* to keep doing what you've been doing all season. Craig, wrap that football up! Matt, don't short-arm your passes. You've got plenty of arm—just throw the ball. I know it's late, you're all a little tired. We aren't going to go much longer.

"Tomorrow we'll just be fine-tuning things," he continued. "Let's make sure that practice isn't our last one of the season."

"Now, *that's* the way to keep us loose," Matt said quietly as the offense retreated to huddle up.

Everyone laughed. But it was nervous laughter. Friday was going to be a long night.

■ ■ ■

As it turned out, Friday was the coldest day of the year, with snow flurries in the air starting at lunchtime.

Christine actually walked Alex down the hall after French class. There was no pep rally because Coach Gordon had decided everyone should go home for a while to rest up, and as he had put it when asked to address a brief morning assembly, "If we need a pep rally to get up for this game, something's wrong!"

Christine caught Alex walking out the door and fell into step with him.

"You think you'll play tonight?" she asked.

"I got my usual snaps in practice, so I'd think so at some point," he said. "It probably depends on how the game's going. I'd love to go in with a big lead."

"Not likely," Christine said. "My dad talked to a couple of the high school writers at the paper. They say Chester's very good."

"That's what Matt said. It's a championship game. You can't expect it to be easy."

"Usually they're much better in basketball," she said. "It's unusual for them to be this good in football."

Alex had actually read a story in the *Inquirer* that morning saying much the same thing.

"Well, we're not playing basketball tonight," he said.

"You nervous?"

"Not yet. I suspect I will be later."

"Especially if you play."

He started to nod, then shook his head.

"Actually, no," he said. "When you get in the game, your nerves disappear. Adrenaline takes over and you just play. I wasn't nervous once during that King of Prussia game. Standing on the sidelines watching, *that* makes you nervous."

"Well, I'll be a little bit nervous watching from the press box tonight."

"That's nice of you," he said. "I mean that."

"Don't get me wrong. I'd like to see you win because this is my school, so that's part of it."

"Part of it?" he asked.

She smiled. "If you guys win, I get to cover the playoffs for the *Inquirer* next week. One of their high school guys read some of my stories and recommended me as a stringer if we're playing."

"A stringer?"

"Someone who writes for the paper but doesn't work for them full-time."

"Well," he said as they reached the steps where they went in different directions—she to the newspaper office, he to his locker—"here's hoping you get to be a stringer next week."

"Don't ruin my career," she said cheerily, turning and heading down the hallway.

They hadn't really talked about the holiday dance since she had said she would go with him. And there hadn't been much time at all for socializing the last couple of weeks. There had been midterms and football and that had pretty much been it. Still, it made him smile when he thought of going with her to the dance.

That, though, would come later. It was time to worry about a football game. One game to make or break a season.

It was snowing, lightly but steadily, when the game kicked off that night. It was by far the coldest Alex had felt standing on the sidelines, although he was not as miserable as he'd been in the rain at Main Line.

The stadium was packed, and people were standing in any open area they could find.

Alex knew from everything he had read that this was one of those rivalry games that old men talk about twenty, thirty, and forty years after playing in one. Chester was the so-called urban school, Chester Heights the suburban school. Translation: there were only fourteen African American players wearing the Lions' red and white, and probably about the same number of white players in the white uniforms with the black pants representing Chester.

Chester Heights had won six of the last seven meetings

in football. Chester had won eleven in a row in basketball. So this was a chance for Chester to beat Chester Heights at its own game.

Coach Gordon reminded his team that they were now playing a "one-game season."

"If you do your job tonight, you'll have three more one-game seasons in the playoffs," he said. "But none of that can happen if we don't win this one."

The first half was everything you might expect from such a game. Each team had one turnover that set up a touchdown for the other. Matt Gordon was bulling defenders over whenever he carried the ball, but he made a mistake on a play-action pass, overthrowing an open Jonas. One of Chester's safeties grabbed the floating football and carried it to the Chester Heights 19. Matt came off beating himself up, apologizing to Jonas.

"I won't miss that one again," he promised him.

"I know you won't," Jonas said.

They went to the break tied at 7–7. If the thought of putting Alex in the game ever crossed Coach Gordon's mind, he never said it or so much as looked at Alex.

But things changed after halftime. Somehow, Craig Josephs, who had one fumble all season, dropped a simple pitch midway through the third quarter and Chester recovered at the Lions' 23. From there, it took them five plays to score and take the lead, 14–7, with 3:19 left in the third quarter.

As the defense trudged off the field following the extra point, Alex heard Coach Gordon barking his name.

"Myers, over here!"

Alex trotted over to where Coach Gordon was standing. Matt was next to him. The snow had stopped, but the temperature had dropped since kickoff.

"Matt thinks we need a change of pace on offense," Coach Gordon said. "Are you ready to play?"

"Give me three warm-up throws and I'll be set," Alex said.

Coach Gordon nodded and Alex grabbed Nick Munson, one of the JV receivers who was in uniform, and told him he needed to play catch. Munson shucked the cape he had wrapped around his shoulders and walked over to where Alex would be able to throw to him. Alex was actually able to get five throws in before he saw the offense heading onto the field after the kickoff.

"Run 29 toss to start," Coach Gordon said.

Alex nodded. In the huddle, he called the play and looked at Craig Josephs.

"You okay, big guy?" he asked.

It had been 28 toss, the same simple pitch play but going the other way, that had led to Craig's fumble.

"Just pitch it to me, Goldie," Craig said.

He did and Craig wrapped both arms around the ball and picked up nine yards to the 40.

Jonas, who hadn't been in for the first play, sprinted onto the field carrying the next one.

"28 toss, X turn in," he said.

Alex nodded. It was a perfect call. He would fake the same play to Josephs, only going left instead of right, then drop back and look for Jonas—the X receiver running a turn-in pattern over the middle.

The play came off exactly as they had run it in practice—

except for one thing. After Alex hit Jonas in stride at the Chester 42, he ran right through the cornerback's tackle, cut inside on another potential tackler, and wasn't brought down until he reached the 21.

The Chester Heights crowd, which had been silent for a long time, was suddenly roaring as the Lions sprinted downfield to huddle up again. The huddle was alive with chatter. After hearing the next call, Alex stepped in and looked around.

"Everyone calm down," he said, realizing he was giving orders to ten players—Jonas was out of the game again—who were all two or three years older than he was. It didn't matter. He was the quarterback. As Matt had told him repeatedly, it had to be *his* huddle. Clearly, it was just that. Everyone quieted as he called the play.

Twice in a row they ran options where Alex had to decide as he got to the corner whether to turn upfield or pitch to Josephs. Both times he kept it himself because the defense was keying on Josephs—which made sense. Alex picked up fifteen yards on the two plays to a first down at the six. From there, Josephs did the rest behind the offensive line, bulling to the 2-yard line on first down and then into the end zone.

The quarter ended as he scored. The extra point made it 14–14.

The sideline was alive as the offense came off the field.

"Good job, Myers, very good job," Coach Gordon said. "Stay ready."

That meant Matt would be back in on the next offensive series. Alex wasn't surprised, but he was a little disappointed. Jake, having heard what Coach Gordon said, came up and gave Alex a high five.

"He should keep you in there," he said.

Alex was surprised. Jake wasn't just Matt's best friend; he was also Coach Gordon's biggest supporter on the team—bigger, Alex often thought, than Matt.

"Matt's the quarterback—you know that."

Jake shook his head. "You got us down the field."

"I threw one pass that you or any of the JV guys would have completed too, and Jonas turned it into a big play."

"You're being modest and you know it, Goldie. Jonas was covered pretty well. Matt—or any of us—might not have made the throw. And you made two good option decisions. Coach is right about one thing: you need to stay ready."

Neither offense could do much as the fourth quarter began. It was snowing again and the field was getting slippery. Once, when Matt got to the outside and looked to have a lane, his feet went out from under him. He came up screaming in frustration.

Then, with the clock ticking under five minutes, disaster struck. The Lions had just picked up a first down at their own 46 on another Josephs run. Coach Gordon decided to go with a play-action pass on first down: something he hadn't called all game—an element of surprise.

Matt expertly pulled the ball out of Josephs's stomach on the fake, dropped back, and wound up to throw. Out of the corner of his eye, Alex could see that both Jonas and Tom Revere were running behind their defenders. Matt just had to choose which receiver to throw the ball to.

He never got the chance. As he cocked his arm, the ball slipped from his grip. Panicking, he tried to dive on it as it hit the ground, but it squirted loose. A huge pileup ensued, with much screaming and yelling in the pile. When the officials finally picked everyone off one another, the referee stood up and pointed in the wrong direction.

It was Chester's ball at the Chester Heights 34. The far side of the field erupted. Alex felt the kind of rush you feel when fear suddenly hits you. He looked at the clock: it was at 4:44. If Chester scored now, it would take something approaching a miracle to save the season.

Matt looked to be near tears as he came to the sideline, tearing the helmet off his head. "I'm sorry, I'm sorry!" he said. "*Two* guys open and I blew it!"

Coach Brotman was the first one to meet him. "You didn't blow anything, Matt. The ball slipped. Stay calm. We'll get another chance."

Alex wasn't so sure about that. Chester picked up a first down at the 21 on two straight rushing plays. Alex remembered hearing the coaches say their kicker had made a forty-two-yard field goal. This might be different, though, because of the conditions. Still, the clock was slipping away. Chester was content to keep running the ball.

The quarterback, Todd Austin, who wasn't much of a runner, did run—twice—picking up a total of six yards.

The clock was at 2:40 as he was brought down at the 15.

"We've got to use a time-out or we'll have almost nothing on the clock after they score," Jake said.

Coach Gordon read his mind and called time-out—Chester Heights' second of the half—with 2:36 to go.

"We have to stop them here," Alex said. "Or they'll run the clock all the way down. We've only got one time-out left."

Jake didn't say anything.

Chester's coach, Mike Byrnes, apparently had a lot of faith in his field goal kicker, because he ran a straight dive play to get the ball to the middle of the field on third down. The ball was sitting on the 13 and the field goal team came on. Coach Gordon decided to save his last time-out. Chester let the play clock run down to two seconds before snapping the ball. The snap and the hold were perfect—the ball had been dried off by the officials before the play at the request of Chester's center—and the kick was perfect too. It sailed through the uprights with 1:52 on the clock, making the score 17–14.

Everyone congratulated the defense for holding the Clippers to three, but it wasn't with much enthusiasm. The Lions would need to drive the ball a long way—barring a long kickoff return—to try to get a tying field goal.

The one-game season was in serious jeopardy.

■ ■ ■

As the kickoff return team took its place, Alex looked over and saw Coach Gordon with his arms crossed. Matt had his helmet on and was talking to the offense. Surprisingly, Coach Brotman wasn't talking to the players, but to Coach Gordon.

"Alex, he's going to put you in," Jake said softly. "There's no choice. We have to throw the ball. Matt can't do it."

For once, Alex didn't answer. Jake was right. But there was Matt, helmet on, clearly ready to go back on the field. Before he could say anything, Alex heard Coach Brotman call his name—or nickname, anyway.

"Goldie," he said. "Over here."

He jogged over to where the two coaches stood.

Coach Gordon looked at him. "Are you ready to do this?" he asked.

Alex glanced over at Matt, who was a few yards away, hands on his hips. He knew it would break his heart to be taken out at this point. He was tempted to say, *Matt's the quarterback, Coach.*

Instead, he said very quietly, "If you want me in, Coach, I'm ready."

Coach Gordon nodded. "We have one time-out left. Two play calls at a time, just like in the King of Prussia game. Do *not* use the time-out unless I signal for it. We need to get at least to the 20."

"Yes sir."

Coach Gordon glanced at his son, who had taken his helmet off. He called two plays and sent Alex onto the field.

The kickoff had been returned to the 33. Alex stepped into the huddle and saw all eyes locked on him. No one said a word. "Two plays at a time," he said. "And *no one* calls a time-out except Coach. We've only got one left."

Alex could see Chester lying back, willing to give him anything over the middle that wasn't deep. Twice, he took exactly that: a circle pass to Josephs that picked up nine yards, followed by a quick come-back pass to Alan Fitzgerald that picked up another nine. They were in Chester territory at the 49. But the clock was at 1:05 and ticking.

"Spike!" Alex heard Coach Gordon scream. He ran to the line, took the snap from Will Allison, and spiked the ball. Exactly a minute to go.

In came Jonas with two more plays. The first was a draw, which scared Alex. Even if it picked up yardage, it would keep the clock running. But he wasn't going to argue at this point. The hole was huge—everyone on defense was dropping back for a pass—and Josephs picked up thirteen yards to the 36.

"Spike!" Coach Gordon yelled again.

Alex complied. There were thirty-nine seconds left.

Coach Gordon sent in a second play call to add to the one already called. Alex thought for a second he saw Crenshaw open over the middle but then saw the safety creeping up and looked away. He saw Jonas, who had been running a deep route, running back in his direction, hand up. He rifled a pass, which Jonas dove for and caught at the 25.

First down.

"Spike!"

Alex spiked the ball and looked up. There were twenty-two seconds left, twenty-five yards to go. But they were almost in field goal range.

The next call was for Josephs, the circle play that had worked so well. But he slipped coming out of the backfield. Alex scrambled quickly to his right and aimed a pass at Fitzgerald near the sideline. It sailed just over his hands. That stopped the clock at sixteen seconds.

Third down. They needed to pick up at least five yards— ten would be a lot better—and then use their time-out to get Pete Ross on the field for the field goal. Coach Gordon was thinking just that and called a double-slant route for Jonas and Revere. Each player was to try to go downfield five yards and slant to the middle, and—with luck—one would open up at about the 15 at either the left or the right hash mark.

It wouldn't be a perfect angle, but Ross was deadly accurate within his range.

As soon as Alex took the snap, he was in trouble. Knowing he wasn't going to throw deep, the Chester defensive coordinator had blitzed both safeties. Alex saw them coming before he even had a chance to look downfield. He tried to step up between them, but one of them got to him. Alex pulled his arm down so he wouldn't fumble and went down in a heap at the twenty-nine-yard line.

Even though he knew he was supposed to let Coach Gordon call the last time-out, he didn't wait to hear anything from the sideline because he knew if he didn't call time-out the clock would run to zero.

"TIME-OUT!" he screamed.

The referee waved his arms to signal a time-out.

The clock stopped at six seconds. They were outside of Ross's range by a good fifteen yards. It was fourth and fourteen.

When Alex trotted to the sideline to consult with the coaches, he was greeted by three people: Coach Gordon, Coach Brotman, and Matt Gordon. Pete Ross was standing a couple steps away in case the coaches decided their best chance was a very long field goal.

"Any chance you can get it there, Pete?" Coach Gordon was saying as Alex arrived.

"If I hit it exactly right," Pete answered—without a lot of confidence in his tone.

That did not appear to be the answer Coach Gordon was looking for. He turned to Coach Brotman, Matt, and Alex.

"What do you think?"

"Dad, scramble 5 is our only chance," Matt said. "Alex has to make a fast choice—throw one to the sideline quickly and hope we get out of bounds in time, or go for it all."

Coach Gordon was nodding; so was Coach Brotman.

Alex too. Scramble 5 was one step short of the old Hail Mary in terms of desperation. The Hail Mary meant you threw the ball into the end zone and hoped against hope one of your guys came down with it. Scramble 5 meant you sent five wide receivers down the field. Two would run short routes to the sideline. If Alex thought he could get the ball to either of them and be close enough for a field goal *and* the receiver could get out of bounds before the clock hit zero, he would throw the ball there. The other three receivers would run deeper, to the end zone. Two went down and out, and the third ran a straight post pattern, literally running down the middle toward the goalpost. If Alex decided the short receivers were not open, he would have to go long. But if he did that, the clock would run out by the time the play was complete. There'd be no second chance. When they ran the play in practice, it took anywhere from five to six seconds to complete . . . when it worked.

"Okay," Coach Gordon said after what felt like an eternity. "Scramble 5."

Coach Brotman was waving the extra wide receivers over, saying to each, "Scramble 5, let's go."

Coach Gordon put his hand on Alex's shoulder. "They won't rush more than three, maybe only two. That will give you time to go deep, but you *must* decide right away if you want to go short. You know that, right?"

Alex nodded. He knew. Boy, did he know.

■ ■ ■

The official was telling them to get back on the field. "Starting the play clock now, Coach," he said.

The play clock was no longer an issue. The play was already called. They just had to make it work.

Matt, who hadn't said a word to Alex throughout the fourth quarter, grabbed him as he started back.

"You can do this, Goldie," he said. "No one else—you."

Alex thought his eyes looked wet, but it might have been the snow, which had started again. He ran to the huddle. "You heard," he said, stepping in. "Scramble 5. Fitzgerald, Revere, run those short cuts tight. On three."

Calling for the snap on the third sound didn't matter one way or the other with the clock stopped. Alex just wanted one extra deep breath once he was standing in the shotgun behind Allison.

They came to the line and Alex heard nothing—even though he knew everyone in the stadium was on their feet.

"Red!" he shouted—the first sound. Then, "White!" He was in a patriotic mood. Finally: "Blue!"

The ball came back to him as if on a string. He took a quick step back and looked for Fitzgerald and Revere. The safeties and an extra linebacker were all over them. He would have to force the ball to get it to one of them.

No, he thought, can't do it. He dropped another step. As Coach Gordon had predicted, he had time—Chester had only rushed two players. He could almost *hear* his heart pounding as he looked down the field.

All he could see for a moment was a crush of bodies in red tops and white tops going in all different directions. Then, suddenly, he saw Jonas running straight for the goal line, his arm in the air.

He saw a white uniform right in front of Jonas and two

waiting for him on the goal line. Still, Alex had no choice. He stepped up and threw the ball as hard as he could, hoping to hit Jonas in stride just behind the first defender and—somehow—just in front of the two waiting at the goal line.

He knew he had thrown it as well as he could as he stepped into it, and he saw the ball speeding at Jonas. Then, one of the Chester defenders got a hand on his legs and the two of them went down in a heap.

Alex heard a roar, but he couldn't really tell what direction it was coming from. He and the Chester defender untangled and sat up. Alex heard a profanity come from the defender's mouth. Squinting down the field, he saw Jonas rising from the ground, the football in his hands. The official had his arms in the air, signaling a touchdown.

OH MY GOD, Alex thought, scrambling to his feet. A split second later, he was buried again—this time by a red wall of his teammates screaming his name. A moment later, he was on their shoulders. Jonas was getting the same ride in the end zone.

He looked down and saw Matt Gordon right there, holding his left leg. There were tears streaming down Matt's face. Alex knew they had nothing to do with the snow.

■ ■ ■

It wasn't until the next morning that Alex got to see what had happened on the last play. As he had thought when he released the pass, he had thrown the ball as well as he possibly could. It had just cleared the grasping hand of a defender at about the four-yard line and had whistled into Jonas's hands as he reached the two-yard line going full speed. Even though the two defenders who were no more than a half step from him were right in front of him, his momentum had forced them backward just enough to get him across the goal line.

Alex was watching Comcast SportsNet–Philadelphia, which always repeated its late-night sports show in the morning. "Watch this remarkable throw by freshman quarterback Alex Myers," the anchor said as the replay came up for a second time. "If the Eagles had a quarterback who could throw with that kind of accuracy, they wouldn't be three and five!"

Alex laughed, but he loved the line. The anchor then said, "Let's go now to our Lisa Hillary, who spoke to the man with the golden arm after the game."

Alex had talked to a lot of people after the game, but he remembered Lisa Hillary, in part because of whom she worked for but also because she seemed both pretty *and* smart. The latter of which, as his dad often pointed out, wasn't always a criterion for getting a job in TV.

"I'm with Alex Myers, who will be forever remembered at Chester Heights for what happened here tonight," she said in her opening. Then, turning to Alex, she said, "Were you surprised when Coach Gordon sent you in to take Matt Gordon's spot for the last series?"

Alex's answer was honest. "Yeah, a little bit," he said. "Matt got us to the point where we had a chance to win the conference tonight. I think it was just a matter of time on the clock and our need to throw the ball."

"What kind of nerves come into play when you're put into a situation like that?"

Alex smiled. "Honestly, none. You don't have time to be nervous. You just have to do it."

"Coach Gordon told us that it was up to you whom to throw to and whether to go deep or short and try for the field goal. Why did you decide to throw the ball to Jonas Ellington? Your coach said it was probably the toughest throw of the options open to you."

Alex nodded. "Well, the short throws just weren't open," he said. "When I looked downfield, Jonas had his arm up and I saw a little seam in the defense. He's made tough catches all season. I just thought it was our best chance." He paused. "I haven't seen the catch because I got knocked down, but I'm pretty sure the real hero is Jonas."

Hillary thanked him, then turned back to the camera. "Neil, as you can tell, being a hero has *not* gone to Alex Myers's head. Back to you."

Alex replayed the final play and the interview three times before his mother walked into the room. She was holding the phone.

"It's your dad," she said.

Alex had seen a text—one among what seemed like hundreds—from his dad the night before and hadn't answered, not because he was angry but because he'd had so much to do in the aftermath, including the entire team going back on the field in uniform to take a picture in front of the scoreboard.

He took the phone from his mom.

"Congratulations," his dad said. "I texted you last night."

"I know, Dad, sorry. There was just so much going on."

"I can imagine. Your mother said if I was a good father my first question would be about your French quiz yesterday."

Alex laughed. "Believe it or not, I think I did well," he said. "I'm getting better."

His dad, having done his duty, came back to football.

"Do you think you'll start the playoff game next week?"

Alex hadn't thought about that. "I don't even know who we play," he said. "We'll find out tomorrow. I would think Matt will start, and if I'm needed—"

"To bail Matt out . . ."

"Dad, Matt Gordon's a really good quarterback. Plus, he's been my biggest supporter all season. You haven't been here, so you don't know. Don't put him down."

He was surprised at how sharply the words came out of his mouth.

"I'm sorry," his dad said. "You're right. And I'm sorry I haven't been there more. That's going to change—soon. And I mean it, not just more empty words."

Alex didn't say anything, so his dad plowed on. "I have to go to Chicago this Friday to see a client. But if you guys win, I'll be there the next week."

"That would be nice, Dad."

His mom was standing in the kitchen doorway when he hung up.

"You barked at your dad a little bit there," she said.

"Mom, he hasn't been here at all; he doesn't get it," Alex answered.

"I know, I know. But your dad and I are *both* responsible for this. I'm sorry it's been tough for you and Molly."

She changed the subject suddenly, pointing at the TV,

where Alex and Lisa Hillary were frozen on the screen at the point where Alex had hit the pause button.

"She's pretty, isn't she?" she said.

Alex looked again. "She looks like you, Mom."

"Oh come on, Alex, I don't look anything like that."

She turned and walked back into the kitchen, not wanting to return—no doubt—to the conversation about his father but smiling at the thought that she might look like Lisa Hillary.

Alex looked back at the TV. He wondered if his dad was dating anyone. He hoped not, although he couldn't say why he felt that way. It didn't really seem to matter that much one way or the other.

He hit rewind again and watched the throw for a fourth time.

30

The only problem Alex had when he went back to school on Monday was trying to get from one class to another on time. Every single person in the place—teachers, students, janitors—had to stop him to congratulate him, tell him they knew all along that he could do it and exactly what they were doing at the moment he threw the pass to Jonas.

And they all wanted to know, "How good is York Central?"

Alex had no idea. All he knew was that their opening playoff game would be played on Friday at eight o'clock at home, the starting time moved back an hour because Comcast–Philly had decided to televise the game, not just because of the amazing finish the previous Friday but also because Chester Heights was now the number eight team in the country according to the *USA Today* poll. Alex found that amusing, since his team had been one miraculous play away from finishing the season unranked and not in the post-season at all.

Everyone had received a text on Sunday night telling them that the team would meet at noon—with lunch being brought in from outside—to go over the plans for the coming week.

"How's *your* day been, Goldie?" Jonas asked when they were en route to the meeting.

They hadn't seen each other all morning, although they had talked on the phone over the weekend. As far as Alex could remember, Jonas had never called him by his nickname before.

"Probably a lot like yours," he said. "I couldn't take two steps in the hallway without someone stopping me."

Jonas shook his head. "Some people stopped me. Most just waved and said, 'Nice going.' All I did was catch the ball. You threw it."

Alex laughed. "If you don't catch, my throwing it doesn't mean much."

"Yeah, well," Jonas said. "I guess everyone is kind of all over the story of Coach benching his own son with the game on the line. That's gotta be tough on Matt."

Alex had thought about that a lot over the weekend. He'd even thought about calling Matt. Then he'd realized there wasn't much he could say.

Pizza was waiting when the players walked into the meeting room. Alex grabbed a box marked CHEESE and sat in one of the back rows. Jonas and Jake slid in on either side of him.

"How's life as a hero?" Jake asked.

"Exhausting," Alex answered.

Coach Gordon got right down to business, explaining that he and the coaches had already looked at tape of York Central. "They're all tough kids. They won't be scared or intimidated. We haven't played them before, but they've been in the playoffs four of the last five years, so they're very experienced. They start nine seniors on offense and nine on defense."

He went through the practice schedule for the week, which would be a bit lighter than normal because it was late in the season and everyone was tired.

"You guys who love the weight room, love it a little less this week," he said. "If you aren't strong enough to compete by now, you aren't going to get there. Let your bodies rest a little."

He also announced that the players would be excused from their afternoon classes on Friday. "There will be a pep rally at lunchtime. Then you've got the afternoon off to go home, get off your feet, and relax," he said. "We'll want you back here at six o'clock.

"If anyone has a test, try to work it out with your teacher. If you have a problem, talk to your position coach." He smiled. "I doubt there will be any issues."

He paused.

Coach Brotman waved a hand from the side of the room.

"Coach," he said. "Drug testing?"

"Right," Coach Gordon said. "Thanks, Coach. Most of you guys are probably unaware that last year the state high school board voted to drug-test in all sports during statewide competition. All of you will be tested after practice on Wednesday, as will the players from the other seven schools who have qualified.

"This won't sound like good news to some of you who don't like needles, but a blood test is better than a urine sample because it's more accurate and the results come back sooner.

"I know none of you are stupid enough to be doping, so I'm not worried about this at all. Just so you know, if we win, a random sampling of the team will be tested again next week, and then again before the championship game. It's a minor nuisance, but it shouldn't be anything more than that.

"Any questions?"

He nodded when no hands went up. "Okay, then. Practice at the regular time today. Finish your pizzas and head to class."

"You clean, Goldie?" Jake asked, laughing as most of the team stood to leave. Fifth period was ten minutes away.

"Unless there's something in the pizza or in a McDonald's hamburger, I should be all right," Alex said.

Jonas leaned in and said softly, "We've got some big linemen. You think they're all clean?"

Jake stood up. "Guess we're going to find out. You might be able to beat a urine test or claim there was a mistake. Pretty tough with blood testing. 'Course, it's only a problem if we win Friday and someone's test comes back positive next week."

"What's the penalty for a positive test?" Alex asked.

"No idea," Jake said. "Let's hope we never find out."

■ ■ ■

Coach Gordon hadn't addressed the other lingering question: who would start at quarterback in the York game? Alex got the answer that afternoon at practice when the team scrimmaged. It was business almost as usual: Matt got about two-thirds of the snaps and Alex the rest—except for one final series when Jake came in.

The scrimmage was shorter than normal and so was practice. The weather was relatively warm—probably around fifty degrees at the start of practice. But when the sun began to set at quarter to five, it got cold quickly. Coach Gordon reminded them of the schedule again before he sent them inside. Tuesday would be the last all-out practice of the week. Wednesday's practice would be shortened to allow time for the drug testing, and Thursday would, as usual, be briefer than the rest of the week.

"We'll be more about preparing for the opponent than practicing anything new or anything hard this week," he said. "You third-teamers and JVs are going to be crucial running scout team plays, so please study what we've given you on York. This is your chance to really contribute to this team."

Based on what they were seeing from the scout team, York was a very aggressive defensive team—frequently blitzing linebackers and even safeties to try to keep the quarterback from getting into any sort of rhythm with either a running game or a passing game. That meant quick-hitting passes against what would often be one-on-one coverage should be effective, as would counter plays—starting in one direction, then going in the other to take advantage of an aggressive defense.

Alex couldn't help but notice that Matt was struggling with his short, quick throws. The football was frequently a half step or a full step off target. He was clearly frustrated when he missed on a pass—even when it was caught. On one play, Jonas reached out and made a catch. When he came back to the huddle, Matt said, "I gotta get the ball in your stomach, Jonas. If I don't, someone's going to kill you reaching for it."

"No worries," Jonas said. "We made the play."

"*You* made the play," Matt said.

The counter plays were Matt's forte. He was such a quick, strong runner that the defense had to respect him anytime he took off with the ball. He never seemed to make a wrong decision on those plays: If the defense stayed back, he took off. If it chased him, he was ready to make a pitch, a quick counter handoff, or even a reverse.

It was apparent to Alex that the offense would focus on running the ball—unless he got into the game. No one said anything to him about what his role might be.

"They'll get you in for one series in the second quarter," Jake predicted as they walked off the practice field on Wednesday. "How much you play the rest of the night will depend on how the game's going."

It occurred to Alex that Jake might not be much of a quarterback, but he was an amazing mind reader.

"Yeah," Jonas put in. "As in, if we need to throw, you're in there, Goldie. Matt's never been that good a passer, but he's been brutal the last couple days."

Jake nodded. "I'm not sure what's up with him," he said.

Matt's throwing hadn't been very good—even by his

standards—but Alex thought he had also been uncharacteristically quiet: hard on himself as always, but not in his joking, self-deprecating way. At one point, after another bad throw, he had looked at Alex and said, "You better be ready, Goldie. I have a feeling we're going to need you."

He'd said almost the exact same thing before, but it had been in more of a "Come on, let's go" tone. This was more of an almost resigned "I'm just not that good" tone. Alex wondered if having his dad take him out for the final series last week—and then watching Alex help win the game—was the reason for his mood. He thought about asking him but decided the week of the state quarterfinals wasn't the right time.

■ ■ ■

The drug testing didn't take very long. They were called into the training room alphabetically. Teams of testers were drawing blood, labeling the vials with each player's name, and making sure they were stored properly for shipment.

The players had been told to bring their school ID with them. Apparently, there had been cases where someone taking PEDs had tried to send someone else in his place to give the sample. Even if the other players saw there was a non-team-member giving blood, they weren't likely to say anything. Code of the locker room: you don't turn in your teammates for anything.

When Alex showed his ID to the nurse, she looked at the photo, then looked at him and smiled.

"Last week's hero, right?"

"I'm the backup quarterback," Alex said, causing Jimmy Marshall, two tables away, to shout, "He's our closer!"

If the nurse knew what that meant, she didn't show it. She handed Alex back his ID and the other tech found a label with his name on it and stuck it on a vial.

"Okay," the nurse said as she swabbed his arm with alcohol. "You'll feel a quick pinch and that will be it. Make a fist—keep it closed until I tell you it's okay."

Alex did as he was told, and thanked them.

"We'll have the results back in a week," the tech said. "Needless to say, no news will be good news."

Alex said thank you once more and walked back to the locker room. A funny thought occurred to him: the one thing he wanted right now was to be drug-tested again in a week. It would mean they were still playing.

Jake Bilney's prediction about how much Alex would play against York was deadly accurate. The night was cold and blustery and both teams had a tough time moving the ball. York Central's defense was, as expected, aggressive and tough. Their strategy was apparent: key on Matt Gordon and make him give up the ball. If he wanted to pass, that was fine—especially given the windy conditions.

The closest anyone came to scoring was at the end of the first half, after Craig Josephs had gotten outside on a counter play in the final minute with the York Central defense lying back because of the clock. Josephs had broken out a thirty-one-yard run to the York Central 20, and with time running out, Matt had spiked the ball.

Pete Ross came on with four seconds left to attempt a thirty-seven-yard field goal, but it was dead into the wind and well short. The score was 0–0 at halftime.

"This is exactly the kind of game we expected," Coach Gordon said during the break. "They're good on defense and so are we. We just need to make sure we don't turn the ball over, because I guarantee you they will. Be patient and we'll be fine."

Alex thought the cheers for the team as it came back on the field were somewhat muted. No one was scoring and no one was roaring. The band was playing, but the notes seemed to drift away in the wind. This was November football and nothing about it was easy.

The punt-fest continued in the third quarter. With 4:48 left and York Central facing a third and ten from its own 31, Coach Brotman called Alex's name. Jake, who had been standing next to Alex, looked surprised.

"What's he doing—" Jake started to say, but Alex jogged over to Coach Brotman before he finished the sentence.

"Warm up," was all Coach Brotman said. "You may be in if we get a stop."

Alex did as he was told. The defense held, and as the York punt team went on the field, Alex noticed that Matt had not—as he normally did—put his helmet back on. The kick, with the wind, was downed on the Chester Heights 23. Play stopped for a TV time-out.

"Myers!" It was Coach Gordon. "You ready to go?" he said as Alex jogged up to him.

"Yes sir."

"Are you sure?" he asked, almost as if he wanted Alex to really think about it.

"Absolutely," Alex said.

"Okay, then." He put his arm around him for a moment.

"The short passes have been there all night." He paused. "Matt hasn't been able to make the throws. Start with 33 swing and we'll go from there."

Alex nodded and trotted in. By now, no one in the huddle was surprised to see him. He called 33 swing, a simple out route to Josephs off a play fake, and brought them to the line. He could hear the York Central defenders yelling at one another: "Passer, passer! New QB—watch the pass!"

Alex took the snap, made a motion as if to throw the ball over the middle, and then swung it to Josephs, who caught it in stride, dragged a defender for a couple yards, and picked up twelve yards to the 35.

Coach Gordon was right: the short passes were there. Alex kept taking what the defense was giving until, on third and one at the York Central 37, he saw an opportunity. York Central had nine players in the box—the area right behind the line of scrimmage and on the line itself. Alex hadn't even considered an audible since the debacle at Bryn Mawr. Now, seeing Jonas lined up wide with one cornerback on him, he called one.

He yelled "Black!" to tell his teammates he was changing the play, and then called "Z no-fly!"—that was the audible call for a fly pattern off a play fake. Alex took the snap and turned to Josephs, who lunged as if he were trying to get to the first-down marker, selling the fake brilliantly. Alex pulled the ball out of Josephs's stomach and took two quick steps back. The cornerback had completely bought the fake and Jonas was wide open. Alex put a little extra on the ball because of the wind and watched as Jonas still had to slow a bit to wait for it. He was so wide open it didn't matter.

He raced into the end zone with four seconds left in the quarter.

Coach Gordon was almost smiling when Alex came to the sideline. "Funny thing," he said. "I was almost going to call that play there."

"I could see the defense, Coach," Alex said. "You couldn't when you sent the play in."

Coach Gordon batted him on the head and Matt, standing right there, hugged him.

"Goldie," he said, "I don't know what we'd do without you."

■ ■ ■

Seven points felt like a huge lead in this game. And then Gerry Detwiler put it away. With York Central at midfield, he read an out pattern perfectly, stepping in front of the receiver at the 45-yard line. He was gone down the sideline, untouched. The extra point made it 14–0 and seemed to drain all the fight from York Central.

Matt went back in and, with the York Central defense suddenly looking tired, put together a time-killing seventy-two-yard drive that ended with Josephs scoring from the 1-yard line with 4:11 left in the game. The final was a very deceiving 21–0.

As the clock wound down, Alex patted Matt on the shoulder. "That was a great last drive," he said. "You put the game away."

Matt smiled for the first time in what felt like a week. "Long as I can run the ball, I'm okay," he said. "You think this one was tough? Wait until next week." He returned the

pat on the shoulder. "Gotta be ready, Goldie. We're not winning this thing without you."

Alex grinned in return. It was good to hear Matt sounding
like Matt again.

■ ■ ■

The news that Allentown would be the opponent came down
as the players were dressing after the York Central game. No
one was surprised. Allentown had lost one game all season,
a nonconference game at Beaver Falls, who were the defending state champions and the only undefeated team in the
tournament other than Chester Heights.

"I'm not just saying this—they'll be really tough," Matt
said as he carefully combed his hair. "We played Beaver Falls
last year in the semis and they beat us pretty easily. They
have most of their key guys back and they needed overtime
to beat Allentown—even with a home-field advantage."

He turned to Alex, who had just put his shoes on. "I
meant what I said, Goldie. You better be ready."

"I'm always ready," Alex answered with a grin.

Matt nodded. "That's what I want to hear. Gotta roll."

"Where are you rushing off to?" Jake asked.

"Have a date," Matt said. "You'll have one someday, Jakey,
don't worry about it."

"Hey!" Jake shouted at Matt's back. "I've got a date too!"

"Do you really have a date?" Alex asked, a little nervous.

Jake sat down on the bench in front of his locker. "No,"
he said. "But I could if I wanted to."

Alex didn't doubt that. Everyone laughed. It had been a
fun night.

• • •

Alex wasn't surprised when he got a phone call from Christine Whitford the next morning.

"I played one series last night," he said in semi-mock protest. "Why would you want to talk to me?"

"Because you saved the season a week ago and your one series decided the game last night," she said.

He decided it would be more fun to argue with her while looking at her across a table at Stark's, so he told her he would meet her there at noon.

"Jake's coming too," she said.

Alex slumped. Apparently, he didn't have a date either.

"Why?" he asked.

"Because he's honest."

"I'm not?"

She paused. "You're careful," she said finally. "See you at noon."

They were both sitting at the back table waiting for him when he walked in one minute late.

Jake looked at his watch.

"You get lost?" he said. "Or were you doing a TV interview?"

"Not too many second-string quarterbacks get interviewed on TV," Alex said, sliding into a chair.

"Unless they should be starting," Christine said. "That's what Steve is writing for Wednesday."

"Oh jeez," Alex said.

"Here's the thing," Jake said. "Matt did some things well last night—especially on the last drive. Problem is, Allentown North will take away the run just like York Central did. I don't think Matt has much confidence in his throwing right now."

"So do you think Coach should bench him?" Alex asked, knowing how much faith Jake had in Coach Gordon.

"No," Jake said. "I think he should keep doing what he's doing. We need Matt. But we'll need you too."

"But you'll have to pass to move the ball," Christine put in.

"Can't fool you," Alex said, causing her to give him a dirty look. "But seriously—fine, if Matt struggles to throw, then Coach will put me in."

"He only puts you in if he *has* to," Christine said. "He almost waited too long in the Chester game out of loyalty to an inferior player."

"Why are you so tough on Matt?" Alex said, feeling a little bit angry. "Why is Garland so tough on Matt? The guy gives everything he has every day. He encourages everyone on the team—no one more than me—he's a brilliant strategist, and he's a very good player."

"He's still not as good as you are," Christine said. "Everyone knows that. Don't you *want* to play?"

"Of course I want to play," Alex said. "I *have* played. You haven't answered my question. Why are you so hard on Matt?"

"Because they don't like his father," Jake said.

"That's not true," Christine said hotly.

"You mean you *like* his father?" Jake said. "No one likes his father."

"Except you," Christine said.

"I *respect* him," Jake said. "The team is eleven and oh and you want to rip him!"

"That's not why we're hard on him," she said, then caught herself. "I mean, we're *not* hard on him. We're just being fair."

"Everyone has a different definition of 'fair,'" Alex said.

"I will say this," Jake said, looking around as if he didn't want anyone to hear. "I hope Matt lightens up next week. I've never seen him as uptight before a game as he was last night."

"He was uptight last week?" Christine asked.

Jake and Alex both nodded.

"I think he was feeling as if he had failed the team against Chester, and Goldie had to bail us out," Jake said. "He's that kind of guy."

"Well, he may be uptight again this week," Christine said. "Because Steve sent me his column this morning. The lead is pretty direct."

"What's it say?" Alex asked.

"It says, 'If Matthew Gordon wants to coach a state-championship team this season, he's going to have to bench his son.'"

"Great," Alex moaned.

"Yeah, great," Jake added. "That won't make Matt up-tight. But it will make his father crazy."

■ ■ ■

Alex didn't get to find out how upset Coach Gordon was with Garland's column. In fact, the subject never came up.

He was sitting at lunch on Wednesday with Jake, Stephen,

and Jonas discussing what Garland had written, not to mention Christine's feature on Allentown North quarterback Ken Jackson, in which she had gone on at length about his 4.0 grade point average and how he had been voted king of the junior prom the previous spring.

"You gotta give her a hard time about that," Jonas said. "King of the junior prom? Seriously?"

"She's just trying to be a good writer," Alex said.

"She's not," said Jake, who had surprised them by sitting with them. Usually he only came over when Matt did. "That is *not* good writing," he continued. "That is flirting in print. Dude, you need to protect your turf."

"My turf?" Alex said. "You're the one who showed up early Saturday to hang out with her."

"Easy, tiger," Jake said. "You know she and I are old news. Actually, we were never news. Anyway, we need you cool and calm this week."

The sentence was barely out of Jake's mouth when Alex noticed Coach Brotman walking in their direction.

"Myers," Coach Brotman said, pointing a finger. "Need you right now in Coach Gordon's office."

Alex glanced at his watch. Fifth period started in fifteen minutes.

"Now, Coach?" he said. "But—"

"*Now,*" Coach Brotman said with a kind of firmness that sent a shiver through Alex.

He picked up his tray and his books. "Leave the tray," Coach Brotman said. "The other guys can take care of it."

Now Alex was really baffled. He put the tray down and followed Coach Brotman, who was half running, half walk-

■ 282 ■

ing out of the room. When they got into the hallway, Alex pulled even with him and said, "Coach, what's up?"

Coach Brotman simply held up a hand and kept walking.

■ ■ ■

When they got to Coach Gordon's office, there were two other men in the room whom Alex didn't recognize.

"Myers, this is Mr. Turgeson from the Pennsylvania state school board," Coach Gordon said.

Alex took a step in Mr. Turgeson's direction to shake hands, but the man recoiled as if Alex were carrying some kind of virus.

"And this is Mr. Lyons, from LabCorp."

Mr. Lyons, who was standing against the wall, didn't even nod at him, so Alex didn't bother with attempting a handshake.

"Coach, what is this about?" Alex said. He was now both baffled and scared.

"What this is about, Mr. Myers," the school board guy said, stepping forward, "is the results of your drug test from last week."

"Drug test?" Alex said. "What about my drug test?"

The school board guy—Mr. Turgeson—took another step forward, almost into Alex's face, before he answered.

"You tested positive for a synthetic testosterone called"— he said some name that Alex never heard—"and your level was high enough that, even allowing for the possibility that you have an abnormally high level, it's clear you have been taking steroids. If by some chance"—he was sneering now— "the B sample comes back clean, then you'll be cleared. But the chances of that are close to zero. As of now, pending the B sample result, you are suspended from playing football—or any other high school sport—in the state of Pennsylvania."

Alex realized his mouth was hanging open. He closed it and shook his head, thinking he'd wake up from the nightmare he was clearly having. He didn't.

"There's no way," he finally said. "There has to be a mistake. I've never taken *any* drugs in my life, unless you count aspirin."

Turgeson laughed in a very unfunny way. "Are you a sports fan, Myers?"

"Yes."

"Have you ever heard an athlete who has tested positive come out and say, 'Yeah, I did it?' Of course not. You're all innocent."

"There is still the B sample," Coach Gordon said. "I thought you didn't consider someone guilty until you got the B sample back."

"We can't prosecute anyone legally without the B sample," Turgeson said. "We *can* suspend."

"What's the B sample?" Alex asked.

"We draw enough blood for two tests. If the first test comes back positive, we can retest with the remainder. On rare occasions it will show a different result. *Very* rare occasions. If the B sample comes back positive, we will then decide whether you should be prosecuted or face expulsion from school—or both. In the meantime, you won't be playing on Friday."

Alex felt all the color drain from his face. He was scared and he was angry—angry because he knew someone had make a mistake and yet this Turgeson guy was acting as if he were Barry Bonds and Alex Rodriguez rolled into one.

He turned to Coach Gordon, who looked very upset too.

"Coach, I'm telling you, this can't be right," he said. "I don't even know what these guys are talking about. There's got to be something you can do. I'll give another sample right now. This man"—he pointed at the man from LabCorp—"can test it right away and prove I'm innocent."

Coach Gordon shook his head. "Alex, it doesn't work that way. I'm sorry. I believe you—I really do. We'll wait for the B sample and hope it shows that this is a mistake." He pointed at Alex but stared at Turgeson. "Does this look to you like an athlete on steroids?" he asked. "What do you weigh Alex—160?

"One-sixty-six," Alex said.

"Some steroid user," Coach Gordon said. "Use your eyes."

"We use science," Turgeson said. "And his test is positive. Do you want to tell him or should I?"

Coach Gordon glared at Turgeson for a moment and then sighed. "Myers, until further notice you are suspended from the football team. You may not come into the locker room or be on the sideline during the game on Friday." He looked at Turgeson. "Happy?" he said.

"Overjoyed," Turgeson said. "Mr. Myers, we'll be in touch."

He turned and walked out, followed by the man from LabCorp.

The next few hours were a blur for Alex.

Coach Gordon explained to him that the school would have to announce that he had been suspended due to a positive drug test. If it didn't, the board of education and the state high school athletic association would make the announcement.

"We don't have to do it until tomorrow," he said. "Tomorrow at noon, to be exact. I'd recommend you go home and talk to your parents so they know. If you want to take tomorrow off from school, I think your teachers will understand. If you want, I can talk to them for you. Once the announcement is made, you're going to get mobbed. I wish I could tell you different, but it's true."

Alex wasn't thinking about that. He was trying to figure out *how*.

"Coach, how could this have happened?" he asked. "I don't even take vitamins."

He knew that many of the players took vitamin supplements that they bought at GNC. After the drug testing had been announced, several had been nervous that there might be a banned substance of some kind in one of them.

"Did anyone else test positive?" he asked.

Coach Gordon shook his head. "No, thank God," he said. "I'll be honest, Alex, I wouldn't have been shocked if a couple of the other guys had some kind of supplement or something in their system, but not you. Can you think of *anything* you might have taken to make your testosterone level shoot up like that?"

Alex was shaking his head as he spoke. "Nothing," he said. "Unless there's testosterone in a Stark's burger or McDonald's French fries."

Coach Gordon put a hand on his shoulder. "Go back to class, try to get through the day."

He walked back to his desk and opened a drawer. He took out a pad and wrote something on it. "Here's a late slip for fifth period." He paused. "I'm really sorry this happened."

Alex believed him. He hadn't been this nice all season. He would rather *not* have seen this side of his coach.

■ ■ ■

Alex was completely zoned out during his history and English classes. If someone had screamed that the building was on fire, he probably wouldn't have budged. Walking down the hall to French class half dazed, he heard someone calling his name. He turned and saw Jonas.

"Hey, man, have you lost your hearing? I called your name like five times."

"Sorry."

"So what happened with Coach?"

"Nothing."

"What do you mean nothing? You don't get called to his office in the middle of lunch for nothing."

The two-minute warning bell was ringing. "I'll tell you later," Alex said. He had been thinking of a lie to tell but realized it was pointless. Jonas would know soon enough. Everyone would know soon enough. As he watched Jonas walk off looking a little bit miffed, it occurred to him they might not be teammates anymore.

"Us versus them," he said to himself as he walked down the hall. "I'm not *us* anymore."

He brooded about that throughout French class. At one point he realized that the whole class was staring at him.

"*Monsieur Myers!*" Mademoiselle Schiff was saying, apparently not for the first time. Everyone was giggling.

"Oh," Alex said. "Sorry. I mean, *pardonnez-moi.*"

"*Monsieur Myers. Êtes-vous malade?*"

She was asking if he was sick.

"*Non, Mademoiselle,*" he replied. "*Je suis très fatigué.*"

"*D'accord,*" she said. And then in English, "Try to pay attention, Monsieur Myers. The game isn't until Friday."

More giggling. Mademoiselle Schiff speaking English was never good. It meant she was really angry.

"*Oui, Mademoiselle,*" he said. And then, again, "*Pardonnez-moi.*"

Mercifully, she moved on.

By the time class ended, Alex had made a decision. He followed Christine out the door and called her name. She stopped and waited for him.

"Boy, did you space out in there," she said. "What was—"

He waved a hand at her to stop. "Listen, I have to talk to you," he said.

"Why don't you call me after practice," she said.

"No," he said. "I have to talk to you now. Not here—somewhere away from school. But right away."

She was looking up at him with concern on her face.

"What's wrong?" she asked. "*Are* you sick? You know we can't talk now. You can't be late for practice."

"I'm not going to practice today," he said. "I may not be going ever again."

"Walk with me," she said.

■ ■ ■

"Where are we going?" he asked as they unhooked their bikes.

"I'm not sure yet," she said. "Just follow me."

They rode in the opposition direction of Stark's and the other places where kids hung out after school, including the McDonald's.

They finally turned into a neighborhood with yards starting to fill up with fallen leaves. Christine wound down a road called Trotter's Lane for a little while, then veered right onto the cleverly named Trotter's Court. She pulled into the driveway at the third house, a comfortable-looking, two-story redbrick house.

There was a screened-in porch off the side of the house and she rode around to it and pulled open an unlocked door. He followed her and they parked their bikes inside.

"When in doubt, go home," she said.

She used a key to open a door that led from the porch into the kitchen. "My mom is at work until six o'clock," she said. "Do you want something to drink?"

"Coke?" he asked.

She opened the refrigerator and pulled out two bottles of Coke. Then he followed her to a family room. He was cold and winded from the bike ride and the shock of the day, but the Coke felt good going down. He sat on the couch and breathed deeply for the first time in hours.

"So," she said, leaning forward. "What in the world is going on?"

He started to say their conversation had to be off the record, then realized it didn't matter. He took another deep breath and told her everything.

Her mouth was hanging open when he finished. "Are you *sure* you didn't take *something* by accident?" she said. "Matt told me a lot of the guys take supplements."

"Matt?" he said. "You talk to Matt a lot, don't you?"

"Just sometimes," she said, reddening suddenly. "He's helped me—and Steve—out sometimes."

That bothered Alex in a way he couldn't completely put his finger on.

"So?" she said.

He snapped back from his thoughts about Matt and

Christine talking to one another. "No, there's no way," he said. "The guy said my level was so high that it had to be some kind of steroid."

Christine took another sip of her Coke.

"Then there has to be some kind of mistake," she said.

"But how?" he asked. "I mean, how can you make a mistake like that?"

"That's the question we have to find the answer to."

"And how do we do that?" he asked.

She shook her head. "I have no idea. This is a little bit over my head. Actually, a lot over my head."

They sat in silence for a moment.

"I can ask my dad—"

"No!" Alex said. "You can't tell your dad!"

Then he stopped. He kept forgetting that everyone would know by the next day anyway. "I'm sorry—you're right. But you said he's a news editor. Does he know about sports?"

"He's friends with a lot of the guys in sports. But this isn't a sports story anyway. This takes someone who knows how to be a real reporter."

"You're good," he said, meaning it. "I trust you."

"I'm good for a high school freshman doing it for the first time. I wouldn't even know where to begin on a story like this."

"Okay," he said. "If you think your dad could help . . ." Alex felt lost—he wasn't sure anyone could help.

"You should go home and tell your mom. I'll talk to my dad and call you later."

He had almost forgotten about telling his mom. He took

a long sip of his Coke and put it down. His stomach felt like it was going to explode. So did his head.

■ ■ ■

His mom was stunned, then confused, then angry. After asking him several times if there was *any* way he could be guilty, she stood up and said, "I'm calling your father. They can't do this to you if you're innocent."

"Mom, I *am* innocent," he said.

"I believe you," she said. "Let me talk to your father."

His mom came right back, saying Alex's dad must be on a plane because his phone said he was "unavailable."

"What a shock," Alex said.

He expected his mom to defend his dad, but instead she just sighed and said, "Yeah, no kidding."

She said she was going to make some calls and suggested he go upstairs and try to do some homework. Alex did, but it was a waste of time. He would start to read a phrase in French and then, ten minutes later, realize he was still staring at the same phrase, thinking about what it would be like at school when word got out about the test.

He shut the book and checked his phone for messages. Practice would be just ending. He expected to start hearing from people soon. Of course, some of them had to be drug-tested again first because it was Wednesday.

His phone vibrated as he was looking at it. He saw Christine's number pop onto the screen.

"I talked to my dad," she said.

"What did he say?"

"That there are ways to find out more about what happened. I just wanted to let you know we're working on it. I'll call if I know more tonight. Or else I'll see you tomorrow, okay?"

"Yeah, okay. Thanks, Christine."

He went to tell his mom the update and she was just getting off the phone with Coach Gordon. He had apparently suggested that Alex might want to stay home from school the next day, but she disagreed.

"You're going to have to face it sooner or later. Might as well get it over with."

He didn't argue. He could barely think. And he figured she was probably right.

He went to bed without eating much dinner and without doing any studying. He wasn't sure when he finally fell asleep, but he awoke before the sun was up in the middle of a dream in which Christine was marrying Matt. He lay back in bed and almost smiled. He wished that a dream like that was the worst of his problems. Sadly, it wasn't even close.

The announcement would be made at noon. Alex had talked to Jonas and Stephen Harvey the night before but had sworn them to secrecy so he could at least get through the morning.

Alex had found Coach Brotman when he first got to school and asked him if there was any way he could eat lunch in the football offices. Coach Brotman had shaken his head.

"I'm really sorry, Alex," he said. "The rules say you can't be in the locker room, the offices, anywhere around the football team. You're allowed inside the stadium at the game tomorrow and that's about it."

There was no way Alex was going to go to the game and sit in the stands with everyone staring at him.

He was sitting at his usual table in the cafeteria when Matt Gordon walked over and sat down. It was noon straight up and Alex knew that all hell was about to break loose in his life.

"I'm your new bodyguard, Goldie," Matt said. "People are going to be coming over here demanding to know what happened in"—he looked at his watch—"about five minutes would be my guess. Just let me do the talking."

Alex wasn't too surprised that Matt knew.

Matt looked Alex in the eye. "You didn't do it, right?"

"NO," Alex said vehemently.

Before he could say anything else, Matt held up his hand. "That's all I need."

Matt's prediction was off by one minute. At 12:04, Alex saw kids starting to stand up and show one another their phones. Then he saw them starting to look in his direction. And then, the stampede began.

Matt stood up to intercept people as they came to the table holding up their phones. Alex could hear a chorus of voices. . . .

"Is it true?" "What happened, Myers?" "Are you taking steroids?"

And on and on. Matt put up a hand and, in effect, made an announcement.

"A mistake has been made," he said in a loud voice. "Goldie hasn't done anything wrong. This will be fixed soon."

Someone called out, "In time for tomorrow's game?"

The confident look on Matt's face disappeared. "We hope so," he finally said. "Now, do me a favor and give my teammate some space."

"But is he still your teammate?" another voice called out.

There were probably a hundred kids around the table. They had appeared that quickly, as if by magic.

Matt flared angrily at the question. "Of course he is," he

said. "Someone messed up. My dad is working on finding out who and how right now."

That was the first Alex had heard about that. He suspected it wasn't true. But the crowd began to dissipate, for which he was grateful.

"Thanks," he said as Matt sat down. "I really needed that."

"And we need you, Goldie," Matt said softly. "Anybody hassles you, just say you aren't allowed to talk about it." He got up to go. "Sorry—I have to go figure out how we can possibly win without you tomorrow."

He wasn't smiling even a little bit when he said it.

■ ■ ■

Alex followed Matt's advice the rest of the day. As soon as anyone approached him, he put up a hand and said, "I'm not allowed to talk about it."

That got him through French class. Christine played unofficial bodyguard for him from the classroom to the bike rack.

"What now?" he asked.

"I have a lot of phone calls to make," she said. "My dad gave me a list."

"Like who?"

She shook her head. "I need to get started while people are still at work. When I have something, I'll call."

He had turned off his phone, as required by school rules, once lunch was over. Now he turned it back on and gasped: he had 104 new text messages.

He had given his cell phone number to a few media members after his late-game heroics earlier in the season. Now it appeared that every single media member in the state of Pennsylvania had his cell number.

There was one from someone named Stevie Thomas, who sounded familiar. Then he remembered: he was the teenage sports reporter who had broken a bunch of big stories at major events along with his partner, Susan Carol Anderson.

The first few words on the screen said, *You're not the only one.* Curious, Alex opened it and read the rest of the message, which said, *There were eleven positive tests in all among the eight teams, six from guys on teams still playing. Two from Allentown North—both on the O-line. If you want to talk or need help with this, call me . . . .*

Alex showed the text to Christine.

"I've met him a couple of times through my dad," she said. "He's doing work for the *Daily News.* He seems like a good guy.

"It figures there would be more than one failed test. I wonder if anyone else who tested positive is innocent."

She got on her bike. "I'll add Stevie to my call list and see if he has any ideas."

Alex was tempted to stop at McDonald's on the way home but realized it would be packed with kids from school. His mom and Molly weren't home when he arrived, so he found some bread and salami and made himself a sandwich.

His phone kept buzzing while he ate. Each time he picked it up, he saw a number he didn't recognize and ignored it. Finally, just as he was finishing, he saw Christine's number and grabbed the phone.

"I may have something," she said.

"Really?" he asked, surprised.

"Yes. What's your blood type?"

"No idea," he said.

"Ask your mom," she said. "And make sure she tells you if you're positive or negative. I'll meet you at your house, okay?"

■ ■ ■

Alex's blood type was O-positive, according to his mom, who naturally wanted to know why he was asking. He told her he wasn't sure yet, but that Christine seemed excited.

When he opened the door to Christine fifteen minutes later, she was already talking.

"Did you find out your blood type?"

He nodded and told her as he took her coat. "O-positive. Why's it matter?"

Christine whooped and seemed ready to jump out of her skin. "It matters because you're innocent—and we can prove it!"

"What?" Alex asked. "How? Why?"

"Because the blood type on the sample that came up positive is O-*negative*," Christine said. "It can't possibly be your blood!"

Alex gaped at her for a moment and then wrapped her in a hug that might have been a little too tight. When she squeaked, he let her go and grinned.

"So . . . so someone really just made a mistake?"

Christine's smile faded. "Or," she said, "someone didn't."

They sat in Alex's kitchen with mugs of hot chocolate and Christine explained that she had called a football coach last night whose name had been given to her by Dick Jerardi, a longtime *Daily News* columnist. Christine had told the coach she was convinced something was amiss with Alex's test, and he said he'd see what—if anything—he could find out.

The coach's athletic director sat on the board of the state high school athletic association—part of the reason Jerardi had recommended calling him. It was the AD who had called Christine back that afternoon.

"He can't be quoted on any of this," she said. "He said he'd look into it as a courtesy to his coach but he doubted there would be anything to find because a positive test is almost never a mistake."

"So how am I off the hook?"

"I'm trying to tell you. He called me back a little while

ago and said he had the Chester Heights results in front of him. He said occasionally there's a false positive if a kid has an unusually high testosterone level naturally. But that yours was sky-high.

"I told him we'd heard that and it was one reason we were suspicious. You're not an offensive lineman who weighs three hundred pounds.

"He agreed that seemed weird, but that the test was clear— the only thing unusual about it was that you had O-negative blood," Christine said. "I asked him why that was significant and he said it really wasn't, except that O-negative blood is rare. He could see that only four Chester Heights players had O-negative blood. I looked it up and less than ten percent of the U.S. population has O-negative blood. So I thought it was worth asking if you had it."

"But I don't."

"Exactly!" Christine said. "Which means it wasn't your blood that tested positive."

"But.... *someone* from the team with O-negative blood did test positive, right?"

Christine nodded. "Yes. And once we establish that you *aren't* the person who tested positive, they're going to have to figure out who *is*. But that comes later. *First*, we prove to the state it wasn't your blood and clear your name. *Then* we find out how this happened."

■ ■ ■

According to Christine, Chester Heights would have to file a formal appeal on his behalf. Since the appeal would be based on the fact that he didn't have the same blood type as the blood that had come back positive, Alex would have to produce proof of his blood type and then submit to another blood test because they would want to see proof that his *real* blood was clean. Once that was established, he would be cleared.

"Great!" Alex said. "Can I take the test tomorrow, before the game?"

"You can take the test, yes," Christine said. "You'll have to go to Harrisburg, which is where the state athletic association has its headquarters. Since you are appealing, the responsibility lies with you to get the documentation, bring it to them, and be tested."

"But if I pass the test, can I be cleared in time to play?"

Christine shook her head. "No," she said. "I'm sorry—it takes nearly a week to get the results back—three or four days if they rush it. There isn't time."

Alex sagged. For a split second he had seen himself in uniform for the game in Allentown, cleared of all wrongdoing and helping the team win. He knew the team was boarding a bus to Allentown at lunchtime tomorrow. He wouldn't be going with them.

He drained the last of his cocoa and tried to think of something else. "How do you think this happened? The vials must have been mislabeled, right?"

Christine crossed her arms. "Yeah," she said. "But that's not supposed to be possible. Unless someone who has possession of the blood samples does it on purpose."

"Why would anyone do that?" Alex asked.

Christine shrugged. "That's a good question. If we figure out why, we might figure out who. . . . We figure that out, we solve the mystery."

■ ■ ■

Alex and Christine explained the situation to his mom when she and Molly got home that night.

The more Christine talked, the more Alex's mom smiled, and in the end she wrapped Christine in a hug nearly as tight as her son's. "Thank you!" she said. "I don't know how to thank you."

Christine grinned, clearly pleased, and said she should get going.

Alex tried to call his dad to give him an update. He knew his mom had filled him in because he'd gotten a text that morning saying, *Hang in there, this will get straightened out.*

When Alex got his voice mail, he didn't bother leaving a message. If his dad cared, he'd see the number and call back.

Meanwhile, his mom was trying to track down Mr. White, the principal. He'd left for the day, but his email was in the school's online directory, so she sent him an email with the subject line "URGENT—PLEASE CALL RIGHT AWAY."

About thirty minutes later, Mr. White called and Alex's mom explained that they needed a meeting first thing in the morning because they had proof that a mistake had been made with Alex's drug test and they needed the school to file an official appeal.

Alex could only hear his mom's side of the conversation.

"No, Mr. White, this *can't* wait," she said. "We need to see you first thing in the morning, before school starts."

She paused, nodding. "Of course," she said. "That's perfectly fine. He should be aware of what's going on too. But I'm told I need your signature on the letter requesting the appeal."

Another nod as she listened. "Fine, we'll see you at seven o'clock."

She hung up.

"He thinks Coach Gordon should be there too," she said.

"Why?" Alex said. "He has to sign the appeal note, not Coach Gordon."

"I know," she said. "But he said since it was a football issue in addition to a school issue, Coach Gordon should be there. I said fine."

She paused for a moment. "I don't think we should tell them what proof we have," she said finally. "All we have to do is say we want a retest."

Alex was surprised. "You don't trust him?" he said.

"Right now," she said, "I don't trust any of them."

There was steel in her voice when she said it, a kind of steel Alex couldn't remember ever hearing before. He suspected Mr. White was going to have a tough morning.

■ ■ ■

They dropped Molly off at her school early and got to Mr. White's office at 6:57. Mr. White's assistant told them she would let the principal know they were here and offered Alex's mom some coffee.

"I'm fine, thank you," she answered. "It's 6:58. I hope we're going to get started on time."

Whoo, boy, thought Alex.

Mr. White opened his door at 7:01, just as his mom was looking at her watch again, and waved them in. Coach Gordon was already inside and he stood and shook her hand.

"Did Mrs. Appleman offer you coffee?" Mr. White asked as they all sat down.

"Yes, she did. Thanks."

Mr. White looked at Coach Gordon. Clearly, there had been a discussion about how to handle the meeting.

Coach Gordon leaned forward and smiled. Alex wasn't sure if he had ever actually seen the coach smile before.

"Mrs. Myers, this has, of course, been upsetting for all of us . . . ," he began.

"Not as upsetting for you, Coach, or for you, Mr. White, as it's been for my son and for me," Alex's mom said.

Tone set. Message delivered.

Coach Gordon's smile faded.

"I understand that," he said. "Believe me, we need Alex on the field tonight. But the charge against him is—"

"False," said Alex's mom. "And we're leaving for Harrisburg to prove it just as soon as Mr. White signs the letter of appeal on school letterhead that we are required to bring with us. That's what we're here for, Coach. Not for coffee *or* conversation."

Coach Gordon looked at Mr. White.

"Mrs. Myers, we're one hundred percent behind you even if overturning a test like this is a long shot. And I will gladly sign the appeal letter—"

"Good."

"But we want you to understand what's involved. First,

you'll be required to pay for the costs involved. It could be as much as five hundred dollars."

"You don't think I'd pay five hundred dollars to clear my son of a baseless charge?" she asked.

Alex was, at that moment, in complete awe of his mother.

"Of course you would. And I'm just trying to make you aware of everything involved. But I should ask you, with all due respect, are you *sure* the charge is baseless? I have no doubt Alex didn't intentionally take an illegal substance, but as you know—"

Alex's mom stood up. "Mr. White, you're wasting my time. How long will it take you to write the letter of appeal and sign it?"

Mr. White looked at Coach Gordon. He appeared to be staring at something on the wall behind Mr. White's desk.

"Can you give me fifteen minutes?"

"I'd prefer ten," she said. "We'll wait outside. And yes, I'd like some coffee now while we wait."

Alex hadn't opened his mouth during the whole meeting.

■ ■ ■

Thirty minutes later, they were in the car with the directions to the state high school athletic association offices in Harrisburg punched into the GPS. Mr. White had promised to contact James Newsome, the director of the association, to let him know they were on their way. They had gotten Mr. Newsome's phone number as backup. Mr. White had also given them the number for Mr. Turgeson, the very unpleasant man from the board of education who had informed Alex of the positive test, so they could let him know they were officially filing an appeal.

"I don't know what time the office opens," Mr. White had said.

"Leave a voice mail," his mom said. "I'll do the same thing once we're in the car."

The office was apparently open early, because a cheery voice answered the phone on the second ring, saying, "Pennsylvania High School Athletic Association, good morning."

"Good morning," Alex's mom said, talking on the car's Bluetooth so that Alex could hear both sides of the conversation. "I'm calling for Mr. Newsome."

Surprisingly, the receptionist didn't even ask who was calling. A moment later, a voice said, "James Newsome."

Alex's mom explained the situation and told Mr. Newsome that she and her son were en route to Harrisburg. Perhaps Mr. Newsome had already spoken with Mr. White, because he didn't seem surprised by the call.

"I understand completely," he said. "As soon as I hang up I'm going to call Dr. Novitsky, who is the head of our drug-testing program. Either he or one of our other doctors will re-administer the test this morning. When you get here, I'll have a name and the address of where you need to go. The only thing I have to tell you is that you will have to pay for the testing service, since this sort of thing isn't in our budget. Of course, if there's been a mistake made, your money will be refunded. And before you pay for the test, I'd like to talk to you face to face about what the chances are of finding the kind of error needed to overturn the initial finding."

"That's fine," she said. "We'll see you in about ninety minutes."

"What do you think will happen when we get there?" Alex asked after she had hung up.

"I think we'll show him the card validating your blood type and then the doctor will draw your blood," she said. "Once they get the test back, you'll be cleared."

"The season may be over by the time they get the tests back," Alex said, feeling glum at the thought.

His mother sighed. "We'll get them to rush it as much as they can," she said. "We'll do our best."

James Newsome looked like someone who had played football once upon a time. He appeared to be in his midforties and was a couple inches taller than Alex. He looked as if he could still jump into uniform and play that night. He offered them something to drink and ushered them into his small office, which confirmed what Alex had suspected: on the wall were photos of him in a University of Pittsburgh uniform.

"Did you play at Pitt?" Alex asked as they sat down, pointing at the photos.

Mr. Newsome nodded. "I played on the last Pitt team that was an independent," he said. "The year after I graduated we joined the Big East."

"When was that?" Alex's mom asked, clearly being polite.

"I graduated in 1991," he said.

They got down to business. Mr. Newsome had pulled

Alex's file, and he asked his mom to go through everything that had happened even though he had been briefed.

When she got to the part about the blood types not matching, his eyes widened.

"Well, if that's true, then a major injustice has been done," Mr. Newsome said. "Unfortunately, even if we retest your blood today, the earliest we can get results back is Tuesday—I've already checked on that. That's with a rush on it. If you're cleared, Alex, you could play in the state championship game—if Chester Heights wins tonight."

"That's a big if," Alex said.

"No doubt," Mr. Newsome said. "And if a mistake has been made"—he sighed and tapped his pen on his desk—"there's just nothing that can be done. I don't have the authority to clear you to play without the blood confirmation."

"How could this have happened?" Alex's mom asked, her tone not unfriendly but not warm either.

Mr. Newsome dropped the pen and spread his hands, which Alex noticed were huge.

"I have no idea," he said. "If Alex's blood was somehow switched with someone else's, our next step will be to figure that out."

He stood up. "For now, let's get you to Dr. Novitsky's office and get this sample so we can get the results back as soon as possible. It's probably easiest if I just drive you there, rather than having you navigate your way through Harrisburg."

"That's very nice of you," Alex's mom said. For the first time since the test results had come back, she smiled.

■ ■ ■

Dr. Novitsky was expecting them. He had a nurse make a copy of Alex's medical forms, which showed his blood type, and ushered them into a small examining room.

As the doctor went through the ritual of drawing Alex's blood, Alex's mom quizzed him about how the mix-up could have happened.

Dr. Novitsky had clearly been thinking about it too. "If a mistake was made, it must have been in labeling whose blood was whose, though I don't see how that could happen. It's possible the lab mixed up the samples . . . but they have strict handling protocols to guard against that, so that seems even more unlikely. I'm afraid I just don't know.

"I'll call you myself as soon as we get a result back," he added. "It should be before noon on Tuesday."

They thanked him and headed for home. They were quiet for a while before Alex's mom said, "Do you have any interest in going to the game tonight? I could take you if you want."

Alex shook his head. "No, thanks," he said. "It would kill me to be there and watch from the stands. Plus, I'd have to deal with all the people asking me questions."

He thought about that for a minute, staring out the window as the car pulled onto the Pennsylvania Turnpike, heading east. Thinking about his teammates running onto the field without him depressed him for a moment. Then he brightened.

"The good news is I can watch on television," he said. "And it's supposed to rain or maybe even snow tonight. At least we'll be dry and warm."

His mom reached over and patted him on the leg.

"I'm really proud of how you've handled this," she said.

"And in case you don't know it, your dad has been texting me constantly for updates."

"Did you tell him about the blood type? And that we were coming here?" he said.

"Yes," she said.

"What'd he say?"

In response, she picked up her cell—which was sitting in between the two of them—hit a button quickly, and handed it to him.

I knew he didn't do it, the text said. *We should sue the board of ed. Tell him I love him.*

"You should call him," she said.

"I do," Alex said. "He can never talk."

"He *does* care."

"I know he cares. I'm just not sure how much."

They rode in silence for a long while after that. The next thing he heard his mother say was, "McDonald's in five miles. Hungry?"

"Starving," Alex said. He thought for a moment and then added, "And tired. Really, really tired."

■ ■ ■

Before the game started, Alex called his dad.

"Congratulations, Alex. Mom texted me the news," his dad said.

"Nothing's done yet, Dad," he said. "And if we lose tonight, it won't really matter that much."

"Of course it matters. Even if you don't get to play again this season, it means your name is cleared—which is the most important thing of all."

Alex sighed. His dad was right. Life would be a lot easier at school once people knew he hadn't taken any steroids. But if the team lost tonight because he couldn't come off the bench and bail them out if needed, it was going to hurt.

He changed the subject.

"When are we going to see you, Dad?" he asked.

There was a pause. "Well, I have to be in California again this coming week," he said. "Business."

"On Thanksgiving?"

There was a pause. "I'm flying home on Thanksgiving."

"So if we make the championship game on Friday and I'm cleared, you can come down?"

Another pause.

"Of course. I wouldn't miss it."

Alex sensed his dad was saying yes because he didn't expect to have to make the trip, but he didn't push it, and a minute later they hung up. Alex's dad had never traveled much in the past. Now he seemed to be on the road all the time.

Alex decided not to think about it. The game was about to start.

■ ■ ■

As soon as Alex turned on the TV, any small, lingering doubts he might have had about not making the trip to Allentown disappeared. The opening on-camera shot was of something that looked like sleet or wet snow coming down steadily. The field already looked white.

"It's going to be a cold, wet night in the Lehigh Valley," Alex heard a voice say. "This mixture of snow and sleet is expected to continue until around midnight, but it will hardly be noticed by the young men of Allentown North and Chester Heights who will be competing here for the right to play in next week's state championship game."

At that point the camera shifted from the field to a shot of the two announcers, both bundled up in ski jackets. Alex didn't recognize either one of them, although the color commentator looked like he had once been a lineman. They welcomed the viewers to "Goodman Stadium, on the campus of Lehigh University," and went through the usual ritual about how exciting the game was likely to be and the fact that the two teams had a combined record of 21–1 coming into the state semifinals.

Then they showed close-up shots on a split screen of the starting quarterbacks, Matthew Gordon and Ken Jackson, both prime candidates for state player of the year and as Division I prospects in the future.

"And we have to mention," the play-by-play guy said, going from cheery to somber without missing a beat, "that both quarterbacks will be under a little extra pressure tonight because of some very unfortunate circumstances."

"You're right, Jeff," the ex-lineman said as pictures of Alex and two other guys came up on the screen.

"Michael Akers and Joe Burness have been Allentown North's starting tackles all season. Alex Myers is Matthew Gordon's backup and has come off the bench on a couple occasions to lead critical drives for the Lions. None of the three will play tonight because they are among eleven players who tested positive this week for performance-enhancing drugs."

The cameras cut back to the two announcers, both shaking their heads sadly. "These are the times we live in, Jeff," the ex-lineman was saying. "We can only hope these young men will learn from the mistakes they've made. Speaking as an ex-player, if I were a teammate of any of these guys, I'm not sure I'd ever be able to look them in the eye or respect them again."

"Well said, Armand," said Jeff. "Well said. Now let's turn our attention back to those who earned the right to play tonight—"

Alex didn't hear the rest of the sentence because he was screaming. He was so angry he had tears in his eyes. His mother raced into the room.

"What is it, Alex?" she said.

"They just called me a cheat on TV!" he yelled. "They showed my picture and said my teammates should never speak to me again. Didn't someone from the school tell them there might have been a mistake? Or that we've filed an appeal?"

"Maybe they're not allowed to?" she said.

"Or maybe they are," Alex said.

He was as angry as he could ever remember being. He paced the room like a caged . . . Lion. Suddenly he felt very alone. His dad was MIA, his teammates were playing without him, he'd been labeled a cheat on TV, and no one was standing up for him. Then he looked at his mom—and went over and gave her a hug.

"Thanks, Mom," he said softly.

"For what?"

"For being here."

She didn't say anything, but he knew she understood.

■ ■ ■

The next three hours were torture for Alex. The good news was the announcers never brought his name up again—

probably on orders, he figured: get the cheats out of the way early and then forget about them.

The bad news was, no one could score. Hanging on to the ball was almost impossible. Staying on your feet was just about as difficult. Both star quarterbacks struggled: neither seemed able to grip the ball to throw with any consistency and both teams fumbled almost constantly.

With under six minutes left in the fourth quarter, Chester Heights finally put together a mini-drive after taking over on a Ken Jackson fumble at the Allentown North 42-yard line. Sticking to basics—Matt turning and handing the ball off to Craig Josephs on just about every play *or* faking to Craig and then following him straight into the line—the Lions steadily moved the ball to a first down at the Allentown North 8-yard line.

The clock was under two minutes. The Raiders had already used two of their time-outs. Alex wondered if Coach Gordon would try to punch the ball into the end zone or take a chance on Pete Ross making a short field goal, kicking a wet ball off a frozen field. It was apparent that Allentown North was saving its final time-out to make Ross think about the kick if he had to try to make it.

On first down, Josephs went up the middle and was tackled for no gain. The clock ticked down to 1:35 before Matt handed to Josephs again. This time he picked up two yards to the six. It was pretty clear that Allentown North was jamming the middle, and so trying to score by going straight into the line would be impossible. If Josephs carried again, it would come down to a field goal. The clock was under a minute as Matt brought the team to the line.

Coach Gordon clearly understood that another handoff to Josephs was going to result in a field goal attempt in very difficult conditions and decided to take a different sort of risk. On third down, Matt looked like he was going to hand to Josephs again. But he pulled the ball out of his stomach and dropped to pass. He raised his arm to throw, then pulled it down. Apparently, no one was open, because he took off on a scramble. He dodged one lineman, then two. A third Raider seemed to have him but fell on his face when Matt cut outside.

At the 2-yard line, two defenders waited to cut him off. Matt lined them up and then leaped right into their arms—pushing them backward with his sheer power. The three of them fell in a heap right on the goal line. The official raced in, arms in the air, signaling a touchdown.

Alex jumped off the couch, shaking his fist. "Way to go, Matt—way to go!" he screamed as he watched his teammates pummel their quarterback. Alex could see the clock at the bottom of the screen: there were thirty-eight seconds to go.

Ross came in to kick the extra point, but the snap went way over the holder's hands and the ball rolled loose for an agonizing few seconds until a Lion smothered it. Coach Gordon had been right not settling for the field goal. Allentown North tried two long passes after the kickoff. The second was intercepted by Tony Riley—who was in as a sixth defensive back—and the game came to an end. Final: Chester Heights 6, Allentown North 0.

They were in the state championship game. Alex took a deep breath and thought, Maybe, just maybe, my football season isn't over.

It wasn't until some sideline announcer interviewed Matt after the game that Alex found out what happened on Matt's touchdown run.

"I got lucky," Matt said in typical Matt fashion. "The call was for a play-action fake and then for me to throw it to Jonas Ellington in the end zone. He was wide open, but when I tried to cock my arm to throw, I realized I didn't have a good grip on the ball. I was afraid I'd miss the throw, so I just took off."

"That run wasn't lucky," the sideline reporter said.

Matt shrugged. "On a night like this, anything good that happens is lucky. We were just luckier than they were to-night."

Alex knew that was true. It was also true that Matt had made a spectacular play, figuring out a way to pull the ball down rather than having it wobble out of his hand and end up—at best—falling incomplete. At worst, it might have been intercepted.

His mom walked into the room. She had been upstairs reading in bed as she always did after Molly went to sleep but had heard Alex shouting after Matt's touchdown run.

"What happened?" she asked.

"We won," Alex said.

As happy as he had been when Matt scored, he didn't feel overjoyed anymore. Chester Heights would play in the championship game. That thrilled him. But the uncertainty about what would happen to him—what if they somehow screwed up the test again? what if they refused to admit their mistake?—was weighing on him.

His mom had apparently not thought about any of that. Or didn't show it.

"That's *great*!" she said. "This means you get to play next week!"

"Maybe," he said. "If I'm cleared. But Matt's still the starter. He saved the game tonight."

"What do you mean *if* you're cleared?" she said. "You're going to be cleared."

Alex told her his fears. She was shaking her head as he spoke. "I'm very good on gut feelings," she said. "You know that. Mr. Newsome is an honest man. He won't let anything like that happen."

"I hope you're right," he said.

"I know I'm right," she said, crossing the room to give him a kiss on the forehead. "Get some sleep now. You should be able to sleep well tonight."

He nodded. "You're right."

He went to bed still full of adrenaline, thinking about the possibility of playing in the state championship game. His mom was right—the state *had* to clear him. Then a thought that had been nagging at him all day popped back into his mind one more time: if it wasn't his blood that had tested positive, whose blood had it been? It had to be one of the linemen, he thought. He lay awake trying to figure out which one it had been.

Finally, after he'd run through all the names, he slept.

■ ■ ■

He had texted both Christine and Jonas on the way back from Harrisburg and Christine suggested they all meet at Stark's for lunch on Saturday.

When Alex walked in, the others were sitting in the back booth that now felt like home to Alex. Both were drinking milk shakes.

"I would think after last night you'd never want anything cold again," he said, hugging Jonas as he stood to greet him.

"You're not far wrong," Jonas said. "Christine talked me into it."

"Was it as bad as it looked?" Alex asked as they sat down.

"Worse," Jonas said. "You know me, I think I can catch anything. But I was never so happy in my life as when Matt pulled that ball down. I was convinced he was going to throw it to me and I was going to flat-out drop it. I was soaked *and* shivering by then."

Christine had barely said a word as the two boys talked.

Her hair was tied back and the brightness in her eyes that was usually so evident seemed missing.

"You okay?" Alex asked, turning to her finally.

"Fine. Just *very* tired," she said. "We couldn't drive home last night because of the weather, so we checked into a hotel and got up at six to come home. I've been doing homework most of the morning since we got back."

The waitress came over and Alex, still cold from the bike ride over, opted for hot chocolate.

Christine got down to business.

"The *Daily News* has asked me to write this story as soon as you're cleared on Tuesday," she said.

"That's a pretty big deal for a high school freshman reporter, isn't it?" Jonas said.

"It is," Christine said. "But Stevie Thomas has been writing for them since he was my age, so they've done it before. Plus, my dad showed the sports editor some of my stuff and he thought it was pretty good."

"Glad to be of service," Alex said, hoping he didn't sound too sarcastic. If he did, Christine didn't pick up on it.

"There's still one important fact missing."

"What's that?" Alex said.

"Whose blood was it?" Christine said. Her tone made it clear she was a little stunned he didn't know the answer.

"Right," he said.

"The good news is, there are only a handful of guys on the team who have O-negative blood," Christine said. "The bad news is, the state can't be sure which is the one who tested positive."

Alex said, "But isn't there someone out there with

O-negative blood whose test came back clean, showing O-positive blood because it was mine?"

"That makes sense," said Jonas, who had been listening intently. "But tell me if I'm wrong, Christine. Won't they first try to figure out *how* someone else's blood ended up marked with Alex's name? Figuring out whose blood it really was only comes after figuring out how the system broke down. Otherwise, how do they trust *any* of the results? There might be more than one mix-up. Sounds to me like it's very unlikely they'll figure out who it is before Friday."

Alex thought about it for a minute. "Actually, it's not all bad. It means we won't lose a key lineman for the championship game."

"So you're okay with having someone play who's a cheat as long as it helps you win?" Christine asked, shooting him a disgusted look.

"I didn't mean it that way."

"Yes, you did."

"What makes you so sure it's a lineman?" Jonas said, much to Alex's relief—although Christine was still shooting daggers at him with her eyes.

"Gotta be one of the big guys up front, right?" Alex said. "Every other positive test in the state was a lineman."

"That makes sense," Jonas said.

"It's also not fair that he plays," Christine said.

"He's already been playing," Alex said. "Whoever it is, whether by accident or not, has beaten the system. I'll just be glad to put this behind me."

"*That*," Christine said, "you're entitled to."

■ ■ ■

The next couple of days dragged for Alex. The school was electric on Monday as everyone geared up for Thanksgiving break—which started after school on Tuesday—and for the championship game, which would be played at Heinz Field, the home stadium of the Steelers, in Pittsburgh on Friday night. It would be televised on Comcast SportsNet–Philadelphia, which meant it would be broadcast statewide and up and down the Northeast Corridor.

Chester Heights was in its third state title game but its first in seven years. Their opponent, Beaver Falls High School, was not only the defending state champion but had also produced the great Joe Namath, among others. The Tigers probably weren't ever going to have anyone as good as Namath play for them again, but they did have a senior quarterback named Johnny Washington who was being recruited by a lot of big-name schools. He had been nicknamed "Little Johnny Football" by the media covering the team in honor of "Johnny Football" Manziel, the 2012 Heisman Trophy winner.

If anyone at Chester Heights was concerned about facing Little Johnny Football and the 12–0 Tigers, it didn't show in the hallways, the classrooms, or the cafeteria on Monday.

Alex, Christine, and Jonas decided to tell no one about his retest—better to be cleared officially and *then* spread the news.

Alex moved around school on Monday almost as if he were in a bubble: people either pointedly looked the other way or barely nodded at him. The fact that Matt had been the savior on Friday while he had been in exile had returned him to the early days of the fall when he had felt like the invisible man.

During lunch, Matt came over and sat down with Alex, Jonas, and Christine. No one else had come anywhere close to the table.

"How you holding up, Goldie?" he asked.

Alex shrugged. "I'm doing okay." He forced a smile. "I'm doing a lot better thanks to you making that play Friday night."

"We could have used you," Matt said. "On a field like that, your arm strength would have helped a lot. I just couldn't grip the football well enough to get it where it needed to go. If we'd been able to throw—if *you'd* been there to throw—we'd have won easily."

"Sorry."

Matt leaned forward. "I didn't mean it that way—you know that."

"I know."

Alex wondered if Coach Gordon had told Matt about the retest. He knew that Mr. Newsome had sent Mr. White an email informing him of the retest and the reason for it, because he had sent a copy to Alex's mom with a note attached, saying, "I hope this turns out well. Alex seems like a very nice young man."

Alex figured that Mr. White would have told Coach Gordon and that Coach Gordon would have told Matt. But if Matt knew anything, he wasn't saying.

Matt stood up. "Hey, thanks for the text. It meant a lot."

Alex had texted Matt late Friday to congratulate him. He had texted back a brief *Thanks . . . . missed you* in response.

"You think he knows?" Christine asked as Matt walked away.

"Has to," Jonas said. "The old man had to tell him."

"If he does, it seems like he would have said something in his text," Alex said.

"Something's a little off here," Jonas said.

Alex agreed. His gut told him that Matt's father hadn't told him. Coach Gordon was hard to figure out—in more ways than one.

■ ■ ■

A pep rally and assembly had been scheduled for last period on Tuesday since it was the last day of school before Thanksgiving—and the championship game. Alex had decided he was only going to go if he had been cleared to play by then. He was telling his mom about that decision when his phone rang late Monday night.

"We need to meet—six-thirty in the morning, at the bike rack."

It was Christine. "Oh God, why? And why there and why so early?" Alex asked. "Can't we do it somewhere indoors and closer to the start of school? I mean, what's the big deal now?"

"We can't meet that close to school starting," she said. "People will see us. You're a celebrity now, for better or worse. People will recognize you. At six-thirty at the bike rack we'll be alone."

"But—"

"Alex, just meet me. This is important."

"How important?"

"That coach I talked to last week—remember him? He

knows the guy who runs the high school athletic association. . . ."

"Mr. Newsome?"

"Yeah, him. The coach apparently talked to him." She paused for a moment and then said, "You've been cleared."

Alex's heart leaped. "Are you sure?" he said. "That's just great . . . amazing!" He realized his heart was going about a thousand beats a minute. He had known this *had* to be the outcome, but now he *really* knew.

He paused for a moment, still catching his breath. Then he said, "Why haven't they called me? Why do we have to meet so early . . . ?"

"Because there's more. I want to make a couple more calls to people to try to be absolutely sure this guy has it right before I fill you in. I need a little more time."

"What in the world are you talking about?"

"Alex, *please*. Just trust me a few more hours and meet me tomorrow at six-thirty."

Alex went from thrilled to baffled and back in about ten seconds. At this point, other than his mom there was no one in the world he trusted more than Christine.

"Okay," he said finally. "I'll see you in the morning."

"Do *not* be late."

He hung up and stared at the phone, then realized he had almost forgotten the most important thing. He was going to play Friday. He raced upstairs to tell his mom.

Even though Alex was on time—two minutes early, in fact—
Christine was waiting for him when he rode up to the bike
rack. She was holding two large cups in her hands.

"I thought you might want some hot chocolate," she
said, handing him a very hot cup after he had chained his
bike.

Holding the hot chocolate in her left hand, she put out
her right hand—which was gloved. "Congratulations," she
said. "I'm glad you were finally proven innocent."

"Because of *you*," Alex said. "I don't know how to thank
you."

Still holding the cup of hot chocolate, he attempted an
awkward one-armed hug. She returned it, smiling—even if
they both almost lost their balance for a second.

"Listen to the rest of the story," Christine said. "There's
still a lot more we have to do."

They sat down on a very cold bench next to the rack. Alex put both hands on the hot chocolate and took a sip. It had cooled just enough that it was perfect.

"It's a little bit dangerous, actually," she said. "We could both get in big trouble."

Alex laughed. "Trouble is my middle name," he said.

"More like *in* trouble," Christine said.

"I've been looking into how the blood samples get processed," she continued. "The people at the lab have very strict rules about how samples are handled. I talked to one of the nurses who drew blood, and assuming he's telling the truth, there's only one way your blood could have been confused with somebody else's."

"How?" Alex asked.

"Someone had to switch the labels *before* the samples went to the lab."

"You mean on purpose?" Alex asked.

"Had to be," Christine said, sipping the hot chocolate. "You can't peel a label off one vial of blood and put it on another by accident."

Alex sat back on the bench, its coldness shooting through him as he did.

"So someone tried to frame me?" Alex said.

"Or was trying to get someone else off the hook and happened to pick your sample," Christine said.

"Or both?" he said. "That's possible too, isn't it?"

They looked at one another.

"But who?" Alex asked.

"That's where the danger comes in," she said.

■ ■ ■

The plan was extremely dangerous—and potentially brilliant.

Christine was going to talk to Mr. Hillier and ask him if he could find out exactly who had been in charge of the blood samples once the nurses had taken them from the players. Apparently, once the samples had been taken and sealed, it was the responsibility of the school to deliver them to the lab.

"Doctors and nurses don't do that sort of work," Christine explained. "They're not messengers. The labs have messengers who are paid to pick up blood samples and deliver them. We need him to find out who called for the pickup and who handed over the samples to the messenger."

"That could be the guy who did it," Alex said.

"Maybe," she said. "One step at a time. Freshmen went last—isn't that what you told me? Do you remember what time you were finished?"

Alex thought about it for a moment. "It was about six-thirty. We showered after practice and then waited to be called. I remember calling my mom when I was on my way home because I was later than normal for dinner."

"Good," Christine said. "I bet I can find out from Lab-Corp what time they picked up the blood."

"Why would they tell you that?" Alex asked.

She smiled. "Because once the announcement is made that a blood test got screwed up, they're going to want to be sure no one thinks *they're* responsible. They'll be happy to account for every second the blood was in their possession—I'm pretty sure of that. In fact, I'll make it clear to them that I'm writing a story for the *Daily News* and the more specific information I have, the better it will look for them."

"Okay, so far so good," Alex said, checking his watch. People would be showing up very soon. It was almost seven.

"Right," Christine said. "That's actually the easy part. Here's the hard part. We have to find out who the four guys on the team are who have O-negative blood."

"Doesn't the state know that?" Alex said.

"Sure they do," she said. "But they can't reveal that information to anyone—it's confidential student info. We have to find out."

"And how do we do that?" Alex asked.

"Everyone's health form must be on file in the football office," Christine said. "And no one is ever in there from first period until lunchtime."

"Are you saying we break in?" Alex asked.

She shook her head. "Oh no. I can get Mr. Hillier to give me a key. You have study hall third period—"

"Are you kidding!" Alex exploded.

"We'll get Jonas to help," she said. "He has study hall that period too. It shouldn't take too long."

"Should we get Jonas involved in this?" he said.

She gave him a look. "What do you think he'll say when we ask him?"

"This is nuts," Alex said.

"I know." She grinned. "So let's do it."

■ ■ ■

Alex didn't hear a word anyone said in either of his first two classes. Christine and Jonas were waiting for him outside his history classroom after second period.

"I told him," Christine said.

Alex remembered she and Jonas were in the same math class.

"What do you think?" he said to Jonas.

"I think we should get going," Jonas said.

Alex turned to Christine. "Do we have the materials we need for our experiment?" he asked, just in case someone walking by might overhear them.

She nodded and held up her hand so he could see that a key was inside the palm. People were rushing by them, heading for third-period classes. A couple of heads turned in Alex's direction, but most people were focused on getting where they needed to go.

"Come on, then," Alex said.

They walked down the steps to the first floor and down the hall that led to the back of the building and the athletic facilities. Alex's heart was already pounding. He'd come up with a decent excuse for missing study hall: he could say he'd gotten a call from his mother to tell him about the results from the second blood test.

The gym, where classes would be going on, was on the other side of the building. They could hear noise from there, but no one was around.

"So Mr. Hillier was okay with giving you the key?" Alex asked.

"I told him this was the only way to find out who *did* test positive. He finally agreed that we needed to know."

They reached the door marked CHESTER HEIGHTS LIONS FOOTBALL. Instinctively, Alex tried the handle—locked. Christine handed him the key. Heart pounding, he put the key into the lock. He turned it and pushed—and nothing happened. Had Mr. Hillier given Christine the wrong key? Were they being set up somehow?

He looked at Jonas, panicked.

"Turn it the other way," Jonas said quietly.

Alex did—and this time the door opened.

The lights in the hallway that led to the offices were on, so they had no trouble finding their way. Mr. Hillier had told Christine that the players' records were kept in an old-fashioned file cabinet in Coach Gordon's office. When they found the coach's door ajar, Alex got scared again: what if Coach was there? But he pushed the door open and poked his head in—empty. The file cabinet had no locks on it, and in the top drawer, there it was: VARSITY/JUNIOR VARSITY—2014, HEALTH FORMS.

"Bingo!" Christine said.

They each took a stack of forms and looked for a place to sit. Christine sat on the floor. Jonas plopped down behind Coach Gordon's desk, which made Alex nervous. He said nothing and sat down in the chair across from the desk with his set of forms on his lap.

Christine was already ahead. "Blood type is two-thirds of the way down the page," she said. "Right-hand side."

Alex's first form was for Timothy P. Maxwell. He recognized the name: a JV player. Only a handful of the JVs— the ones who had suited up—had been tested. He wished the varsity and JV forms had been separated out. There were probably close to a hundred forms to go through.

Maxwell had type A blood. Alex put his form on the desk in front of him and moved on. The next one was Jonas's. He also had type A blood.

He was about eight forms in when he heard Jonas say, "Got one—Terrence Gaston."

"Backup slotback," Alex said.

Christine gave him a look as if to say, *I know that*, then took out a notebook and asked Jonas for details.

"He's five eleven, 148," Jonas said. "Anything's possible, but it doesn't seem likely."

She nodded. They kept looking. Alex found the next one: Alan Tribble, an outside linebacker. Tribble was certainly a more likely candidate than Gaston. He was listed as six two, 215 pounds.

Alex also found the next one: it was a JV player, Kenny Holtzman.

They were all now nearing the bottom of their piles. Alex glanced at his watch: fifteen minutes were left until the end of third period. He kept going. He only had four forms left when he heard Jonas say, "Oh my God!" in about as loud a whisper as was possible.

"What?" Alex asked.

Jonas was holding up a form in the air. "I think we may have it," he said.

"Well, who is it?" Alex asked.

Jonas put the form down on the desk and pushed it across to Alex. "Read it yourself," he said.

Alex gasped when he saw the name at the top of the page: MATTHEW GORDON JR.

His eyes darted downward. BLOOD TYPE: O-NEGATIVE.

Christine leaned over his shoulder and gave a little gasp too.

They were all staring at one another when they heard

a door open. Jonas pointed at the small bathroom that adjoined Coach Gordon's office. He put a finger to his lips, and as quietly and as quickly as possible, they dashed into the bathroom.

If Jonas was scared, he didn't show it. Christine looked the way Alex felt: terrified. Jonas had grabbed his backpack and his forms and carried them into the bathroom. When Alex saw that Jonas had the forms, he gasped again: he'd taken Matt's, but the rest of his were on Coach Gordon's desk.

He started to go back, but Jonas seized his arm. It was too late. Someone was walking into Coach Gordon's office.

"Alex? Are you in here? Christine?"

Jonas looked at Alex and mouthed the word *who?* As in, who could possibly know that Alex was in here?

They listened again.

"Guys, it's okay," the voice said. "It's me. Mr. Hillier."

Alex breathed a huge sigh. Christine almost collapsed into his arms in relief. The three of them walked out of the bathroom.

"I figured I'd better check on you guys," Mr. Hillier said. "Coaches usually don't come in before eleven, but if someone came in a little early—"

He stopped, looking at the form in Alex's hand.

"You find something?" he asked.

Alex nodded and handed him Matt's form.

Mr. Hillier looked and whistled. "You think he's the one?"

"He's the only one of the four O-negatives that makes any sense," Christine said. "The others aren't that important or aren't that big, or aren't either."

Mr. Hillier nodded and read from the file. "Matt's six two, 195 pounds. To be honest, I'd say he's more like 210."

Alex was shaking his head. "I can't believe Matt—"

"Would take steroids?" Mr. Hillier asked. "I can. Think of the pressure his father puts him under. What I *don't* believe is that he had anything to do with switching the labels on the vials. For one thing, I don't think he'd have the opportunity. But even if he did, this isn't who Matt Gordon is."

"Then who?" Christine asked.

Mr. Hillier looked around. "We need to put these files back and get out of here. You three all need to get to fourth period. Let's all meet in my office at lunchtime."

They didn't argue.

As they walked out of the office, Alex's head was spinning. Matt? It had to be a mistake. Then again . . .

■ ■ ■

When Alex, Christine, and Jonas walked into the newspaper office at lunchtime, Mr. Hillier was ready.

"Let's go," he said. "As soon as word gets out that Alex has been cleared, people are going to start trying to hide."

"Where are we going?" Alex asked.

"To see Buddy Thomas," Mr. Hillier said.

They all just followed him.

Buddy Thomas was alone in the training room, opening up boxes of the tape he wrapped players' ankles with.

When he looked up and saw the four of them coming, he didn't say a word. Instead, he turned his back, pulled down another box, and said, "Coach Hillier, all due respect, we don't allow girls in the locker room."

"Buddy, we only need a minute," Mr. Hillier said, ignoring the comment about Christine.

"Haven't got it," Buddy said, opening another box of tape.

"You can talk to us right now," Mr. Hillier said. "Or to the police in about an hour."

Buddy looked up quickly. "The police?" he asked. "About what?"

"About tampering with blood samples. About falsifying evidence against an innocent student."

Buddy looked truly baffled.

"Coach, I swear I don't know what you're talking about," he said, his tone completely different than it had been thirty seconds earlier.

"When the blood samples were taken from all the players two weeks ago, you were left in charge of them until Lab-Corp picked them up," Mr. Hillier said. "I know that from the other coaches. And we found out from LabCorp that your signature is on the form for turning the samples over to the messenger."

"So?" Buddy said. "What does that have to do with falsifying evidence? I never touched the stuff. It just sat in the training room until the guy came to pick it up."

"How long was that?" Christine asked.

Buddy shrugged. "I don't know." He thought for a second. "Maybe an hour. What's going on?"

Christine didn't answer, just plowed on. "Were you in the training room the whole time?" she asked.

Buddy shook his head. "No. I had work to do. Once all the nurses cleared out, I called the lab for the pickup and worked on stuff in my office. What is this, an episode of *Law and Order?*"

"Was anyone else around?" Christine asked.

Buddy actually thought about that one, then shook his head.

"No. I'd already sent the kids who help me here home. Everything was done. Coaches had all left. Except for . . ."

He stopped.

"Except for who, Buddy?" Mr. Hillier asked.

"No one," Buddy said. "No one. Look, I've got work to do. . . ."

Alex hadn't said a word until then.

"Buddy, please. Someone switched the labels on the vials in there. That's why my blood came up positive—because it wasn't mine. *Someone* had to switch them. Please tell us who was here that night."

Buddy looked at Alex.

"I never thought you were guilty, Myers," he said. "I really didn't."

"Who was here, Buddy?" Mr. Hillier said very softly.

Buddy leaned on top of the training table. "I had no idea why he went into the training room," he said. "I really didn't. He said he'd left something behind."

"*Who?*" they all said.

"It was Jake," Buddy finally said. "Jake Bilney."

■ ■ ■

Alex actually felt faint for a moment. Clearly, Christine did too. Mr. Hillier and Jonas simply stared at Buddy.

"Are you *sure?*" Mr. Hillier said.

"Of course I'm sure," Buddy said. "That doesn't mean he did anything. But he was in there a few minutes. Said he'd taken his watch off for the blood test and then couldn't find it."

Christine shook her head. "Jake doesn't wear a watch."

Alex realized she was right. Jake was always looking at his cell phone for the time.

"Buddy," Mr. Hillier said. "I don't want to accuse Jake of anything unless you're sure."

"I'm *not* lying," Buddy said. "And I did *not* touch that blood."

He was, if nothing else, convincing.

"Now what do we do?" Jonas asked.

"We go see Jake in the cafeteria," Mr. Hillier said. "Except for you, Christine. You're going to go talk to Matt."

Christine reddened a little. "Why should I go talk to Matt?" she said.

"Because he'll tell you the truth," Mr. Hillier said. "Hmm . . . , now that I think of it—Alex, Jonas, you guys go talk to Jake without me. If I walk in with you, Jake'll freak out. Tell him what you know—and be firm about it. See what he says."

Alex still wasn't sure what was going on. He had sensed, at times, that it bothered Jake that he had come in and moved ahead of him on the depth chart. But Jake had never said it was wrong—in fact, he'd made a point of saying it was the right thing to do, not so much because Jake was a bad player (he wasn't) but because he was Matt lite running the offense and Alex brought a completely different dimension to it with his arm.

Jealous of him? Sure, Alex could buy that. Defensive about Coach Gordon? Absolutely. But this? He still couldn't believe it.

Lunch period was winding down when they walked in. Alex spotted Jake sitting with a bunch of juniors—none of them football players.

Matt was standing at a table on the other side of the room with some of the guys on the team. The room was buzzing more than normal: five days without school loomed, as did the pep rally and the game Friday night. Christine took a deep breath and walked in Matt's direction without saying a word to Alex or Jonas.

Alex took a deep breath too, and he and Jonas headed for Jake's table. If any of this was making Jonas uptight, he didn't show it. He was as cool now as in the closing seconds of the games they had pulled out during the regular season.

"Hey, Goldie," Jake said. "Where've you been?"

"Actually, I've got some news. You got a minute?" Alex nodded in the direction of the table where he and Jonas usually sat.

"Absolutely," Jake said, sitting up from his usual slouch and then standing. The three of them went to the table and sat down. Alex knew all eyes from the football table were on them.

"So," Jake said. "Tell me you got some good news—please tell me that."

"In about two minutes, they're going to announce I've been cleared," Alex said. "There was a mistake."

"That's *great!*" Jake yelled. "Goldie, I guarantee we're going to need you Friday. What happened?"

Alex walked through how he had learned about how the blood samples had somehow been switched. He watched Jake's face carefully as he talked.

"So how in the world did they get switched?" Jake asked. At that moment, his cell phone began pinging. He picked it up. "Google alert on you, Goldie," he said. He hit a couple of buttons. "Here it is: 'State clears Chester Heights QB. Blood test was compromised.'"

He looked up, smiling.

"Congrats, Alex," he said. "But I still don't understand how it happened."

"Why don't *you* tell us?" Jonas said, his tone a little bit menacing.

For the first time, Jake's face betrayed some fear. "Me?" he said. "How would I know anything?"

Jake was clearly lying—the look on his face now was a dead giveaway. Alex could feel his anger swell.

"Hey, Jakey, what time is it?" he asked.

Jake looked at his phone. "It's 12:01. Why?"

"You told Buddy Thomas you needed to go back into the training room on the day we were tested because you left your watch in there," Alex said. "Problem is, Jake, you don't wear a watch."

Jake's face lost all color. "So?" he said, knowing he was caught but trying to bluster through somehow.

"Why, Jake?" Alex asked. "How could you do that to me?"

"Let me answer that one, Jakey," a voice said behind Alex. "I'm pretty sure I know exactly what happened."

Alex looked behind him. Matt Gordon was standing there with Christine. He grabbed two empty chairs from the next table. Christine sat in one, Matt the other. The bell rang. No one moved.

"Let me begin at the beginning," he said.

"A lot of this is your fault, Alex," Matt said, looking right at Alex and calling him by his real name for just about the first time since he'd put "Goldie" on him way back in August. "It started, really, when I first saw you throw a football in preseason. You *do* have a golden arm. I looked at you and thought, he's just a freshman—by the time he grows and gets stronger, he's going to be a better quarterback than I can ever dream of being."

"But—" Alex said.

Matt held up a hand to stop him. "I had two goals this summer: for us to have a great season *and* to put myself in a position by the end of the season to be a big-time D1 recruit. When I saw you, I knew I was a lot farther from being the kind of player I needed to be to get recruited than I'd thought."

He paused. They were all staring at him. No one said a word. The cafeteria was emptying. None of them noticed.

Matt looked down at the floor. "I panicked," he continued. "I knew I could never throw the ball like you do—I just don't have that kind of arm. But I could use my speed and build my strength to the point where I could be a very good college quarterback. There are 126 Division I schools. Maybe twenty have quarterbacks with legitimate NFL arms each year. I didn't have to be one of those guys. I could be a poor man's Tebow: big enough and athletic enough to be a very good college QB. If I got to that point, maybe I could even be an NFL tight end or fullback or H-back.

"But I needed to get better—fast. In a fair competition, Goldie, you might have beaten me out by midseason."

"Not true," Alex said.

Matt again held up a hand. "You play football well, Goldie, but you don't *know* football like I do. You aren't a coach's son. You haven't studied the game your whole life. I still had an edge there. But I needed more.

"So I went looking for help—and I found it."

"Isn't it hard to find steroids?" Christine asked.

Matt laughed and shook his head. "Not even a little bit. Every team, including ours, has guys on it who know people who know people. You just ask around a little. Took me about a week to make a connection.

"I screwed up twice. First, I didn't know about the new drug-testing rule. Of all people, I should have known. I found out when my dad got a reminder memo and I happened to see it on his desk. By then it was too late to cycle off before the first test.

"And you know the worst thing about steroids? They work. That's why so many guys take the risk. I put on fifteen pounds of solid muscle. I could work out twice a day and not feel tired or sore.

"But when I realized I was caught, I thought I owed it to my dad to let him know." He looked Alex right in the eye. "I told him I'd quit before they did the test. I said I'd confess to the team and quit, and he could play you instead. It would probably come out sooner or later what I'd done, but at least I wouldn't have a positive test on my record.

"He said I should just play. He said maybe everything I'd read was wrong and I'd test clean if I got off what I was taking right away. So I stopped. And when my test came back clean, I was stunned.

"But then I heard you tested positive, Alex, and I knew something had happened. I knew there was no way you were taking anything. For one thing, you can't lift five pounds. For another"—his eyes were starting to glisten—"I know you."

They were all listening now, mouths agape.

"I went to my father the day they announced you were suspended. I told him it had to be a mistake. He said there was nothing to be done and that it wasn't my concern. I got angry with him and said it *was* my concern because Alex was my teammate and my friend.

"He waved me off. Then I really got angry and asked him if he'd had anything to do with it. He was furious. He couldn't believe I'd question his integrity that way, even if there *was* a way to mess with the test—which there wasn't, he said. He threw me out of his office."

"But he was lying," Christine said. "Right, Jake?"

Jake also had tears in his eyes. The bell for fifth period was ringing. They all just stared at him.

"Yes," Jake said slowly. "He was lying. He called me in the Monday after we beat Chester. He said he needed me to do something that was awful but would be better for everyone on the team in the long run. When he told me what it was, I said no, absolutely not, no way. He said he'd make certain Alex wouldn't be punished beyond missing the playoffs this year.

"I said it'll jeopardize his chances to get a scholarship. He insisted it wouldn't, that as long as Alex tested clean the next three years, colleges would overlook it because he was so talented. He pointed out that a lot of kids with serious criminal records get scholarships because they're good."

"That's true, actually," Matt said.

Jake nodded. "I still said no. Then he told me that he would *guarantee* that he would get a coach at either a D1 school or at least a Patriot League school to scholarship me in a year. The Patriot League thing got my attention. I know I'm not good enough to play at a big-time school, but a place like Lehigh or Lafayette? I could have a chance at those places."

"Do they give scholarships?" Jonas asked.

"Yes," Matt said. "You have to be a good student too, unlike at a lot of the big-time schools, but the scholarships are the same."

Jake continued. "Coach said, 'Jake, do this for me and you'll be *my* son when it comes to a scholarship.' I asked how I could trust him to follow through on his promise. He just said, 'If I don't, you'll go public with the story, and my career is over.'

"I told him I'd think about it."

He was looking at Alex now. "There's no excuse for what I did—none. All I can tell you is I did it because I really need a scholarship if I'm going to go to college. And Coach was guaranteeing it."

"But why Alex?" Christine asked. "If Coach Gordon was just trying to save Matt, why not switch vials with someone who doesn't play? Why bring Alex down when he may have been needed in the playoffs?"

"I think I can answer that one," Matt said. "My dad wanted Goldie gone. He knew that by next year *everyone* would be saying he should start instead of me. He figured if Goldie tested positive, he'd have to transfer someplace because of the public humiliation."

He paused and looked Jake in the eye. "And with Goldie gone, you'd have gotten to play more next year too—right, Jakey? It wasn't *all* about my dad wanting to get rid of Alex. You didn't mind the idea either."

Jake looked at Alex. "God, I'm sorry," he said. "I've been sorry since the day they nailed you with this. Matt's right. I thought I was going to play this year. I'd even thought about not playing next year and coming back a fifth year to be the starter when Matt graduated. Once you showed up, that was out the window."

"And so you walked into the training room and just switched the labels on the vials," Matt said. "I'm off the hook, Alex is a dead man walking, and you get a scholarship *and* the chance maybe to start in two years."

Jake nodded. "It was easy. I just told Buddy I'd left my watch behind. He didn't care if I went back in there—why should he? I just switched the two labels. Took about five minutes because I was nervous and I was being very careful."

A teacher Alex didn't recognize walked in and did a double take when she saw the group sitting around the table. "You're all late for fifth period!" she said. "What do you think you're doing! Get going!"

They were about to stand up when the door opened again and Mr. Hillier walked in.

"It's okay, Ms. Cohen," he said. "I called this meeting. The kids all have permission to be here."

"Oh," she said, clearly startled. "I'm so sorry. I didn't know."

"No problem," he said, smiling.

"I can give you all late slips," he said after she left. "But are you close to a resolution? You can fill me in on details later, but tell me what happens next."

Again they all looked at one another. It was Matt who finally spoke.

"Well, now that I know what happened, it seems pretty clear," he said. "I'm going to tell Mr. White that I was doping and that my father arranged to get the samples switched. I'd rather not tell him about Jake. . . ."

"But, Matt, I'm guilty. . . ."

"I know you, Jake. And I know my dad. He's . . . persuasive. I believe you do feel guilty for what you did," Matt said, "and even if we don't make it public, I expect the team will figure it out—and that you'll pay a pretty steep price. I think that's enough—unless you disagree, Alex."

Alex thought about how the team was likely to react. "No, I agree," he said.

"Christine, are you willing to keep Jake's name out of print?" Matt asked.

They looked at one another. "Can't use his name if no

one goes on the record," Christine finally said. "I'm guessing no one here's going to go on the record with that part of the story?"

Jake was shaking his head. "I don't deserve this," he said.

"Shut up, Jakey. You'll suffer plenty—I guarantee it," Matt said, now clearly in charge again.

"After I tell Mr. White what happened, I'm going to tell the whole school at the pep rally," Matt said. "I don't want there to be any doubt that Goldie was completely innocent. I'll take my lumps and try to move on."

"You don't have to do that," Alex said.

"I'd *rather* do that. I'd rather everyone hears it from me firsthand than people hear about it secondhand. What is it you told me, Christine, back when my dad wasn't letting anyone talk? 'It's always better to get your version on the record.'"

"You know that once you tell Mr. White, he's going to have to fire your dad," Mr. Hillier said.

Matt was clear-eyed now. "I know," he said. "He deserves it."

■ ■ ■

By the time the pep rally began, the word was all over the school. Something big was going on, but no one knew exactly what it was. The rally was supposed to start at two-thirty, as soon as seventh period was over, but it was almost quarter to three before Mr. White—looking grim—walked onto the stage.

There were no announcements—nothing about how to buy tickets for the bus ride to Pittsburgh and for the game. There was no cheerleading, no promises of victory on Friday. Instead, Mr. White said simply, "Ladies and gentlemen of Chester Heights, I have an announcement. At two o'clock this afternoon, I accepted the resignation of football coach Matthew Gordon. I would now like to introduce to you our acting football coach, Tom Hillier."

That sent a loud buzz through the entire audience as Coach Hillier walked onstage. He waited a second, then said, "The sooner we get quiet, the sooner you'll know what's going on."

That worked. Coach Hillier continued, "Will all of you please welcome the members of the Chester Heights football team that will be representing you this Friday night in Pittsburgh in the state championship game."

There were no exclamation points in his tone. The side door opened and, one by one, the players walked in. Quietly they lined up behind Coach Hillier. The applause was—if possible—confused. No one knew what to do: Clap? Roar? Stand and cheer? Clearly, something was going on.

Once the players were all assembled, standing shoulder to shoulder behind Coach Hillier, he leaned into the microphone again.

"And now, Matt Gordon has requested to speak to his fellow students."

The applause for him was louder, because he was Matt Gordon and because they were thinking he was going to clear up all the confusion. He walked to the microphone and gestured for quiet.

"What I'm about to tell you is exactly what I told my teammates a few minutes ago. The most important thing you need to know is that Alex Myers did not test positive for steroid use—I did."

Gasps broke out all over the room. Matt plowed on. He told everyone what he had told Alex, Christine, Jonas, and Jake in the lunchroom. He made a point of saying that there wasn't a single excuse for his behavior—or for his father's. He didn't mention Jake, saying only that his father had "arranged" for the samples to be switched. Finally he turned to Alex and said, "I'm so sorry for this, Alex. No one will be cheering you on louder than I will on Friday night. You're a great quarterback and a better person. I'm proud to call you a friend."

He turned and walked in Alex's direction. Alex stepped forward and Matt wrapped him in a bear hug, tears streaming down his face.

Someone in the audience started to clap as they embraced. Then someone else. And then, in an instant, everyone in the room was on their feet, clapping and cheering for the two quarterbacks. The rest of the team joined in.

Finally Matt walked back to the podium, his arm still around Alex.

"I hope, someday, I can earn your forgiveness for this," he said. "For now, I plan to be in the stands on Friday, leading the cheers for Goldie and this great team."

He turned to the back of the stage and put his arm up in the air. The entire team moved in to surround him and Alex. "On three—state champs," Matt said.

They put their hands in the air and leaned into the circle, pushing against one another to get as close as they possibly could.

Gerry Detwiler said, "One, two, three . . ."

And the whole school roared, "STATE CHAMPS!"

The next few hours were a blur for Alex.

Once the pep rally was over, the team headed straight for the locker room to get ready for practice. While Buddy Thomas was taping Alex's ankles, Coach Hillier—back in his coaching gear—asked him to come into his office for a moment.

When Alex walked into the small office, Coach Hillier was in there along with Gerry Detwiler and Mr. White.

"Mr. Myers, I haven't had a chance to see you yet," Mr. White said, shaking Alex's hand. "I'm glad you were cleared. I'm sorry for doubting you. And I'm very sorry this happened."

"There was no way for you to know, Mr. White," Alex said.

Coach Hillier jumped in before an extended silence could turn awkward.

"Alex, we've been discussing how to handle the publicity. Obviously, what's happened is all over social media. We think we should hold some kind of press conference after practice, with you and Gerry speaking for the players, me speaking as the acting coach, and Mr. White speaking on behalf of the school."

Alex nodded, looking at Gerry, who he guessed had been briefed already.

"Okay?" Alex said, as they seemed to want an answer.

"The thing is, we all have to be careful about what we say about Coach Gordon," Mr. White said. "He's apparently refusing all media requests and isn't going to admit any wrongdoing publicly. . . ."

"He covered up for his son," Detwiler said. "Matt's already said it publicly."

"Still," Mr. White said, "if you are asked about the things Matt said about his father at the pep rally, just say the person to talk to about that is Matt. We've asked Matt to steer clear of any media until after the game. Then he can say anything he wants."

Alex nodded. "Got it," he said.

"Anything else?" Mr. White said.

"Yeah," Detwiler said. "Any way we can play this game tomorrow instead? This is going to be a long three days."

■ ■ ■

The press conference was a zoo. The soap opera nature of the story had attracted national attention, and Alex saw cameras from both CNN and ESPN in the audience along with all the local ones. Reporters were asked to identify themselves before asking questions. One stood up and said he was from the *Washington Post*. Another was from the *New York Times*. Alex recognized the teen reporter Stevie Thomas sitting next to Christine in the third row.

Alex and Gerry let Coach Hillier and Mr. White take any questions about Coach Gordon. Gerry nicely described how the team felt, Alex thought.

"We miss Matt already," he said. "I'm the captain for now, but he's our leader. He's the guy we look to for a pickup when we're down. But once we get on the field, we all have faith in Alex. Every time we've needed him this season, he's come through. I have no doubt he'll do it again Friday."

A little shudder went through Alex as Gerry spoke. He had started two games earlier in the season, but they had been against second-tier opponents. Now he would be starting the state championship game against another undefeated team.

And Matt would be in the stands. He wouldn't even have his counsel on the sideline. Jake would be his backup. Coach Hillier had agreed Jake should stay on the team—at least through Friday's game. At that moment a reporter stood up and asked Alex how he felt about being *the* quarterback under these circumstances.

"How do I feel? I'm beyond happy to have been proven innocent," Alex said. "This last week has been brutal. I hope the guys who did the telecast of the semifinal game will announce my innocence as loudly as they did my supposed guilt. . . .

"But worse than that was feeling cut off from my team. There's no place I'd rather be than on the field with them on *any* Friday night. So I feel excited to have the chance to play.

"And I also feel . . . sad. Because I'll miss Matt Gordon."

■ ■ ■

Alex had a long talk on the phone with his father on Wednesday and felt better than he had in months. Dave Myers not only said that he'd be at the game on Friday night but also that he was going to get to Philadelphia much more often.

"Those are empty words until it actually happens," he told Alex. "But I'm going to make them real."

He told Alex how proud he was of the way he'd handled himself and asked him if he ever thought he could look Jake Bilney in the eye again.

"Matt, I can understand," his dad said. "He didn't set out to sabotage you. Bilney did."

Alex sighed. He'd thought about that a lot since Tuesday.

"I hear you, Dad," he said. "But I think Coach Gordon knew just what button to press to get him to cooperate. And I honestly believe he's sorry he did it. Sometimes guys are sorry they got caught. I really think Jake is sorry for what he did."

"Well, you're a lot more forgiving than I am," his dad said.

Alex smiled for a moment even though his father couldn't see him. "I guess," he said, "that's a good thing for you too, Dad."

"Touché, young man," his father said. "I'll see you Friday in Pittsburgh."

■ ■ ■

Thanksgiving was going to be an early dinner with just Alex and his mom and Molly, because Alex had to be at school at 5:00 p.m. to get on a bus to Pittsburgh. The team would stay in a hotel Thursday night so they would be rested for the game on Friday.

His mom and Molly were both in the kitchen and Alex was just about to turn on the Lions–Packers game when the doorbell rang.

On the doorstep, all grinning broadly, stood Matt, Jonas, and Christine.

"What the . . . ?"

"Alex, who's there?" he heard his mom call.

"Friends," Alex said, realizing the three of them were just that.

He waved them in. His mom was as surprised as he was to see them.

Matt explained, "It's a Thanksgiving tradition in my family to play touch football before we eat. But to be honest, I'm not all that fired up about playing football with my dad right now."

"Oh, yes, I can see that," Alex's mom said.

Matt shrugged. "I'm having dinner at Jonas's house because his mom and dad invited me. Anyway, the three of us thought we'd come over and see if Alex wanted to play a little touch, start a new tradition with his new friends in Philly. Nothing too intense. We have to make sure he and Jonas are ready for tomorrow."

Alex's mom looked at him. "Think you can handle that, Alex?" she said.

"I'll grab a ball from the garage and meet you guys outside," he said.

As he walked to the garage, it occurred to him that for the first time since they had arrived in Philadelphia, he felt truly at home.

They played for about an hour and then went inside for hot chocolate. Christine left first because she had relatives coming over. Matt and Jonas lingered a bit longer, watching the game.

"Hey, Goldie, there are two things I have to tell you before you leave for Pittsburgh, since I won't be allowed to be around the team before the game," Matt said.

Alex turned to Matt. "Okay," he said. "What've you got?"

"The second most important thing is this: just be yourself tomorrow and you'll be fine. You've got a bunch of good receivers and"—he looked at Jonas—"one great one. You can make all the throws, and you know how to deal with pressure. I've seen you do it."

Alex nodded. "Thanks. I wish you could be there on the sideline. . . ."

"I do too, Goldie. I do too."

"What's the most important thing?"

Matt grinned.

"You're taking Christine to the holiday dance on Saturday, right?"

"Yeah," Alex said. "How'd you know?"

"Because I asked her—too late."

Jonas was smiling now too.

"So here's the deal. You guys win tomorrow night, and I'll be a good boy and settle for Hope Alexander this weekend and in the future. But if you lose . . ."

"What?" Alex said.

"I won't coach you up on how to be a good boyfriend," Matt said. "You're on your own. And trust me, you *need* coaching."

Matt and Jonas dissolved in laughter. And pretty soon Alex did too.

■ ■ ■

Even though they all slept late on Friday, the day crawled by.

Alex and Jonas were rooming together, and they killed time watching football games on TV for a while and then went for a walk around downtown. It was too cold to go very far, so they went back inside quickly. At three o'clock they all ate a pregame meal together in one of the hotel's ballrooms. Everyone was quiet, thinking about what lay ahead that evening. Finally, at five o'clock, they got on the buses for the short ride to the stadium. It was dark and Alex could see the stadium lights from the bridge. He took a deep breath as the bus followed the police escort motorcycles into the parking lot and pulled into the tunnel underneath the stadium.

He wished he could just relax and enjoy the experience. But his stomach was tied in knots.

They had gotten lucky with the weather. It was cold—the forecast had been for thirty-three degrees at kickoff—but there was no snow and the wind was brisk but not biting. They all suited up, trying to make this pregame feel like any other.

Just before they left the locker room, Coach Hillier called them into the center of the massive room.

"Fellas, I know what a long and crazy week it's been," he

said. "But now you get to do what you love to do and what you all do best—play football. And you get to play in front of about thirty-five thousand people here and a whole lot more watching on television.

"You should be unbelievably proud of the fact that you're here right now. Very few high school players get to do anything like this. Take a second to feel a chill when you run down that tunnel. We're all going to remember tonight for the rest of our lives. So give every single bit of effort you have inside you once the game starts. Every last bit. If you do that, regardless of the score, you can walk out of here tonight feeling proud."

He paused for a moment and grinned. "Of course I have no doubt we're going to win the game. No doubt at all. How about you?"

He stepped into the middle of the room and put his arm in the air. They crowded around.

"On three," he said.

Everyone put their arms in. "One, two, three—state champions!"

They were about to pull their arms down when Alex said, "Hey, one more thing: for Matt!"

Their arms pushed even closer to one another, as did their bodies.

"For Matt!" they repeated.

They turned and headed for the field.

■ ■ ■

Alex did feel a chill as they came down the tunnel and ran through a cordon of Chester Heights cheerleaders onto the field. The band was playing, and he heard a roar from the near side of the stadium. A moment later, he heard a cheer from the far side and saw the Beaver Falls players racing from their tunnel to their sideline.

Then they were all standing at attention on the sideline for the playing of the national anthem. Alex thought he'd never heard it sound quite so sweet.

Beaver Falls won the coin toss and chose to defer, so Chester Heights would get the ball first.

They lined up for the kickoff, with everyone in the stadium—or so it appeared—on their feet. Alex looked around, wondering exactly where his parents were and where Matt was, and remembered to take it all in one more time.

A split second later, he heard Jonas's voice.

"Let's go, QB," he said. "It's time."

The kickoff had been returned to the 28-yard line. Alex pulled on his helmet and trotted onto the field and into the huddle. Coach Hillier had already called the first play.

"Everybody ready?" he said.

Will Allison looked across the huddle and pointed a finger at him. "We're golden, Goldie," he said. "Long as we have you. Call the play."

"Ninety-four pitch," Alex said, his voice rising above the crowd. "On three."

They broke the huddle and came to the line.

This is forever, Alex thought.

He called out three colors, took the snap, felt the ball in his hands, and set his sights on the goal line.

Football.

Basketball.

Baseball.

Whatever the sport, Alex Myers always has
his game face on. . . . Here's a sneak peek of
The Sixth Man, book 2 in the Triple Threat series.

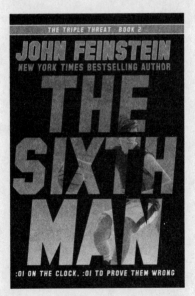

It was apparent very quickly that Max Bellotti was the real deal.

Alex noticed it in the shooting drills Coach Archer ran them through before they started to scrimmage. The ball came off Max's hands softly as it arced toward the basket. He stepped into three-point shots with the confidence most players showed when going in for an open layup. Even when he missed, the ball seemed to go around the rim several times before dropping off.

Coach Archer put both Max and Alex with the white team when they started to scrimmage. Max was still feeling his way a little bit, learning the offense, and Alex was pretty tentative on his first day back practicing. Even so, when they were both in, the whites held their own against the reds.

Coach Archer pulled Alex to rest him on several occasions

so that he didn't try to do too much too soon. And even with Early at point, Max managed to score.

As they walked off the court at the end of practice, Holder caught up to Alex and Jonas.

"Fellas," he said, "I think we might just have ourselves a basketball team."

Zane Wakefield, walking a couple of steps in front of them, turned when he heard that. He started to say something but apparently thought better of it, then kept walking.

■ ■ ■

The first sign of trouble came Monday morning, when Alex walked out of his third-period math class and was almost thrown against the wall by Hope Alexander.

He had actually been enjoying the morning—thinking about how nice it was to start a new semester at a school where he now had friends, knew his way around. Plus, he couldn't wait to get to basketball practice.

And then Hope literally put her hand on his chest and pushed him up against the lockers.

"Okay, who is he?" she asked. "And don't give me any runaround."

Alex thought that Christine Whitford was the prettiest girl in the school. But Hope Alexander was tops on a lot of other guys' lists. She was tall (at least five ten) and impossible to miss as she sashayed down a hallway with her long blond hair appearing to blow in the wind—even indoors.

Now she was looking him right in the eye—which was a little unnerving—and saying, "Did you hear me, Alex? I want details."

Alex was genuinely confused. "Who are you talking about?" he asked.

"The Greek god walking around with Steve Holder," Hope said in a tone that implied Alex was perhaps the densest person she had ever met.

Ah. Alex probably should have predicted this. "You mean Max?" he said casually, as if he were talking about his cat. "He's the new kid from Detroit. Transfer. Plays basketball. He's a good shooter; I think he's going to help us—"

"Who *cares* if he's any good," said Lisa Vantoff, who was standing just off Hope's shoulder. "Do you know if he's dating anyone?"

"Since he just moved here, I doubt it," Alex said. "But I really don't know. I only met him for a few minutes yesterday before practice. Seems like a good guy—"

"Introduce me," Hope said instantly.

Alex looked at her for a second and smiled. "You're not shy, Hope. Introduce yourself," he said. "And while you're at it, introduce him to Matt too."

Hope and Matt Gordon had been dating since the middle of football season. Alex had actually been impressed that even after Matt's fall from grace, Hope had stuck with him.

Her face clouded for a second; then she brightened. "Maybe he's got a sister for Matt," she said.

"Maybe he's got a twin brother," Lisa said.

Alex had heard enough—more than enough. "I gotta go," he said. He squirmed free from Hope's grip and fled down the hall.

■ ■ ■

It got worse at lunch.

Alex was sitting at his usual table with Jonas, Matt, and Christine when he saw Steve Holder and Max approaching. Maybe it was his imagination, but he swore he could hear sighing as Max and Steve carried their trays through the cafeteria.

"Wow," Christine murmured. "Hope wasn't kidding. . . ."

"Max, I know you've met Alex and Jonas," Steve said. "This is Matt Gordon and Christine Whitford."

Max said hello and Alex was convinced his smile had widened when he saw Christine. Which was understandable.

"So, word is you're going to turn our basketball team around," Matt said as Steve and Max sat down.

Max laughed. "Well, I hope I can help," he said. "From what Coach Archer has told me, getting Alex back will be key too."

"Very modest of you," Christine said. "But you were averaging twenty-one points a game before you transferred—"

"How did you know that?" Alex said, breaking in.

She shrugged. "It didn't take a genius to go on the Internet and check out the stats for Wildwood High School in Detroit," she said, giving Alex her *you're too stupid to live* look. She looked directly at Max and gave him her megawatt smile. "I work for the student newspaper, the *Weekly Roar*. Would you be up for an interview?"

"For you?" Max said, returning the smile. "Of course."

Alex was feeling a little bit sick.

"Great," Christine said. "Give me your number and I'll call to set up a time."

Alex was staring at his green beans as if they held the

secret of life. Inside his head, Alex heard the words of an old Grateful Dead song his parents both loved: "Trouble ahead, trouble behind. . . ."

He kept staring at the green beans. It felt like the right thing to do.

■ ■ ■

The good news was that Alex felt great at practice that afternoon. He still wasn't one hundred percent, but he felt more confident handling the ball and shooting than he had on Sunday. He had no trouble dealing with Zane Wakefield when the second team was on offense. Coach Archer started the day with Alex and Max still in white but then began giving each time with the red team.

Max seemed to be feeling more comfortable today too. There was no doubt about it—Max was the best player on the court. Even Holder, easily the team's best defensive player, couldn't guard him. Max was giving away a couple of inches to Holder, but he was a lot quicker.

Alex's mind was racing: With Max, they could be a good team—compete, he thought, with just about anyone in the conference. At the same time, he envisioned Max making game-winning plays while the entire female population of Chester Heights—including Christine Whitford—swooned.

Before practice was over he had gone through the five stages of "about to lose a girlfriend" grief. For a while he was in denial: Christine liked him; she wouldn't fall for another guy just because of his looks. Then came anger: she better *not* fall for him because of his looks. He bargained: maybe he could convince Max that he was better off with Hope

Alexander; maybe the tall girl would appeal to him more than the petite one. Depression set in while the team was shooting free throws: *why* did this have to happen? He was just starting to feel confident with Christine and then *this* guy shows up. And finally, acceptance: if she wanted to dump him for Max, there was nothing he could do.

He'd just focus on basketball and move on.

Or at least try to.

■ ■ ■

Coach Archer called them all to the center jump circle at exactly 5:29—meaning he had one minute before the girls' team would take over the court.

"Good practice today, guys," he said. "I think we all agree we're a better team with Alex healthy and Max wearing red or white. I don't want some of you guys on the second team to get discouraged because you think you're going to lose playing time. We're going to need everybody here right now if we want to have a chance to win the conference.

"But we *can* win the conference with the thirteen of you standing here right now. . . ."

He paused for a moment.

"Be here at five o'clock tomorrow," Coach Archer added. "Starters will be Holder, Bernstein, Ellington, Bellotti, and . . ." He paused a moment before saying, "Wakefield."

Alex could see Wakefield smirking. Apparently he thought he was starting because Coach Archer thought he should, not because Alex wasn't quite ready to play.

Holder walked to the middle of the circle and put his hand in the air. "New year, new start. Let's go one and oh," he said. They all put their hands in with Holder and said, "One and oh," then started in the direction of the locker room. Alex paused to pull his socks up—and so he could linger long enough to talk to Coach Archer.

"You need something, Alex?" he asked.

"Coach, I know we agreed I wouldn't play tomorrow, but I felt pretty good today. . . ."

Coach Archer smiled. "Be patient, Alex," he said. "You dress for the game and we'll see how it goes, but I'd like to give you the extra time."

Alex understood. He just hated the idea that Wakefield thought he was still the starter.

"Did you ask him?" said Jonas, who had waited by the steps and, as usual, could read Alex's mind.

"Yeah," Alex said. "He said I can dress tomorrow, and we'll see as the game goes on."

Jonas smiled. "So that's good, then."

"Yeah, but Wakefield still starts. . . ."

Jonas waved him off. "You know that doesn't matter. Coach knows who his point guard is. We all know who the point guard is."

He smiled and then added, "We've got a real team now. Our boy Bellotti can *play*."

Alex nodded. He was looking forward to being on the same team as Bellotti. Whatever else Max's presence was going to mean, he'd worry about later.

■ ■ ■

In his pregame speech on Tuesday, Coach Archer made a point to remind his team that Main Line had made the state playoffs a year earlier and was off to a 5–2 start. What he didn't mention—as Steve Holder pointed out later—was that they'd graduated four seniors and played in a much weaker conference than the Lions did.

It wasn't as if the Bears were awful. They just weren't good enough to compete with the revamped lineup of the Chester Heights Lions. There were some rough spots—especially on offense, with Bellotti still learning the plays and Wakefield running the offense.

The score was tied in the second quarter when Coach Archer waved at Alex to sit next to him on the bench.

"Tell me the absolute truth," he said. "Are you ready? Because Friday's a lot more important. . . ."

"I'm ready, Coach," Alex said. He wasn't lying. He *knew* he was ready to play.

"Okay," Coach Archer said, pointing to the scorer's table. "Go for Wakefield."

Alex was on his way before the word *go* was out of his coach's mouth.

He put up his hand to give Wakefield a high five as he entered the game, but Wakefield put his head down as if he didn't see him.

Alex felt strong even though his shot, at least when guarded, was a little rusty. He settled for getting the ball to Max, Jonas, and Steve—which proved to be the right thing to do.

The game was close for three quarters, Chester Heights leading by just 49–45. But the fourth quarter began with Bellotti and Jonas making back-to-back three pointers to stretch the lead to 55–45. The Bears didn't give up, but they never got the margin back within single digits, and the Lions won 67–55.

Coach Archer didn't come close to living up to his promise to make sure that the two former starters—Tony Early and Cory McAndrews—would see plenty of playing time. McAndrews got into the game on a number of occasions, and so did Jameer Wilson, who had been the sixth man before the arrival of Alex, Jonas, and Max. Early got in midway through the second quarter, missed a three-point shot, and was back on the bench at the next dead ball. Jonas played thirty of a possible thirty-two minutes. Holder and Bellotti played twenty-eight minutes apiece. Among the starters, only Kenny Bernstein and Wakefield sat for any extended period of time. And Wakefield played more than he probably would in the future, because the coach was going easy on Alex.

Which might have explained the strange dynamic in the locker room after the game. Coach Archer told them he was proud of the way they had all approached the game and that they had a lot of work to do before the conference opener at Bryn Mawr Tech on Friday night. As soon as he walked out of the locker room, the seven players who had gotten serious minutes high-fived one another, then backslapped Bellotti—who had scored nineteen points—and welcomed him to the team. The other five players—all seniors—went to the showers without a word.

Alex and Jonas looked at one another—both thinking the same thing.

"Never a dull moment around here," Jonas said.

"Yup," Alex said. "Winning isn't going to keep those five guys happy."

Which, he had to admit, didn't make him terribly *un*happy.

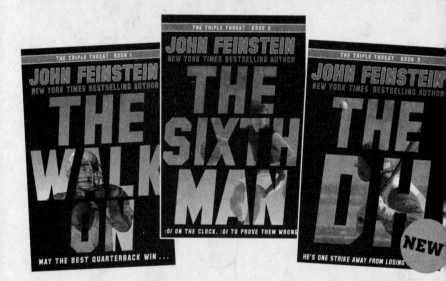

Want to play college ball? Better learn to play the game.

John Feinstein is the author of many bestselling books, including *A Season on the Brink*, *A Good Walk Spoiled*, and *Living on the Black*. His books for young readers—*Last Shot*, *Vanishing Act*, *Cover-Up*, *Change-Up*, *The Rivalry*, *Rush for the Gold*, *Foul Trouble*, *The Walk On*, and *The Sixth Man*—offer a winning combination of sports, action, and intrigue, with *Last Shot* receiving the Edgar Allan Poe Award for best young adult mystery.

He began his career at the *Washington Post*, where he worked as both a political and sports reporter. He has also written for *Sports Illustrated* and the *National Sports Daily* and is currently a contributor to the *Washington Post*, *Golf World*, the Golf Channel, and Comcast SportsNet.

John Feinstein lives in Potomac, Maryland, where he is hard at work on a new book in the Triple Threat series.

Visit him online at JohnFeinsteinBooks.com.